Pearl of Pearl Island by John Oxenham

John Oxenham was the pseudonym used by William Arthur Dunkerley for most of his fiction works including poetry. For journalism he went by the name of Julian Ross.

Dunkerley was born on November 12th 1852 in Manchester. He attended Old Trafford School and Victoria University, both in Manchester.

He married in America and lived they for a short time before returning to these shores, this time to Ealing in West London becoming both the Deacon and teacher at Ealing Congregational Church in the 1880's.

In 1913 he wrote a bestselling book of poems entitled 'Bees In Amber' followed by 'All's Well" in 1916. As a journalist he was a major contributor to Jerome K Jerome's Idler magazine.

In 1922 he moved to Worthing in Sussex and became the town's Mayor.

He died in Worthing on January 23rd, 1941.

Index of Contents

PEARL OF THE PEARL OF THE SILVER SEA!

Pearl Iridescent! Pearl of the sea!
Shimmering, glimmering Pearl of the sea!
White in the sun-flecked silver sea,
White in the moon-decked silver sea,
White in the wrath of the silver sea,—
Pearl of the Silver Sea!

Lapped in the smile of the Silver Sea,
Ringed in the foam of the Silver Sea,
Glamoured in mists of the Silver Sea,—
Pearl of the Silver Sea!

Glancing and glimmering under the sun,
Jewel and casket all in one,
Joy supreme of the sun's day-dream,
Soft in the gleam of the golden beam,—
Pearl of the Silver Sea!

Splendour of Hope in the rising sun,
Glory of Love in the noonday sun,
Wonder of Faith in the setting sun,—
Pearl of the Silver Sea!

Gaunt and grim to the outer world,
Jewel and casket all impearled
With the kiss of the Silver Sea!—
With the flying kiss of the Silver Sea,
With the long sweet kiss of the Silver Sea,
With the rainbow kiss of the Silver Sea,—
Pearl of the Silver Sea!

And oh the sight,—the wonderful sight,
When calm and white, in the mystic light,
Of her quivering pathway, broad and bright,
The Queen of the Night, in silver dight,
Sails over the Silver Sea!

Wherever I go, and wherever I be,
The joy and the longing are there with me,—
The gleam And the glamour come back to me,—
In a mystical rapture there comes to me,
The call of the Silver Sea!
As needle to pole is my heart to thee,
Pearl of the Silver Sea!

Pearl of the Pearl of the Silver Sea!
To some you are Margaret, but to me,
Always and ever, wherever I be,
You are Pearl of the Pearl of the Silver Sea!

J.C.G.

PART THE FIRST

I

If you want murders, mysteries, or mud—pass on! This is a simple, straightforward love-story.

"Jock, my lad," said Lady Elspeth softly, nodding her head very many times, in that very knowing way of hers which made her look like a Lord Chief Justice and a Fairy Godmother all in one, "I've found you out."

And when the shrewd old soul of her looked him gently through and through in that fashion, he knew very much better than to attempt any evasion.

"Ah!" he said meekly, "I was afraid someone would, sooner or later. I've been living in constant dread of it. But it's happened before, you know, between you and me. What is it this time, dear Lady Elspeth?"

"Here have I been imputing grace to you for your kindly attentions to a poor old woman whose race is nearly run, and setting you up above the rest of them therefor, and lo, my idol—"

"Ah!" he said again, with a reproving wag of the head, for he knew now what was coming,—"idols are perverse, camstairy things at best, you know, and a bit out of date too. And, besides,"—with a touch of remonstrance—"at your age and with your bringing-up—"

"Ay, ay, ye may be as insulting as ye choose, my laddie, and fling my age and my upbringing in my face like a very man—"

"There isn't a face like it in all England, and as to—"

"I prefer ye to say Britain, as I've told ye before. Your bit England is only a portion of the kingdom, and in very many respects the poorest portion, notably in brains and manners and beauty. But ye cannot draw me off like that, my laddie, whether it's meant for a compliment or no. I was just about telling you you were a fraud—"

"You hadn't got quite that length, you know, but—"

"Will I prove it to you? Haven't you been coming here as regular as the milkman for a month past—"

"Oh, come now!—Only once a day. I've an idea milkie comes twice, and besides—"

"And what did ye come for, my lad?" with an emphatic nod and a menacing shake of the frail white hand, pricelessly jewelled above, comfortably black-silk-mittened below. "Tell me that now! What did ye come for?"

"To see the dearest old lady in England—Britain, I mean. And—"

"Yes?—And?—" and she watched him, with her head a little on one side and her eyes shining brightly, like an expectant motherly robin hopping on treasure trove.

He smiled back at her and said nothing. He knew she knew without his telling.

"And so I was only second fiddle—" she began, with an assumption of scornful irascibility which became her less than her very oldest cap.

"Oh, dear me, no! Leader of the orchestra!—Proprietor of the house!—Sole director and manager and—"

"Tuts! It was Margaret Brandt you came to see," and the twinkling brown eyes held the merry gray ones with a steady challenge.

"Partly,—and I was just about to say so when you interrupted me—"

"Ay! Were you now? Ye can out with things quick enough at times, my laddie!"

"Well, you see, there are some things one does not speak about until one feels one has an absolute right to."

"You'd have told your mother, Jock."

"Perhaps, I'm not sure,—not yet—not, at all events, until—"

"And wasn't I to take her place when she left you all alone?"

"And so you have. You're just the dearest and sweetest old—"

"Second fiddle! Come away and we'll talk of Margaret, since that's all you come for."

"And isn't she worth coming for? Did you ever in all your life see anything more wonderful than Margaret Brandt?"

And she looked at him for half a minute with a twinkle in the shrewd old eyes, which had surely seen many strange and wonderful things since the first wonders passed and gave place to the common things of life. Beautiful eyes they were still,—of a very tender brown, and shining always with kindly feeling and deepest interest in the person she was talking to.

I do not know how it may be with you, but, personally, I detest people whose eyes and thoughts go wandering away over your left shoulder while you are talking with them. It may be, of course, that you are not much of a talker and are simply boring them, but, all the same, mental squinters are not to my liking.

But Lady Elspeth was never bored—visibly, at all events, and while you talked with her you were the one person in the world in whom she was interested.

Margaret's eyes had something of the same in them, but they were very deep blue, and there was in them just that touch of maidenly reserve which best becomes a maiden's eyes, until, to one at all events, she may lay it aside and let her heart shine through.

Lady Elspeth looked at him, then, for half a minute, with a starry twinkle, and then said, with a finality of conviction that made her dearer to him than ever—

"Never!" and he kissed her hand with fervour,—and not ungracefully, since the action, though foreign to him, was absolutely spontaneous.

"But—!" she said firmly. And he sat up.

"But me no buts," he said. "And why?"

"Well, you see, Margaret is by way of being an heiress—and you are not."

"I'm sorry. But, you see, I couldn't very well be if I tried. Still I'm not absolutely penniless, and—"

"Tuts, boy! What you have is just about enough to pay Jeremiah Pixley's servants' wages."

"D-hang Jeremiah Pixley!"

"D-hang is not a nice expression to use before a lady, let me tell you. What you have, as, I was saying, is just enough to make or mar you—"

"It's going to make me. I can live on it till things begin to come my way."

"Everyone writes nowadays," she said, with a dubious shake of the head. "Who reads all the books passes my comprehension. I suppose you have all just to buy one another's to make a bit of a living out of it."

"Like those washing people! But it's not quite as bad as all that. There are still some intelligent people who buy books—good books, of course, I mean."

"Not many, I'm afraid. They read reviews and chatter as though they'd read the books. And if they really want to read them they get them out of a library. You don't see bought books lying on the tables, as you used to do when I was a girl, and they were scarcer and dearer. How is this last one going?"

"I have reason to believe my publishers are not absolutely broken-hearted over it, which leads me to think that they have probably done pretty well out of it. They are not what you might call a gushing race, you know, but they have given me a kind of cautious half-hint that they might not refuse to look at my next if I offered it to them on my bended knees. But let us get back to our—to Miss Brandt. I had no idea she was an heiress. I have really never thought of money in the matter, except as to how I could earn enough to offer it to her."

"She has a fair portion—about two thousand a year, I believe. Her father was Danish Consul in Glasgow, and had a shipping business there. I should not be surprised if Mr. Pixley had views of his own concerning Margaret's portion and his son—and of course Margaret herself."

"Will you permit me to say, 'Hang Mr. Pixley!' dear Lady Elspeth? It would be such a relief—if you're sure you don't mind."

"You may say 'Hang Mr. Pixley!' though it is not an expression I am in the habit of using myself. But please don't begin it with a D."

"Hang Mr. Pixley, and Mr. Pixley's son, and all his intentions!" he said fervently and with visible relish.

"Yes," she nodded slowly, as though savouring it; and then added, with a delicious twinkle of the soft brown eyes, "There is something in that that appeals to me. Jeremiah Pixley is almost too good for this world. At least—"

"He is absolutely unwholesomely good. My own private opinion is that he's a disreputable old blackg—I mean whited sepulchre."

"Unwholesomely good!" She nodded again. "Yes,—that, I think, very fairly expresses him. 'Unco' guid,' we would say up north. But, all the same, he is Margaret's uncle and guardian and trustee. He is also the kind of man whom nothing can turn from a line he has once adopted."

"I know. Pigheaded as a War-Office-mule," he side-tracked hastily.

For she had looked at him with a momentary bristle of enquiry in the gentle brown eyes, and he remembered, just in time, that her husband had once held the reins in Pall Mall for half a year, when, feeling atrophy creeping on, he resigned office and died three months later.

He hastened to add,—"The ordinary Army-mule, you know, is specially constructed with a cast-iron mouth, and a neck of granite, and a disposition like—like Mr. Pixley's. I imagine Mr. Pixley can be excessively unpleasant when he tries. To me he is excessively unpleasant even to think of, and without any exertion whatever on his part."

"Yes. Mrs. Pixley would rather convey that impression. She is always depressed and apprehensive-looking. But she is very fond of Margaret, and that no doubt is why—But I suppose she really has no choice in the matter, until she comes of age—"

"Mrs. Pixley?"

"Until Margaret comes into her own she is no doubt obliged to submit to her guardian's views. It is difficult to imagine anyone not a Pixley living in the Pixley atmosphere of their own free will. What is the son like? I have only seen him once or twice. Does he take after his father?"

"He's about twice as tall, and several times as wide in some respects, I should say,—certainly in the matter of the enjoyment of life. He's not bad-looking—in a kind of a way, you know,—that is, for those who like that kind of looks,—a trifle fleshy perhaps. But he's a fair dancer, and sings a song well, and can talk about nothing as nicely as any man I ever met. It's an accomplishment I often envy."

"I wouldn't trouble about it, if I were you. There are things more worth doing in the world. And that reminds me. We were talking of your books. I've been wanting to tell you that your love-scenes are not altogether to my liking. They are just a little—well, not quite—"

"Yes, I know," he said sadly. "You see, I lack experience in such things. Now, if Margaret—"

"Don't tell me you want to use her simply as a model," she began, with another incipient gentle bristle.

"I want her as a model and a great many other things besides, dear Lady Elspeth. I love Margaret Brandt with every atom of good that is in me."

"And she?" with a nod and a sparkle.

"Ah! There now—that's what I don't know. She's not one to wear her heart on her sleeve. At times I have dared to hope. Then again I have feared—"

"That is quite right. That is quite as it should be. Anything more, so early as this, would imply unmaidenliness on her part."

"Truly? You mean it? You are, without exception, the most charming old lady in the world! You relieve my mind immensely. You see, she is always so sweet and charming. But then she could not be anything else, and it may really mean nothing. Do you really think I may hope?"

"'White-handed Hope, thou hovering angel, girt with golden wings,'" she quoted, with a smile.

"That's Margaret," he murmured rapturously.

"It's a poor kind of man that gives up hope until he lies in his coffin, and even then—" and she nodded thoughtfully, as though tempted to a descent into metaphysics.

"Let us talk of bridal wreaths. They are very much nicer to think of than coffins when one is discussing Margaret Brandt."

"She is very sweet and very beautiful—"

"There never was anyone like her in this world—unless it was my mother and yourself."

"Let Margaret be first with you, my boy. That also is as it should be. Neither your dear mother nor I stand in need of empty compliments. Margaret Brandt is worthy any good man's whole heart, and perhaps I can be of some help to you. But, all the same, remember what I've said. You may be too late in the field."

"You are just the splendidest old lady in the world," he said exuberantly; and added, with a touch of gloom, "She was talking of going off to the Riviera."

"Ah, then, I suppose I shall be in eclipse also, until she returns."

"Oh no, you won't. We can talk of her, you know," at which Lady Elspeth's eyes twinkled merrily.

"What would you say to convoying a troublesome old lady to the Riviera, yourself, Jock?"

"You?" and he jumped up delightedly,—and just at that point old Hamish opened the door of the cosy room, and announced—

"Miss Brandt, mem!"

"Miss Brandt, mem!" announced old Hamish, in as dry and matter-of-fact a voice as though it were only, "Here's the doctor, mem!" or "Dinner's ready, mem!" and Margaret herself came in, rosy-faced and bright-eyed from the kiss of the wind outside.

Lady Elspeth laughed enjoyably at the sight of her, and touched the bell for tea.

"You are always like a breath from the heather to me, my dear, or a glimpse of Schiehallion," said she, as they kissed, and Graeme stood reverently looking on, as at a holy rite.

"Oh, surely I'm not as rugged and wrinkled as all that!" laughed Margaret. "And I certainly am not bald. How do you do, Mr. Graeme?"

"There is no need to ask you that question, at any rate," he said, with visible appreciation.

"I have loved Schiehallion all my life," said Lady Elspeth. "To me there is no mountain in the world to compare with it. You see how one's judgment is biassed by one's affections. And how is Mrs. Pixley to-day, my dear?"

"She is much as usual, dear Lady Elspeth. She is never very lively, you know. If anything, I think she is, perhaps, a trifle less lively than usual just now."

"And Mr. Pixley is as busied in good works as ever, I suppose."

"As busy as ever—outside,"—at which gentle thrust the others smiled.

"It's all very well to laugh," remonstrated Margaret, "but truly, you know, philanthropy, like charity, would be none the less commendable to its relations if it sometimes remembered that it had a home. I sometimes think that if ever there was a deserving case it is poor Aunt Susan."

"And young Mr. Pixley? Doesn't he liven you up?" asked Lady Elspeth. "He is very good company, I am told."

"Oh, Charles is excellent company. If we didn't see him now and again the house would be like a tomb. But he's not there all the time, and we have relapses. He has his own rooms elsewhere, you know. And I'm really not surprised. It taxes even him to lighten the deadly dulness of Melgrave Square."

"It must be a great comfort to Mrs. Pixley to have you with her, my dear."

"I can't make up for all she lacks in other directions," said Margaret, with a shake of the head. "I get quite angry with Uncle Jeremiah sometimes. He is so—so absorbed in benefiting other people that he—Well, you can understand how delightful it is to be able to run in here and find the sun always shining."

"Thank you, my dear," said Lady Elspeth, with a twinkle in the brown eyes. "Some people carry their own sunshine with them wherever they go."

"And some people decidedly don't," said Margaret, who was evidently suffering from some unusual exhibition of Pixleyism.

"It is generally possible to find a ray or so somewhere about, if you know where to look for it," suggested Graeme.

"I was just accusing Jock of coming here as regularly as the milkman," twinkled Lady Elspeth.

"We have a community of tastes, you see," he said, looking across at Margaret. "I also have a craving for sunshine, and I naturally come where I know it is to be found," and Lady Elspeth's eyes twinkled knowingly again.

"It's a good conceit of myself I'll be getting, if you two go on like this."

"I'm quite sure you will never think half as well of yourself as your friends do," said Graeme.

"Besides, you might even pass some of the credit on to us for the excellent taste we display."

"Ay, ay! Well, it's good to be young," said Lady Elspeth.

"And it's very good to have delightful old sunbeams for friends."

"To say nothing of the young ones," laughed the old lady.

"They speak for themselves."

"We are becoming quite a mutual admiration society," said Margaret. "Have you been dining with your fellow Friars lately, Mr. Graeme?"

"I'm sorry to say I've been neglecting my privileges in that respect. I haven't been there for an age—not since that last Ladies' Dinner, in fact. You see, I'm an infant there yet, and I scarcely know anybody, and I've been very busy—"

"Chasing sunbeams," suggested Lady Elspeth.

"And other things."

"You are busy on another book?" asked Margaret.

"Just getting one under way. It takes a little time to get things into proper shape, but once it is going, the work is very absorbing and sheer delight. You were talking of going abroad again. Are you still thinking of it?"

"I was hoping to get away. I wanted Aunt Susan to come with me to the Riviera, but she flatly refuses to leave home at present, so I'm afraid that's off."

"Well, now, that's curious. I've been feeling something of an inclination that way myself," said Lady Elspeth. "I wonder if you'd feel like coming with me, Margaret. I don't believe we would quarrel."

"Oh, I would be delighted, dear Lady Elspeth, and I'll promise not to quarrel whatever you do to me."

"Who ever heard of sunbeams quarrelling?" said Graeme gaily, with Lady Elspeth's earlier suggestion to himself dancing in his brain. "But think of London left utterly sunless."

"London will never miss us," said Margaret. "It still has bridge, and we are neither of us players."

And then, having an appointment from which he could not escape, and knowing that they always enjoyed a little personal chat, he reluctantly took his leave, and left them to the discussion of their new plans.

III

He had met Margaret Brandt for the first time at a Ladies' Banquet of the Whitefriars Club.

Providence,—I insist upon this. No mere chance set them next to one another at that hospitable board,—Providence, forecasting the future, placed them side by side, and he was introduced to her by his good friend Adam Black, who had the privilege of her acquaintance and sat opposite enjoying them greatly.

For they were both eminently good to look upon;—Margaret, tall and slender, and of a most gracious figure and bearing, with thoughtful, dark-blue eyes, a very charming face accentuated by the characteristics of her northern descent, and a wealth of shining brown hair coiled about her shapely head;—Graeme, tall, clean-built, of an outdoor complexion, with nothing of the student about him save his deep, reflective eyes, and the little lines in the corners which wrinkled up so readily at the overflowing humours of life.

It was Charles Pixley—Charles Svendt Pixley, to accord him fullest justice, which I am most anxious to do—who brought her, and to that extent we are his debtors.

Though why Pixley should be a Whitefriar passes one's comprehension. His pretensions to literature were, I should say, bounded by his Stock Exchange notebook and his betting-book. He had not even read Graeme's latest, though it was genuinely in its second—somewhat limited—edition, and he did not even smile affably when Adam Black introduced them. Graeme, however, had no fault to find with him for that. There were others in like dismal case.

Pixley nodded cursorily at the introduction, with a "How-d'ye-do-who-the-deuce-are-you?" expression on his face. He struck Graeme as not bad-looking, in a somewhat over-fed and self-indulgent fashion, and inclined to superciliousness and self-complacency, if not to actual superiority and condescension. It occurred to him afterwards that this might arise from his absorption in his companion, for he turned again at once to Miss Brandt and began chattering like a lively and intelligent parrot.

Graeme was one of the silent and observant ones, and he could not but think how beneficent Nature is in casting us in many moulds. If we were all built alike, he thought, and all dribbled smart inanities, and nothing but inanities, with the glibness of a Charles Pixley, what a world it would be!

However, it was Charles Pixley who brought Margaret Brandt to that dinner, and Graeme sat on the other side of her there. And so, Charles Svendt—blessings on thee, unworthy friar though thou be!

And presently, Miss Brandt, wearying no doubt of perdrix, perdrix, toujours perdrix,—that is to say of Charles's sprightly chatter, of which she doubtless got more than enough at home,—essayed conversation with the silent one at her other side, and, one may suppose, found it more to her taste, or more of a novelty, than the Pixley outflow.

For, once started, she and Graeme talked together most of the evening—breaking off reluctantly to drink various toasts to people in whom they had, at the moment, no remotest interest whatever, and recovering the thread of their conversation before they resumed their seats.

Only one toast really interested Graeme, and that was "The Ladies—the Guests of the Evening"; and that he drank right heartily, with his eyes on Miss Brandt's sparkling face, and if it had been left to himself he would have converted it from plural to singular and drunk to her alone.

Adam Black, excellent fellow, and gifted beyond most with wisdom and insight, and the condensed milk of human kindness, took upon himself the burden of Pixley, and engaged that eminent financier so deeply in talk concerning matters of import, that Miss Brandt and Graeme found themselves at liberty to enjoy one another to their hearts' content.

They talked on many subjects—tentatively, and as sounding novel depths—in a way that occasioned one of them, at all events, very great surprise. Indeed, it seemed to him afterwards that, for a silent and observant man, he had been led into quite unwonted, but none the less very enjoyable, ways. He went home that night feeling very much as Columbus must have done when his New World swam before his eyes in misted glory. He too had sighted a new world. He had discovered Margaret Brandt.

She had travelled widely over Europe, he learned, and was looking forward with eagerness to another tour in the near future. They discovered a common liking for many of the places she had visited.

She was a wide and intelligent reader. To him it was a rare pleasure to meet one.

"New places, and new books, and new people are always a joy to me," she said, in a glow of naïve enthusiasm. And then she blushed slightly lest he should discover a personal application in the last-named, or even in the last two.

But Graeme was thinking of her, and was formulating her character from the delicious little bits of self-revelation which slipped out every now and again.

"Yes," he said, "new things are very enjoyable, and in these times there is no lack of them. The tendency, I should say, is towards superfluity. But new places—! There are surely not many left except the North Pole and the South. Everybody goes everywhere nowadays, and you tumble over friends in Damascus and find your tailor picnicking on the slopes of Lebanon."

Now, as it chanced,—if you admit such a thing as chance in so tangled a coil as this complex world of ours,—Adam Black had just tucked Charles Pixley into a close little argumentative corner, and given him food for contemplation, and catching Graeme's last remark, he smiled across the table, and in a word of four letters dropped a seed into several lives which bore odd fruit and blossom.

"Ever been to Sark, Graeme?" he asked.

"Sark? No. Let me see—"

"Channel Islands. You go across from Guernsey. If ever you want relief from your fellows—to finish a book, or to start one, or just to grizzle and find yourself—try Sark. It's the most wonderful little place, and it's amazing how few people know it."

Then Charles Pixley bethought him of a fresh line of argument, and engaged Black, and was promptly shown the error of his ways; and Margaret Brandt and Graeme resumed their discussion of places and books and people. And before that evening ended, with such affinity of tastes, their feet were fairly set in the rosy path of friendship.

Now that is how it all began, and that explains what happened afterwards when the right time came.

Chance, forsooth! We know better.

IV

Not long after that dinner, Lady Elspeth Gordon came up to town for the first time after her husband's death.

She had been John Graeme's mother's closest friend, and when he was left alone in the world, the dear old lady, before she had fully recovered from her own sore loss, took upon herself a friendly supervision of him and his small affairs, and their intercourse was very delightful.

For Lady Elspeth knew everybody worth knowing, and all that was to be known about the rest; and those gentle brown eyes of hers had missed little of what had gone on around her since she first came to London, fifty years before. She had known Wellington, and Palmerston, and John Russell, and Disraeli, and Gladstone, and Louis Napoleon, and Garibaldi, and many more. She was a veritable golden link with the past, and a storehouse of reminiscence and delightful insight into human nature.

And—since she knew everyone worth knowing, Graeme very soon discovered that she knew Margaret Brandt, and Miss Brandt's very frequent visits to Phillimore Gardens proved that she was an acceptable visitor there.

Upon that, his own visits to Lady Elspeth naturally became still more frequent than before,— approximating even, as she had said, the record of the milkman,—and, though his dear old friend might rate him gently as to the motives for his coming, he had every reason to believe that her sympathies were with him, and that she would do what she could to further his hopes.

He had never, however, openly discussed Margaret with her until that afternoon of which I have already spoken.

Miss Brandt, you see, was always most graciously kind and charming whenever they met. But that was just her natural self. She was charming and gracious to everyone—even to Charles Pixley, the while he swamped her with inane tittle-tattle, and higher proof of grace than that it would be difficult to imagine.

And, since she was charming to all, Graeme felt that he could base no solid hopes on her gracious treatment of himself, though the quiet recollection of every smallest detail of it would set him all aglow with hope for days after each chance meeting. And so he had never ventured to discuss the matter with Lady Elspeth, and would not have done so that afternoon had she not herself opened it.

The dear old lady's encouragement, however, deepened and strengthened his hopes, in spite of her insidious hints concerning Mr. Pixley's possible intentions. For she was a shrewd, shrewd woman, and those soft brown eyes of hers saw far and deep. And, since she bade him hope, hope he would, though every brick in London town became a Pixley set on thwarting him.

The fact of Margaret's means being, for the present at all events, so much larger than his own, he would not allow to trouble him. It was Margaret herself he wanted, and had wanted long before he heard she had money. The troublesome accident of her possessions should not come between them if he could help it. He did not for one moment believe she would ever think so ill of him as to believe that he wanted her for anything but herself. And in any case, if kind Providence bestowed her upon him, he would insist on her money being all settled on herself absolutely and irrevocably.

Since that never-to-be-forgotten dinner, they had come across one another at Lady Elspeth's with sufficient frequency to open the eyes of that astute old lady to the heart-state of one of them at all events. Possibly she knew more of the heart and mind of the other than she cared to say in plain words; but, as a woman, she would naturally abide by the rules of the game. In the smaller games of life it is woman's privilege, indeed, to stretch and twist all rules to suit her own convenience, but in this great game of love, woman stands by woman and the womanly rules of the game—unless, indeed, she craves the stakes for herself, in which case—

And so—although Lady Elspeth favoured him, that afternoon, only with vague generalities as to the pleasures of hope, and afforded him no solid standing-ground for the sole of his hopeful foot, but left him to discover that for himself, as was only right and proper—his heart stood high, and he looked forward with joyous anticipation to the future.

The radiant sun of all his rosy heavens was Margaret Brandt, and he would not for one moment admit the possibility of its clouding by anything of the name of Pixley.

V

Graeme had not the entrée of the Pixley mansion.

Mr. Pixley he knew, by repute only, as the head of Pixley's, the great law-firm, in Lincoln's Inn. Mrs. Pixley he had never met.

Mr. Pixley was a bright and shining light—yea, a veritable light-house—of respectability and benevolence, and bushel coverings were relegated to their proper place outside his scheme of life. His charities were large, wide-spread, religiously advertised in the donation columns of the daily papers, and doubtless palliated the effects of multitudes of other people's sins.

He was a church-warden, president and honorary treasurer of numerous philanthropical societies—in a word, at once a pillar and corner-stone of his profession, his church, and his country.

He was also a smug little man with a fresh, well-fed face, bordered by a touch of old-fashioned, gray side-whisker, rather outstanding blue eyes, and he carried, and sometimes used as it was intended to be used, a heavy gold pince-nez, which more frequently, however, acted as a kind of lightning-conductor for the expression of his feelings. A pince-nez of many parts:—now it was a scalping-knife, slaughtering the hopes of some harried victim of the law; and again, it was a bâton beating time to a hymn or the National Anthem; possibly it was, in moments of relaxation, a jester's wand poking fun at ancient cronies, though indeed a somewhat full-blooded imagination is required for that. I have heard that once when, in the fervour of a speech, Mr. Pixley dropped his pince-nez among the reporters below, he was utterly unable to continue until the fetish was recovered and handed back to him. It is an undoubted fact that though you might forget the exact lines of Mr. Pixley's face and even his words, you never forgot the fascinating evolutions of his heavy gold pince-nez. Like a Frenchman's hands, it told even more than his face or his words.

He had a good voice, and a deportment which had, without doubt, been specially created for the chairmanship of public meetings. And he was Margaret Brandt's uncle by marriage, her guardian and trustee, and the father of Charles Svendt, on whose account Lady Elspeth had thought well to throw out warning hints of possible paternal intentions respecting Margaret and her fortune.

From every point of view Graeme detested Mr. Pixley, though he had never passed a word with him. He was too perfect, too immaculate. His "unco' guidness," as Lady Elspeth would have said, bordered on ostentation. The sight and sound of him aroused in some people a wild inclination towards unaccustomed profanity and wallowing in the mire. He was so undisguisedly and self-satisfiedly better than his fellows that one felt his long and flawless life almost in the nature of a rebuke if not an affront. He was too obtrusively good for this world. One could not but feel that if he had been cut off in his youth, and buried under a very white marble slab and an appropriate inscription, both he and the world would have been far more comfortably circumstanced. And John Graeme devoutly wished he had been so favoured, for, in that case, he could neither have been Margaret's uncle, trustee, nor guardian, and it is possible that there would also have been no Charles Svendt Pixley to trouble the course of his own true love.

But of Charles Svendt I have no harsh word to say. He could not help being his father's son, and one must not blame him for the unavoidable. And, in most respects, he was as unlike his worthy parent as circumstances permitted.

He was on the Stock Exchange and doing well there. He had very comfortable rooms near St. James's Square, and enjoyed life in his own way and at his own not inconsiderable expense. When Margaret Brandt was at home, however, he was much at his father's house in Melgrave Square.

He made no pretence to unco' guidness whatever. He subscribed to nothing outside the House, with two exceptions—the Dogs' Home at Battersea, and the Home of Rest for Aged Horses at Acton—signs of grace both these offerings, I take it!

To all other demands he invariably replied,—"Can't burn the candle at both ends, my dear sir. The governor charitables for the whole family. He'll give you something if you'll let him head the list and keep it standing."

No, we have no fault to find with Charles Svendt. Time came when he was weighed and not found wanting.

Graeme and he had run across one another occasionally—at the Travellers' Club and elsewhere—but their acquaintance had never ripened to the point of introduction till that night at the Whitefriars' dinner. After that they were on nodding terms, but not much more, until—well, until later.

So, though there was hope in his heart, born of Lady Elspeth's approval and quiet suggestings, John Graeme was still somewhat doubtful as to Margaret Brandt's feelings towards him, and quite at a loss how to arrive at a more exact knowledge of them.

Too precipitate an advance might end in utter rout. And opportunities of approach were all too infrequent for his wishes.

Their chance meetings were rare and exquisite pleasures,—to be looked forward to with an eagerness that held within it the strange possibility of pain through sheer excess of longing;—to be enjoyed like the glory of a fleeting dream;—to be looked back upon with touches of regret at opportunities missed;—to be dwelt upon for days and nights with alternate hope and misgiving, with the rapturous recalling of every tone of the sweet voice, of every word it had uttered, of every gracious gesture, and every most minute and subtle change in the sweetest face and the frankest and most charming eyes in the world.

VI

Their acquaintance had blossomed thus far, when a dire disaster happened and justified all his fears.

He ran gaily up the steps of Lady Elspeth's house one afternoon, brimming with hope that kindly fortune might bring Margaret that way that day, and was hurled into deepest depths of despair by old Hamish as soon as he opened the door.

"Ech, Mr. Graeme!" said the old man, with his grizzled old face tuned to befitting concern. "Her leddyship's awa' to Inverstrife at a moment's notice. She had a tailegram late last night saying the little leddy—the Countess, ye ken—was very bad, and would she go at once. And she and Jannet were off by the first train this morning. They aye send for us, ye ken, when anything by-ordinar's to the fore. It's the little leddy's first, ye understand, and ye'll mind that her own mother died two years ago."

"Well, well! I'm sorry you've had such an upsetting, Hamish. And there's no knowing when Lady Elspeth will return, I suppose?"

"It a' depends on the little leddy, Mr. Graeme. Her leddyship will stay till everything's all right, ye may depend upon that. She told me to give you her kindest regairds and beg you to excuse her not writing. They were all on their heads, so to speak, as ye can understand."

"Yes, of course. Well, we must just hope the little lady will pull through all right. If I don't hear from Lady Elspeth I will call now and again for your latest news."

"Surely, sir. Jannet'll be letting me know, if her leddyship's too busy. Miss Brandt was here about hauf an hour ago," he added, with unmoved face;—to think of any man, even so ancient a man as old Hamish, being able to state a fact so great as that with unmoved face! And there was actually no sign of reminiscent and lingering after-glow perceptible in him!—but Graeme was not at all sure that there was not a veiled twinkle away down in the depths of his little blue-gray eyes.

"Ah! Miss Brandt has been here! She would be surprised too—"

"She was that, sir,—and a bit disappointed, it seemed to me—"

Yes, there was a twinkle in the old fellow's eyes! Oh, he knew, he knew without a doubt. Trust old Hamish for not missing much that was to the fore. He and his old wife, Jannet Gordon, had been in Lady Elspeth's service for over forty years, ever since her leddyship married into the family, and Lady Elspeth trusted them both implicitly and discussed most matters very freely with them. The dilatations of those three shrewd old people, concerning things in general, and the men and women of their acquaintance in particular, would have been rare, rare hearing.

"Well, I'll call again in a day or two, Hamish," and he went away along the gloomy streets, which were all ablaze with soft April sunshine, and yet to him had suddenly become darkened. For he saw at a glance all that this was like to do for him.

PART THE SECOND

I

The rare delight of his meetings with Margaret was at an end. Bluff Fortune had slammed the door in his face, and White-handed Hope had folded her golden wings and sat moping with melancholy mien.

He wandered into Kensington Gardens, but the daffodils swung their heads despondently, and the gorgeous masses of hyacinths made him think of funeral plumes on horses' heads.

He went on into the Park. She might be driving there, and he might catch glimpse of her. But she was not, and all the rest were less than nothing to him.

He found himself at Hyde Park Corner and back again at Kensington Gate. But the door was still closed in his face, and he longed for the sight of somebody else's as he had never longed before.

The post was of course open to him, but, at this stage at all events, he felt that the written word would be eminently inadequate and unsatisfying.

He wanted, when he approached that mighty question, to look into her eyes and see her answer in their pure depths before it reached her lips,—to watch the fluttering heart-signals in her sweet face and learn from them more than all the words in the world could tell. Letters were, at best, to actual speech but as actual speech would be to all that his heart-quickened eyes would discover if he could but ask her face to face.

And besides—he would have wished to make his footing somewhat surer before putting everything to the test.

But, since matters had gone thus far, it was quite out of the question to let them stop there unresolved. Either the precious cargo must be brought safely into port or the derelict must be sunk and the fairway cleared. The question was—how to proceed?

The unwritten laws of social usage would hardly permit him to carry the Pixley mansion by assault and insist on seeing Miss Brandt. Besides, that might expose her to annoyance, and that he would not upon any consideration.

And so, before he reached his rooms, his mind was groping clumsily after written phrases which should in some sort express that which was in him without saying too much too soon,—which should delicately hint his regrets at this sudden curtailment of their acquaintance, and leave it for her to say whether or no she regarded the matter in the same light.

Lady Elspeth's sudden summons to the north furnished an acceptable text. Margaret was not to know that he knew of her call at Phillimore Gardens. It was surely but a friendly act on his part to inform her of a matter so nearly concerning one who was dear to them both.

It took a considerable time, however, and the expenditure of much thought and ink and paper, before he succeeded in producing a letter in any degree to his liking. And even when it was written many perusals only served to deepen his doubts.

In any case, it was the best he could do under the circumstances, and since he could not see her answer in her eyes or in her face, the words she would send him in reply would surely afford his quickened perceptions some indication of her feeling, though nothing to what her presence would have told him.

So he wrote—

"Dear Miss Brandt,—When I called at Lady Elspeth Gordon's this afternoon, I learned, to my very great regret, in which I dare to hope you may participate, that our dear old friend had been summoned to Inverstrife at almost a moment's notice, by the sudden illness of her niece, the Countess of Assynt.

"I trust her visit may not need to be a very extended one, but Lady Elspeth is such a tower of strength to all who seek her help that she is not likely to return so long as she can be of any possible assistance to her friends.

"For reasons which, perhaps, I need not particularise, her sudden departure is to me a loss beyond its apparent magnitude. The hours I have spent at her house have been among the brightest of my life. You also have enjoyed her friendship. I venture to hope that you also will miss her.

"Should I not have the pleasure of seeing you for some little time, I would beg of you to bear me in your kindly remembrance.—Sincerely yours,

"JOHN C. GRAEME."

Did it say too much? Would she look upon it as an overstepping of the limits their acquaintance had reached?

Did it say enough? Could she possibly overlook the things he would so dearly have liked to say but had left unsaid?

Did it say too little? Could she possibly deem it an unnecessary liberty, and cold at that? He did not think she could by any possibility look at it in that light.

But after it was at last surely lodged in the pillar-box, all these doubts came back upon him with tenfold force, and his sleep that night would have been short-commons for a nightingale.

She would get his letter by the first post in the morning. Would she answer it at once? Or would she wait half a day considering it?

Either course held hopeful possibilities. A prompt answer would surely suggest a concurrence of feeling. An answer delayed would without doubt mean that she was pondering his words and reading between the lines. So he possessed his soul in patience, of a somewhat attenuated texture, and waited in hope.

But the whole day passed, and the night, and the next morning's post still brought him nothing,— nothing but an intimation from a publisher of excellent standing that he would not decline to look over the manuscript of his next book if he was open to an offer. And this important document he tossed on one side as lightly as if it were a begging letter or a tailor's advertisement.

What were any other letters, or all the letters in the world, to him when the one letter he desired was not there?

All that bright April day he waited indoors, in order to get Margaret's letter the moment it arrived. For how should he wander abroad, in gloomy-blazing streets or desolate-teeming parks with that anxiously-expected letter possibly awaiting him at home?

The callous passage of the last post, after knocking cheerfully at every door but his own, left him wondering and desperate.

Could he by any possibility have addressed his letter wrongly? It was not easy to make a mistake in No. 1 Melgrave Square.

Could it have gone astray? The Post Office was abominably careless at times. One was constantly hearing of letters slipping down behind desks and monstrously delivered twenty years after date. What earthly good would that letter be delivered when he was forty-seven and Margaret Brandt somewhere in the neighbourhood of forty? Truly, it was monstrous, it was abominable that such carelessness should be permitted in the public departments!

Could Margaret have taken umbrage at anything he had said? He conned his rough draft with solicitous care. It seemed new and strange and crude to him. He feared at each word to come upon the one that might have offended her. But no word, no phrase, nothing even of all that he had left unsaid sprang up before his horrified eyes to choke him with a sense of inadequacy, or inadvertency, or trespass.

No sleep got he that night for cudgelling his tired brains for reasons why no answer had come from Margaret.

Could she be ill? She was well enough, two days before, to call at Lady Elspeth's house. But, of course, even in a day one may take a chill and be prostrated.

The possibility of that was brought home to him next morning by his landlady's surprised stare and exclamation at sight of his face.

"Law, Mr. John!"—she had been handmaid to his mother for many years and he was still always Mr. John to her,—"Have you got the influenza too? Everyone seems to have it nowadays."

He reassured her on the point. But every friend he met that day credited him with it, and suggested remedies and precautions sufficient to have made an end of any ordinary man.

He was vexed to think his face so clear an index of his feelings, but, truly, his spirits were none of the best and the weather was enervatingly warm.

It was quite inconceivable to him that Margaret Brandt should, of knowledge and intention, drop their pleasant acquaintance in this fashion. He believed he knew her well enough to know that, even if she had any fault to find with his letter, she would still have replied to it, and would have delicately conveyed her feeling in her answer.

Then, either she had never received it, or, for some good reason or other, she was unable to reply.

He went down to Melgrave Square to make sure that No. 1 was still there. Possibly he might come across Margaret in the neighbourhood. If he did he would know at a glance if she had received his letter.

But No. 1 offered him no explanations. It stood as usual, large and prim and precise, the very acme of solid, sober wealth and assertive moral rectitude. He was strongly tempted to call and ask for Miss Brandt, but it was only ten o'clock in the morning, and the house looked so truly an embodiment in stucco of Mrs. Grundy and Jeremiah Pixley, that he forbore and went on his melancholy way.

First, to his rooms again, to see if by chance the letter had come in his absence. Then, as it had not, to Lady Elspeth Gordon's for old Hamish's latest news, which, in a letter from his wife, was satisfactory as far as it went, but pointed to a protracted stay. And then, with stern resolution, up to Baker Street and away by train to Chesham, for a long day's tramp through the Buckingham hills and dales, by Chenies to Chorley Wood and Rickmansworth, so to weary the body that the wearier brain should get some rest that night.

The sweet soft air and sunshine, the leisurely life of the villages, and the cheerful unfoldings of the spring, in wood and field and hedgerow, brought him to a more hopeful frame of mind. Every sparrow twittered hope. The thrushes and young blackbirds fluted it melodiously. It was impossible to remain unhopeful in such goodly company. Something unexpected, accidental, untoward, had prevented Margaret replying to his letter. Time would clear it up and set him wondering at his lapse from fullest faith.

Also—he would risk even further rebuff. He would write again, and this time he would trust no precarious and problematical post-office. He would drop his letter into the Pixley letter-box himself, and so be sure that it got there.

If then no answer,—to the winds with Mrs. Grundy and all her coils and conventions! He would call and see Margaret himself, and learn from her own eyes and face and lips how matters stood, and Mrs. Grundy might dance and scream on the step outside until she grew tired of the exercise.

There was joy and hope in action once more. Patient waiting on slowly-dying Hope is surely the direst moral and mental torture to which poor humanity can be subjected. That is where woman pre-eminently overpasses man. Woman can wait unmurmuringly on dying Hope till the last breath is gone, then silently take up her burden and go on her way—or, if the strain has been too great, fold quiet hands on quiet heart and follow her dead hopes into the living hope beyond. Man must aye be doing—and as often as not, such natural judgment as he possesses being warped and jangled by the strain of waiting, he succeeds only in making matters worse and a more complete fool of himself.

To be writing to Margaret again was to be living in hope once more.

If nothing came of this, he would call at the Pixley house.

If nothing came of that—he grew valiant in his new access of life—he would beard Jeremiah Pixley in his den in Lincoln's Inn, state clearly how matters stood, and request permission to approach his ward.

After all, this is a free country, and all men are equal under the law, though he had his own doubts as to whether he would find himself quite equal to that gleaming pillar of light, Mr. Jeremiah Pixley.

So he wrote—

"DEAR MISS BRANDT,—I wrote to you a few days ago, giving you the information of our dear friend Lady Elspeth's sudden summons to Inverstrife, to attend her niece, the Countess of Assynt.

"I hope you will not consider it presumption on my part to express the fear that my letter has somehow miscarried—probably through some oversight of my own, or carelessness on the part of the postal authorities.

"You will, I know, be glad to hear that Lady Elspeth accomplished her journey in safety and without undue discomfort. But Lady Assynt's condition makes it probable that her stay may be somewhat prolonged.

"I venture to hope that you may regret this as much as I do. All who enjoyed Lady Elspeth's friendship and hospitality cannot but miss her sorely.

"I hope, however, that I may still have the pleasure of meeting you occasionally elsewhere. When one has not the habit of readily making new friendships one clings the more firmly to those already made.—Sincerely yours,

"JOHN C. GRAEME."

That letter he dropped into the Pixley letterbox himself that night, and so was assured of its delivery. But two days passed in waning hope, and the afternoon of the third found him on the doorstep of No. 1 Melgrave Square.

II

"Miss Brandt?"

The solemn-faced man-servant eyed him suspiciously as a stranger. He looked, to Graeme, like a superannuated official of the Court of Chancery.

"Miss Brandt is not at home, sir."

"Mrs. Pixley?"

"Mrs. Pixley is not at home, sir."

Was he right or wrong, he wondered, in thinking he detected a gleam of satisfied anticipation, of gratified understanding, in the solemn one's otherwise rigid eye—as of one who had been told to expect this and was lugubriously contented that it had duly come to pass?

However, there was nothing more to be done there at the moment. The polite conventions, to say nothing of the law, forbade him the pleasure of hurling the outcast of Chancery into the kennel and forcing his way in. Instead, he hailed a hansom and drove straight to Lincoln's Inn, boldly demanded audience of Mr. Pixley on pressing private business, and presently found himself in the presence.

Mr. Pixley stood on the hearthrug with his back to the fire, and handled his gold pince-nez defensively.

Here also Graeme had an intuition that he was expected, which was somewhat odd, you know, unless his letters had been handed to Mr. Pixley for perusal, which did not seem likely.

Mr. Pixley bowed formally and he responded—the salute before the click of the foils.

Mr. Pixley stood expectant, but by no means inviting of confidences such as his visitor was about to tender him. Rather he seemed fully armed for the defence, especially in the matter of the heavy gold pince-nez, which he held threateningly, after the manner of the headsman of old towards the victim on whom he was about to operate.

"I have taken the liberty of calling, Mr. Pixley," said Graeme,—and Mr. Pixley's manner in subtle fashion conveyed his full recognition of the fact that liberty it undoubtedly was, and that he had no smallest shadow of a right to be there,—"to inquire after Miss Brandt."

"Miss Brandt?" said Mr. Pixley vaguely, as though the name were new and strange to him. Or perhaps it was an endeavour on his part to express the impassable gulf which lay between his visitor and his ward, and the profound amazement he felt at any attempt on his visitor's part to abridge it. He also made a little involuntary preliminary cut at him with the pince-nez, as much as to say, "If this my weapon were of a size commensurate with my wishes and your colossal impudence, your head would lie upon the ground, young man."

"I have had the pleasure of meeting Miss Brandt at Lady Elspeth Gordon's and elsewhere. I think I may claim that we were on terms of friendship. Lady Elspeth has been called from home very suddenly to the bedside of her niece, Lady Assynt, and I have written twice to Miss Brandt and have had no reply. It struck me that she might be ill and I have called to inquire."

This was all lame enough no doubt, and so he felt it, but it was only in the nature of preliminary feinting. They were not yet at grips.

"Ah!" with ponderous deliberation, "you have called to inquire if Miss Brandt is ill. I have pleasure in informing you that she is not."

"I am glad to hear that, at all events. Might I ask if you are aware of any reason why she should not have received my letters—or replied to them?"

"Two questions," said Mr. Pixley, cutting them in slices with his pince-nez, as though they were to be charged up to his visitor at so much per pound. "There is no reason whatever why Miss Brandt should not have received your letters. There may be the best possible reasons why she should not reply to them."

"So far as I have been able to form an opinion of Miss Brandt it is quite unlike her not to have, at all events, acknowledged them."

"Ah! Your opportunities have probably been limited, Mr.—er—"—with a glance at the card—"Graeme, and you may possibly be—from your calling upon me I judge you undoubtedly are—ignorant of the facts of the case," and the gold pince-nez hammered that into the stolid young man's head.

"Perhaps you would be so good as to enlighten me."

"It would perhaps be as well to do so. To be perfectly frank with you, Mr. Graeme, my ward had the very best of reasons for handing your letters to me and not replying to them herself."

"Really! I would esteem it a favour, Mr. Pixley, if you would enlighten me further."

"Certainly!" with an airy wave of the pince-nez. "I intend to do so. The simple fact of my ward's engagement to my son, and that they are looking forward to the celebration of their marriage in something less than three months, will probably suffice to explain Miss Brandt's disinclination to enter into correspondence with a comparative stranger,"—and the pince-nez shredded Graeme's hopes into little pieces and scattered them about the floor.

"Miss Brandt is engaged to your son?" he jerked, feeling not a little foolish, and decidedly downhearted.

"As I have informed you. It is a union to which we have been looking hopefully forward for some time past—a most excellent conjunction of hearts and fortunes. My ward possesses some means, as you are doubtless aware,"—with an insolent thrust of the pince-nez at the would-be suitor's honour,—"and my son is also well provided for in that respect."

"Then—I am afraid my visit is something in the nature of an intrusion." Mr. Pixley bowed his fullest acquiescence in this very proper estimate of his position, and the pince-nez intimated that the way out lay just behind him and that the sooner he took advantage of it the better.

"I can only say, by way of apology," added Graeme, "that I was wholly unaware of what you have just told me. I will wish you good-day, Mr. Pixley."

Mr. Pixley and the pince-nez wafted him towards the door, and the lumpy cobbles of the courtyard outside seemed to him, for the moment, absolutely typical of life.

He went back home numbed and sore at heart. It was hard to believe this of Margaret Brandt.

And yet—he said to himself—it was wholly he who was to blame. He had deceived himself. He had wished to believe what he had so earnestly desired should be. Possibly he had closed his eyes to facts and indications which might have enlightened him if he had been on the look-out for them. Possibly— well, there!—he had played the fool unconsciously, and he was not the first. It only remained for him now to play the man.

He felt sore, and bruised, and run down, and for the moment somewhat at odds with life. He would get away from it all to some remote corner, to rest for a time and recover tone, and then to work. For work, after all, is the mighty healer and tonic, and when it is to one's taste there are few wounds it cannot salve.

PART THE THIRD

I

Six o'clock next morning found Graeme on the deck of the Ibex as she threaded her way swiftly among the bristling black rocks that guard the coast of Guernsey.

Herm and Jethou lay sleeping in the eye of the sun. Beyond them lay a filmy blue whaleback of an island which he was told was Sark, and it was to Sark he was bound.

And wherefore Sark, when, within reasonable limits, all the wide world lay open to him?

Truly, it might not be easy to say. But this I know,—having so far learned the lesson of life, though missing much else—that at times, perhaps at all times, when we think our choice of ways our very own,—when we stand in doubt at the crossroads of life, and then decide on this path or that, and pride ourselves on the exercise of our high prerogative as free agents,—the result, when we look back, bears in upon our hearts the mighty fact that a higher mind than our own has been quietly at work, shaping our ends and moulding and rounding our lives. We may doubt it at times. We may take all the credit to ourselves for dangers passed and tiny victories won, but in due time the eyes of our understanding are opened—and we know.

Possibly it was the rapt eulogiums of his friend Black—who had spent the previous summer in Sark, and had ever since been seeking words strong enough in which to paint its charms—that forced its name to the front when he stood facing the wide world, that lacked, for him at all events, a Margaret Brandt, and was therefore void and desolate.

"If ever you seek perfect peace, relief from your fellows, and the simple life, try Sark—and see that you live in a cottage!" he remembered Adam Black murmuring softly, as they sat smoking at the Travellers' one night, shortly after that memorable dinner of the Whitefriars'. And then he had heaved a sigh of regret at thought of being where he was when he might have been in Sark.

Graeme knew nothing whatever of Sark save what his friend had let fall at times. "Jersey, Guernsey, Alderney, and Sark," recalled his short-jacket and broad-collar days, and the last of the quartette had always somehow conjured up in his mind the image of a bleak, inaccessible rock set in a stormy sea, where no one lived if he could possibly find shelter elsewhere,—an Ultima Thule, difficult of access and still more difficult of exit, a weather-bound little spot into which you scrambled precariously by means of boats and ladders, and out of which you might not be able to get for weeks on end.

But Sark was to hold a very different place in his mind henceforth. The name of Calais burnt itself into the heart of Queen Mary by reason of loss. Surely on John Graeme's heart the name of Sark may hope to find itself in living letters, for in Sark he was to find more than he had lost—new grace and charm in life, new hopes, new life itself.

He had gone straight home from Lincoln's Inn, and packed his portmanteau, knowing only that he was going away somewhere out of things, caring little where, so long as it was remote and lonely.

Fellow-man—and especially woman—was distasteful to him at the moment. He craved only Solitude the Soother, and Nature the Healer.

He packed all he thought he might need for a couple of months' stay, and among other things the manuscript he had been at work upon until more pressing matters intervened. He felt, indeed, no slightest inclination towards it, or anything else, at present. But that might come, for Work and he were tried friends.

He wrote briefly to Lady Elspeth telling her how things were with him, and that he was going away for a time. He did not tell her where, for the simple reason that at the moment of writing he did not know himself. Sark came into his mind later.

He told his landlady that he was going away for a change, and she remarked in motherly fashion that she was glad to hear it, and it was high time too. He told her to keep all his letters till he sent for them. He had no importunate correspondents, his next book was as good as placed, and all he desired at the moment was to cut the painter, and drift into some quiet backwater where he could lie up till life should wear a more cheerful face.

And so no single soul knew where he had gone, and he said to himself, somewhat bitterly, and quite untruthfully, that no single soul cared.

He had paced the deck all night. The swift smooth motion of the boat, with a slight slow roll in it, was very soothing; and the first tremulous hints of the dawn, and the wonder of its slow unfolding, and the coming of the sun were things to be remembered.

The cold gaunt aloofness, and weltering loneliness of the Casquets appealed to him strongly. Just the kind of place, he said to himself, for a heart-sick traveller to crawl into and grizzle until he found himself again.

As they turned and swung in straight between the little lighthouse on White Rock and Castle Cornet, the bright early sunshine was bathing all the rising terraces of St. Peter Port in a golden haze. Such a quaint medley of gray weathered walls and mellowed red roofs, from which the thin blue smoke of early fires crept lazily up to mingle with the haze above! Such restful banks of greenery! Such a startling blaze of windows flashing back unconscious greetings to the sun! This too was a sight worth remembering. For a wounded soul he was somewhat surprised at the enjoyment these things afforded him.

A further surprise was the pleasure he found in the reduction of a hearty appetite at an hotel on the front. Come! He was not as hard hit as he had thought! There was life in the young dog yet.

But these encouraging symptoms were doubtless due to the temporary exhilaration of the journey. The workaday bustle of the quays renewed his desire for the solitary places, and he set out to find means of transport to the little whalebacked island out there in the golden shimmer of the sun.

There was no steamer till the following day, he learned, and delay was not to his mind. So presently he came to an arrangement with an elderly party in blue, with a red-weathered face and grizzled hair, to put him and his two portmanteaux across to Sark for the sum of five shillings English.

"To Havver Gosslin," said the aged mariner, with much emphasis, and a canny look which conveyed to Graeme nothing more than a simple and praiseworthy desire on his part to avoid any possibility of mistake.

"To Sark," said Graeme, with equal emphasis.

"Ay, ay!" said the other; and so it came that the new-comer's initial experience of the little island went far towards the confirmation of the vague ideas of his childhood as to its inaccessibility.

The ancient called to a younger man, and they strolled away along the harbour wall to get the baggage.

II

"Ee see," said the old gentleman, as soon as they had pulled out past Castle Cornet, and had hoisted the masts and two rather dirty sprit sails, and had run out the bowsprit and a new clean jib with a view to putting the best possible face on matters, and were beginning to catch occasional puffs of a soft westerly breeze and to wallow slowly along,—"Ee see, time's o' consekens to me and my son. We got to arn our livin'. An' Havver Gosslin's this side the island an' th' Creux's t'other side, an' th' currents round them points is the very divvle."

"That's all right, as long as you land me in Sark."

"The very divvle," and the grizzled head wagged reminiscently. "I seen 'em go right up to Casquets and haf-way to Jarsey trying to get across to Sark. An' when time's o' consekens an' you got to arn your livin', you don' want to be playin' 'bout Casquets an' Jarsey 'stid of gittin' 'cross to Sark an' done wi' it."

"Not a bit of it. You're quite right. Try some of this,"—as he began fumbling meaningly with a black stump of a pipe.

He filled up, and passed on the pouch to his son, who was lying on the thwarts forward, and he also filled up and passed it back with a nod.

"What's this?" asked Graeme.

"Jetto. Mr. Lee—Sir Austin 'e is now—brother o' Passon Lee o' the Port," with a backward jerk of the head, "'e rents it."

"Live there?"

"Naw—rabbits."

"And the bigger island yonder?"

"'At's Harm. 'T's a Garman man has that—Prince Bloocher, they calls him. Keeps kangyroos there an' orstrichers an' things. Don't let annybody ashore there now 'cept just to Shell Beach, which he can't help."

They struck straight across to the long high-ridged island in front, and Graeme's untutored eyes found no special beauty in it.

There was about it, however, a vague gray aloofness which chimed with his spirit, a sober austerity as of a stricken whale,—a mother-whale surely, for was not her young one there at her nose,—fled here to heal her wound perchance, and desirous only of solitude.

But, as they drew nearer, the vague blue-gray bloom of the whaleback resolved itself into a mantle of velvet green, which ran down every rib and spine until it broke off sharp at varying heights and let the bare bones through; and all below the break was clean naked rock—black, cream-yellow, gray, red, brown,—with everywhere a tawny fringe of seaweed, since the tide was at its lowest. Below the fringe the rocks were scoured almost white, and whiter still at their feet, like a tangled drapery of ragged lace, was the foam of the long slow seas.

And the solid silhouette of the island broke suddenly into bosky valleys soft with trees and bracken, and cliff-ringed bays, with wide-spread arms of tumbled rock whose outer ends were tiny islets and hungry reefs.

"Brecqhou," said the ancient mariner, as they swung past a long green island with beetling cliffs, and yawning caverns, and comet-like rushes of white foam among the chaos of rocks below.

Then they swirled through a tumbling race, where the waters came up writhing and boiling from strife with hidden rocks below,—past the dark chasm between Brecqhou and the mainland of Sark, through which the race roared with the voice of many waters—and so into a quiet haven where hard-worked boats lay resting from their labours.

There was a beach of tumbled rocks and seaweed at the head of the bay, and there the grim cliffs fell back into a steep green gully which suggested possibility of ascent. But instead of running in there, the sails were furled and the boat nosed slowly towards the overhanging side of the cliff, where a broad iron ladder fell precariously into the water with its top projecting out beyond its base, so that to climb it one had to lie on one's back, so to speak.

The ancient one eyed his passenger whimsically as the boat stole up to the rungs, so Graeme permitted himself no more than a careless glance at the forbidding ladder and asked, "How about the baggage?"

"We'll see to et," grinned the ancient, and stood, hands on hips and face twisted into a grim smile, while the stranger laid hold of the rusty iron and started upwards, with no slightest idea where the end of the venture might land him.

With the after-assistance of a neighbour of somewhat more genial construction,—inasmuch as it at all events stood upright, and did not lean over the opposite way of ladders in general,—the top rung landed him on a little platform, whence a rope and some foot-holes in the rock, and finally a zigzag path, invited further ascent still.

The portmanteaux were hauled up by a rope and shouldered by his guardian angels, and they toiled slowly up the steep.

Each step developed new beauties behind and on either side. At the top he would fain have rested to drink it all in, but his guides went stolidly on,—towards drink of a more palpable description, he doubted not; and he remembered that time was of consekens, and tore himself away from that most wonderful view and panted after them.

The zigzag path led round clumps of flaming gorse to a gap in a rough stone wall, and so to a tall granite pillar which crowned the cliff and commemorated a disaster. It was erected, he saw, to the memory of a

Mr. Jeremiah Pilcher who had been drowned just below in attempting the passage to Guernsey. He had but one regret at the moment—that it was not instead to the memory of Mr. Jeremiah Pixley.

Down verdant lanes—past thatched cottages, past a windmill, past houses of more substantial mien, with a glimpse down a rolling green valley—

"Hotel?" asked the ancient abruptly, from beneath his load.

"No, I want rooms in some cottage. Can you—"

"John Philip," said the ancient one didactically, and trudged on, and finally dumped his share of the burden at the door of what looked like a house but was a shop, in fact the shop.

He went inside and Graeme followed him. A genial-faced elderly man, with gray hair and long gray beard and gray shirt-sleeves, leaned over the counter, talking in an unknown tongue to a blue-guernseyed fisherman, and a quiet-faced old lady in a black velvet hair-net stood listening.

They all looked up and saluted the ancient one with ejaculations of surprise in the unknown tongue, and Graeme stared hard at the gray-bearded man, while they all discussed him to his face.

"Mr. De Carteret," said the ancient at last, with a jerk of the head towards Gray-Beard. "He tell you where to find rooms."

"Thanks! Do you speak any English, Mr. De Carteret?"

The pleasant old face broke into a smile. "I am En-glish," he said, with a quaint soft intonation, and as one who speaks a foreign tongue, and beamed genially on his young compatriot.

"That's all right then. Do you know you're very like Count Tolstoi?"

"I haf been told so, but I do not know him. What is it you would like, if you please to tell me?"

"I want a sitting-room and a bedroom for a month or so, perhaps more,—not at an hotel. I want to be quiet and all to myself."

"Ah—you don' want an hotel. You want to be quiet," and he nodded understandingly. "But the hotels is quiet joost now—"

"I'd sooner have rooms in a cottage if I can get them."

Count Tolstoi turned to the fisherman to whom he had been speaking, and discussed the matter at length with him in the patois.

Then, to Graeme, "If you please to go with him. His wife has roomss to let. You will be quite comfortable there."

Graeme thanked him, and as soon as he had settled satisfactorily with his boatmen, his new keeper picked up both his bags, and led him along a stony way past the post-office, to a creeper-covered cottage, which turned a cold shoulder to the road and looked coyly into a little courtyard paved with cobble-stones and secluded from the outer world by a granite wall three feet high.

And as they went, the young man asked his silent guide somewhat doubtfully, "And do you speak English?"

"Oh yes. We all speak English," he said, with a quiet smile, "except a few of the older folks, maybe, and they mostly understand it though they're slow to talk."

"And your name?"

"John Carré,"—which he pronounced Caury.

"Now that's very odd," laughed Graeme, and stood to enjoy it. "My name is Corrie too, and John Corrie at that."

"So!" said the other quietly, with a glance from under his brows which might mean surprise or only gentle doubt as to the stranger's veracity. And, so odd was the coincidence, that the newcomer saw no necessity to spoil it by telling him that his forebears had left him also the family name of Graeme.

A large brown dog, smooth of hair and of a fine and thoughtful countenance, got up from the doorstep and gave them courteous greeting, and a small, white, rough-coated terrier hurried out of the kitchen and twisted himself into kinks of delight at sound of their voices. And that decided it before ever Graeme looked at the rooms. For if there was one thing he liked when he wanted to be alone, it was the friendly companionship of a couple of cheerful dogs.

And that is how he came,—without any special intent that way, but through, as one might say, a purely accidental combination of circumstances—to be living in that cottage in the Rue Lucas in the little isle of Sark, and under a name that was indeed his own but not the whole of his own. And herein the future was looking after itself and preparing the way for that which was to be.

IV

The cottage was apparently empty. His guide and namesake looked into the kitchen, and called up a stair which led out of it, but got no answer.

"She will be up at the house," he said, and turned and went off up the garden behind, while the dogs raced on in front to show the way.

Through a cleft in the high green bank topped by a thick hedge of hawthorn, they came out into a garden of less utilitarian aspect. Here were shrubs and flowers, palms and conifers and pale eucalyptus trees, clumps of purple iris and clove pinks, roses just coming to the bud, and beyond, a very charming bungalow, built solidly of gray granite and red tiles, with a wide verandah all round. A pleasant-faced woman in a large black sunbonnet came out of the open front door as they went up the path.

"My wife," murmured Carré, and proceeded quietly to explain matters in an undertone of patois.

"I hope you speak English also, Mrs. Carré," said Graeme.

"Oh yess," with a quick smile. "We are all English here."

"Surely you are Welsh," he said, for he had met just that same cheerful type of face in Wales.

"Noh, I am Sark," she smiled again. "I can gif you a sitting-room and a bet-room"—and they proceeded to business, and then the dogs escorted them back to the cottage, to see the stranger fairly inducted to his new abode, and to let him understand that they rejoiced at his coming and would visit him often.

He thought he would be very comfortable there, but why the sitting-room was not the bedroom he never could understand. For it was only a quarter the size of the other, and its single window looked into a field, and a rough granite wall clothed with tiny rock-weeds hid all view of the road and its infrequent traffic. While the bedroom was a room of size, and its two windows gave on to the covered well and the cobbled forecourt, and offered passers-by, if so inclined, oblique views of its occupant in the act of dressing if he forgot to pull down the blind.

The windows of both rooms were set low in the massive granite walls, and being always wide open, they offered, and indeed invited, easy access to—say, a grave-faced gentlemanly brown dog and a spasmodic rough-coated terrier without a tail, whenever the spirit moved them to incursion, which it invariably did at meal-times and frequently in between.

These two new friends of his—for they were never mere acquaintances, but adopted him into fullest brotherhood at sight—proved no small factors in Graeme's extrication from the depths.

Human companionship, even of the loftiest, most philosophic, most gracious, would, for the time being, have jarred and ruffled his naturally equable spirit. Two only exceptions might have been conceivably possible—some humble, large-souled friend, anxious only to anticipate his slightest wish, desirous only of his company, and—dumb, and so unable to fret him with inane talk; or—Margaret Brandt.

The first he could have endured. The latter—ah, God! How he would have rejoiced in her! The spirit groaned within him at times in agonised longing for her; and the glories of the sweet spring days, in a land where spring is joyous and radiant beyond most, turned gray and cheerless in the shadow of his loss. What Might Have Been stabbed What Was to the heart and let its life-blood run.

But, since neither of these was available, a benignant Providence provided him with friends entirely to his taste. For the great brown hound, Punch, was surely, despite the name men had given him, a nobleman by birth and breeding. Powerful and beautifully made, the sight of his long lithe bounds, as he quartered the cliff-sides in silent chase of fowl and fur, was a thing to rejoice in; so exquisite in its tireless grace, so perfect in its unconscious exhibition of power and restraint. For the brown dog never gave tongue, and he never killed. He chased for the keen enjoyment of the chase, and no man had ever heard him speak.

He was the first dumb dog Graeme had ever come across, and the pathetic yearning in his solemn brown eyes was full of infinite appeal to one who suffered also from an unforgettable loss. He answered to his name with a dignified appreciation of its incongruity, and the tail-less white terrier, more appropriately, to that of Scamp.

V

They were on the very best of terms, these two friends of his, possibly because of their absolute unlikeness,—Punch, large, solemn, imperturbable, with a beautifully-curved slow-waving tail and no voice; Scamp, a bundle of wriggling nerves moved by electricity, with a sharp excited bark and not even the stump of a tail. When he needed to wag he wagged the whole of his body behind his front legs.

These two were sitting watching him expectantly as Mrs. Carré brought in his dinner that first day, and she instantly ordered them out.

Punch rose at once, cast one look of grave appeal at Graeme, as who would say—"Sorry to leave you, but this is the kind of thing I have to put up with,"—and walked slowly away. Scamp grovelled flat and crawled to the door like a long hairy caterpillar.

"Oh, let them stop," said Graeme. "I like them by me," and the culprits turned hopefully with pricked ears and anxious faces.

"Mais non! They are troublesome beasts. Allez, Ponch! Allez, Scamp! A couche!"—and their heads and ears drooped and they slunk away.

But, presently, there came a rustling at the wide-open window which gave on to the field at the back, and Graeme laughed out—and he had not smiled for days—at sight of two deprecatingly anxious faces looking in upon him,—a solemn brown one with black spots above the eloquent grave eyes, and a roguish white one with pink blemishes on a twisting black nose. And while the large brown face loomed steadily above two powerful front paws, the small white face only appeared at intervals as the nervous little body below flung it up to the sill in a series of spasmodic leaps.

"We would esteem it a very great favour, if you are quite sure it would not inconvenience you," said Punch, as plain as speech.

"Do, do, do, do, do give us leave!" signalled Scamp, with every twist of his quivering nose, and every gleam of his glancing eyes, and every hair on end.

A click of the tongue, a noiseless graceful bound, and Punch was at his side. A wild scrambling rush, a wriggle on the sill, a patter over the window-seat, and Scamp was twisting himself into white figure-eights all over the room, with tremendous energy but not a sound save the soft pad of his tiny dancing feet.

Then, as he ate, the great brown head pillowed itself softly on his knee, and the eloquent brown eyes looked up into his in a way that a stone image could hardly have resisted. The while Scamp, on his hind legs, beat the air frantically with his front paws to attract attention to his needs and danced noiselessly all over the floor.

He gauged their characters with interest. When he gave them morsels turn about, Punch awaited his with gentlemanly patience, and even when purposely passed by in order to see what he would do, obtruded his claims by nothing more than a gentle movement of the head on his friend's knee; while Scamp, in like case, twisted himself into knots of anxiety and came perilously near to utterance.

The difference between them when, through lack of intimate knowledge of their likes and dislikes, they got something not entirely to their taste, was also very typical. Punch would retire quietly into obscurity, and having disposed of the objectionable morsel somehow—either by a strenuous swallow or in some corner—would quietly reappear, lay his head on Graeme's knee again, and work it up to his lap with a series of propitiatory little jerks that never failed of their object. Scamp, on the other hand, would hold it in his mouth for a moment till he had savoured it, then place it meekly on the floor, bow his head to the ground, and grovel flat with deprecatory white-eyed up-glances, and as clearly as dog could say, would murmur,—"Oh, Man, Lord of all that go on four legs, forgive thy humble little servant in that he is unable with enjoyment to eat that thou hast of thy bounty tendered him! The fault is wholly his. Yet, of thy great clemency, punish him not beyond his capacity, for his very small body is merely a bundle of nerves, and they lie so very close to the skin that even a harsh word from thee will set them quivering for an hour." But, at a comforting word, he was up in a flash dancing and sparring away as gaily as ever.

Then, when Mrs. Carré brought in the next course, they both retired discreetly below the tent of the tablecloth. But she, knowing them of old perhaps, found them out at once and cried, "Ah you! I see you there! You are just troublesome beasts!" But, seeing that her guest was in the conspiracy, she permitted them for that once; and in time, seeing that he really desired their company, she allowed them to remain as a matter of course and without any preliminary harrying.

VI

One other acquaintance he made during these dark days,—perhaps one ought to say an acquaintance and a half, if indeed the half in this case was not greater than the whole, a matter which Graeme never fully decided in his own mind,—a small person of grim and gloomy tendencies, whose sombre humours chimed at times with his own,—and that small person's familiar.

His name was Johnnie Vautrin, and, as far as Graeme could make out, he was about eight years old in actual years, but aged beyond belief in black arts which made him a terror to his kind. And his familiar, in the person of an enormous black cat, which came and went, was named Marielihou.

Johnnie, and presumably Marielihou, lived with an ancient dame who was held by some to be their great-grandmother, and by some to be Marielihou herself. This was a moot and much-discussed point among the neighbours. What was beyond dispute was that Johnnie was said to be grievously maltreated by her at times, and to lead her a deuce of a life, and she him. The family came originally from Guernsey and had married into Sark, and, for this and other reasons, was still looked askance at by the neighbours.

Both Johnnie and his ancient relative were popularly—or unpopularly—credited with powers of mischief which secured them immunities and privileges beyond the common and not a little prudently concealed dislike.

Old Mrs. Vautrin could put the evil eye on her neighbours' cows and stop their milk, on their churns and stop their butter, on their kettles and stop their boiling.

Johnnie claimed equal powers, but excelled in forecasts of bad weather and ill luck and evil generally, and, since there was no end to his prognostications, they occasionally came true, and when they did he exulted greatly and let no one forget it.

He had a long, humorously snaky, little face, a deep sepulchral voice, which broke into squeaks in moments of excitement, and curious black eyes with apparently no pupils—little glittering black wells of ill intent, with which he cowed dogs and set small children screaming and grown ones swearing. His little body was as malformed as his twisted little soul, and he generally sat in the hedge taking his pleasure off the passers-by, much to their discomfort.

Johnnie also saw ghosts, or said he did, which came to much the same thing since none could prove to the contrary. He had even slept one night in an outhouse up at the Seigneurie, and had carefully locked the door, and so the little old lady in white, who only appears to those who lock their doors of a night, came to him, and, according to Johnnie, they carried on a long and edifying conversation to their mutual satisfaction.

He had also a cheerful habit of visiting sick folks and telling them he had seen their spirits in the lanes at night, and so they might just as well give up all hopes of getting better. On payment of a small fee, however, he was at times, according to his humour, willing to admit that it might have been somebody else's ghost he had seen, but in either case his visitations tended to cheerfulness in none but himself. He was great on the meanings—dismal ones mostly—of flights of birds and falling stars and fallen twigs. And he had been known to throw a branch of hawthorn into a house which had incurred his displeasure.

The men scoffed at him openly, and occasionally gave him surreptitious pennies. The women and children feared him; and the dogs, to the last one, detested him but gave him wide berth.

Graeme had very soon run across the little misanthrope and, in his own black humour, found him amusing. They rarely met without a trial of wit, or parted without a transfer of coppers from the large pocket to the small. Wherefore Johnnie made a special nest in the hedge opposite the cottage, and waylaid his copper-mine systematically and greatly to his own satisfaction and emolument. But, like the dogs, though on a lower level, he too was not without his effect on Graeme's spirits, and if he did not lift him up he certainly at times helped him out of himself and his gloomy thoughts.

VII

"You're just an unmitigated little humbug, Johnnie," said Graeme, as he leaned over the wall smoking, to the small boy whose acquaintance he had made the previous day, and who had promptly foretold a storm which had not come.

"Unmitigumbug! Guyablle! Qu'es' ce que c'es' que ça?" echoed the small boy, with very wide eyes.

"You, my son. Your black magic's all humbug. It lacks the essential attribute of fulfilment. It doesn't work. Black magic that doesn't work is humbug."

"Black-mack-chick! My Good! You do talk!"

"What about that storm?"

"Ah ouaie! Well, you wait. It come."

"So will Christmas, and the summer after next, if we wait long enough. On the same terms I foretell thunders and lightnings, rain, hail, snow, and fiery vapours, followed by lunar rainbows and waterspouts."

"Go'zamin!" said Johnnie, with a touch of reluctant admiration at such an outflow of eloquence; and then, by way of set-off, "I sec six black crows, 's mawn'n."

"Ah—really? And what do you gather from such a procession as that now?"

"Some un's gwain' to die," in a tone of vast satisfaction.

"Of course, of course—if we wait long enough. It's perhaps you. You'll die yourself sometime, you know."

"Noh, I wun't. No 'n'll ivver see me die. I'll just turn into sun'th'n—a gull maybe," as one floated by on moveless wing, the very poetry of motion; and the fathomless black eyes followed it with pathetic longing.

"Cormorant more likely, I should say."

"Noh, I wun't. I don' like corm'rants. They stink. Mebbe I'll be a hawk,"—as his eye fell on one, like a brown leaf nailed against the blue sky. "Did ee hear White Horse last night?"

"I did hear a horse in the night, Johnnie, but I couldn't swear that he was a white one."

"Didn' git up an' look out?" disappointedly.

"No, I didn't. Why should I get up to look out at a horse? I can see horses any day without getting out of bed in the middle of the night."

"'Twus the White Horse of the Coupée,"—in a weird whisper.—"I heerd him start in Little Sark, and come across Coupée, an' up by Colinette, an' past this house. An' if you'd ha' looked out an' seen him, you'd ha' died."

"Good old White Horse! I'm glad I stopped in bed. Did you see him yourself now?"

"I've rid him! Yes!—an' told him where to go," with a ghoulish nod.

"Quite friendly with ghosts and things, eh?"

"I don' mind 'em. I seen the ole lady up at the big house. Yes, an' talked to her too."

"Clever boy! Put the evil eye on her?"

"Noh, ee cann't."

"Can't? Why, I thought you were a past master in all little matters of that kind."

"Ee cann't put evil eye on a ghost," with infinite scorn.

"Oh, she's a ghost, is she? And what did you talk about?"

"You coul'n't understan'," grunted Johnnie, to whom his meeting with the White Lady was a treasured memory if a somewhat tender subject.

And Marielihou? Ah, Marielihou was a black mystery. Sometimes she was there, and sometimes she wasn't, and if at such times you asked Johnnie where she was, he would reply mysteriously, "Aw, she's busy."

And busy Marielihou was, always and at all times. If Graeme found her in the hedge with Johnnie, she was busy licking her lips with vicious enjoyment as though she had just finished eating something that had screamed as it died. Or she was licking them snarlishly and surreptitiously, and sharpening her claws, as though just about starting out after something to eat—something which he knew would certainly scream as it died. For Marielihou was a mighty hunter, and her long black body could be seen about the cliffs at any time of night or day, creeping and worming along, then, of a sudden, pointing and stiffening, and flashing on to her prey like the black death she was.

Six full-grown rabbits had Marielihou been known to bring home in a single day, to say nothing of all the others that had gone to the satisfaction of her own inappeasable lust for rabbit-flesh and slaughter.

As to the strange tales the neighbours whispered about her, Graeme could make neither head nor tail of them. But when old Tom Hamon put it to him direct, he had to confess that he never had seen old Mother Vautrin and Marielihou together, nor both at the same time.

"B'en!" said old Tom, as if that ended the matter. "An' I tell you, if I had a silver bullet I'd soon try what that Marrlyou's made of."

"And why a silver bullet?" asked Graeme.

"'Cause—Lead bullets an't no good 'gainst the likes o' Marrlyou. Many's the wan I've sent after her, ay, an' through her, and she none the worse. Guyablle!" and old Tom spat viciously.

"Perhaps you missed her," suggested Graeme, not unreasonably as he thought.

"Missed her!" with immense scorn. "I tell ee bullets goes clean through her, in one side an' out t'other, an' she never a bit the worse. I've foun' 'em myself spatted on rock just where she sat."

"Well, why don't you get a silver bullet and try again?"

"Ah! Teks some getting does silver bullets."

"How much?"

"A shill'n would mek a little wan," and Graeme gave him a shilling to try his luck, because Marielihou's unsportsmanlike behaviour did not commend itself to him.

But it took many shillings to obtain anything definite in the way of results, and Graeme had his own humorous suspicions as to the billets some of them found, and gently chaffed old Tom on the subject whenever they met.

"You wait," said Tom, with mysterious nods.

IX

Graeme's sober intention had been to put Margaret Brandt, and the agonising regrets that clung to every thought of her, strenuously out of his mind. But that he found more possible in the intention than in the accomplishment.

The first shock of loss numbs one's mental susceptibilities, of course, much as a blow on the head affects the nervous system. The bands are off the wheels, the machinery is out of order, and the friction seems reduced. It is when the machine tries to work again that the full effects of the jar are felt.

And so he found it now. As mind and body recovered tone in the whole vitalising atmosphere of the wondrous little isle,—the air, the sea, the sense of remoteness, the placid life of the place, the abounding beauties of cliff and crag and cave,—his heart awoke also to the aching sense of its loss.

All outward things—all save Johnny Vautrin, and Marielihou, and old Tom Hamon, and several others— sang abundantly of the peace and fulness and joy of life, but his heart was still so sore from its bruising that at times these outward beauties seemed only to mock him with their brightness.

In the first shock of his downcasting, wounded pride said, "I will show no sign. I will forget her. I will salve the bruise with work. Margaret Brandt is not the only woman in the world. In time some other shall take her place;"—and he tried his hardest to believe it.

But body is one thing and mind another. The body you may compel to any mortal thing, but the mind is of a different order, and strongest will cannot whip it to heel at times. Forbid it thought of thing or person and the forbidden is just that which will persist in obtruding itself to the exclusion of all else.

And so, in spite of him, the dull ache in his heart at every thought of Margaret murmured without ceasing, "There is none like her—none!" And crush and compel it as he might, the truth would out, and out the more the more he tried to crush it.

And so at times, in spite of his surroundings, his spirits dragged in lowest deeps.

Work he could not as yet, for the work of the writer demands absolute concentration and most complete surrender, and all his faculties were centred, in spite of himself, on Margaret Brandt and his own great loss in her.

He rambled all over the island with his dog friends, risked skin and bones in precarious descents into apparently impossible depths, scrambled laboriously among the ragged bastions of the Coupée and Little Sark, explored endless caverns, loitered by day in bosky lanes, and roamed restlessly by night under the brightest stars he had ever seen.

But, wherever he went—down underground in the Boutiques or the Gouliots; or lying on the Eperquerie among the flaming gorse and cloudlike stretches of primroses; or standing on Longue Pointe while the sun sank in unearthly splendours behind Herm and Guernsey; or watching from the windmill the throbbing life-lights all round the wide horizon;—wherever he was, and whatever he was doing, there with him always was the poignant remembrance of Margaret Brandt and his loss in her.

His heart ached so, at thought of the emptiness and desolation of the years that lay before him, that at times his body ached also, and the spirit within him groaned in sympathy.

Life without Margaret! What was it worth?

Though it brought him riches and honours overpassing his hopes—and he doubted now at times if that were possible, lacking the inspiration of Margaret—what was it worth?

Riches and honours, won at the true sword's point of earnest work, were good and worth the winning. But yet, without Margaret, they were as nothing to him. His whole heart cried aloud for Margaret. Without her all the full rich hues of life faded into dull gray ashes.

With Margaret to strive for, he had felt himself capable of mighty things. Without her—!

And that she should throw herself away on a Charles Pixley!—Charles the smiling, the imperturbable, the fount of irrepressible chatter and everlasting inanities! How could such a one as Charles Pixley possibly satisfy her nobler nature? Out of the question! Impossible! But then it is just possible that he was not exactly in the best state of mind for forming an unbiassed opinion on so large a question as that.

Anyway he was out of it, and Margaret Brandt was henceforth nothing to him. If he said it once he said it hundreds of times, as if the simple reiteration of so obvious a truth would make it one whit the truer, when his whole heart was clamouring that Margaret was all the worlds to him and the only thing in the world that he wanted.

With an eye, perhaps, to his obvious lack of cheerfulness, his namesake and host suggested various diversions,—fishing for congers and rock-fish, a voyage round the island, a trip across to Herm, a day among the rabbits on. Brecqhou. But he wanted none of them. His life was flapping on a broken wing and all he wanted was to be left alone.

In time the wound would heal, and he would take up his work again and find his solace in it. But wounds such as this are not healed in a day. It was raw and sore yet, the new skin had not had time to form.

He recalled Lady Elspeth's dissatisfaction with his love-scenes, and thought, grimly, that now he could at all events enter fully into the feelings of the man who had lost the prize, and would be able to depict them to the life. If the choice had been left to him he would gladly have dispensed with all such knowledge to its profoundest depths, if only the prize had remained to him. But the choice had been Margaret's, and the prize was Charles Pixley's.

If there was one thing he could have imagined without actual experience, it was how a man may feel when he loses. What he could not at present by any possibility conceive was—how it might feel to be the accepted lover of such a girl as Margaret Brandt.

Confound her money! If it were not for that, Pixley would probably never have wanted to marry her. Money was answerable for half the ills of life, and the contrariness of woman for the other half. Confound money! Confound—Well, truly, his state of mind was not a happy one.

X

But there was something in the crisp Sark air that, by degrees and all unconsciously, braced both mind and body;—something broadening and uplifting in the wide free outlook from every headland; something restorative of the grip of life in the rush and roar of the mighty waves and the silent endurance of the rocks; something so large and aloof and restful in the wide sweep of sea and sky; something so hopeful and regenerative in the glorious exuberance of the spring—the flaming gorse, the mystic stretches of bluebells, the sunny sweeps of primroses, the soft uncurlings of the bracken, the bursting life of the hedgerows, the joyous songs of the larks—that presently, and in due season, earthly worries began to fall back into their proper places below the horizon, and a new Graeme—a Graeme born of Sark and Trouble—looked out of the old Graeme eyes and began to contemplate life from new points of view.

It took time, however. Love is a plant of most capricious and surprising growth. It may take years to root and blossom. It may spring up in a day, yet strike its roots right through the heart and hold it as firmly as the growth of the years. And, once the heart is enmeshed in the golden filaments, it is a most dolorous work to disentangle it.

For the first two weeks his mind ran constantly on his loss. Momentarily it might be diverted by outward things, but always it came back with a sharp shock, and a bitter sense of deprivation, to the fact that Margaret Brandt had passed out of his life and left behind her an aching void.

Did he sit precariously among the ragged scarps and pinnacles of Little Sark, while the western seas raged furiously at his feet and the Souffleur shot its rockets of snowy spray high into the gray sky—

through the passing film of the spray, and the marbled coils of the tumbling waves, the face of Margaret Brandt looked out at him.

Did he stride among the dew-drenched, gold-spangled gorse bushes on the Eperquerie, while the sun came up with ever fresh glories behind the distant hills of France—Margaret's face was there in the sunrise.

Did he stand above Havre Gosselin in the gloaming, while the sun sank behind Herm and Guernsey in splendours such as he had never dreamed of—just so, he said to himself, Margaret had gone out of his life and left it gray and cheerless as the night side of Brecqhou.

Wherever he was and whatever he did, it was always Margaret, Margaret,—and Margaret lost to him.

By the end of the third week, however, the tonic effects of the strong sea air and water began to work inwards. Healthy body would no longer suffer sick heart. He had taken his morning plunge hitherto as a matter of course, now he began to enjoy it and to look forward to it—certain index of all-round recovery.

His appetite grew till he felt it needed an apology, at which Mrs. Carré laughed enjoyably. He began to take more interest in his surroundings for their own sakes. His thoughts of Margaret, with their after-glow of tender memory, were like the soft sad haze which falls on Guernsey when the sun has sunk and left behind it, in the upper sky, its slowly dying fires of dull red amber and gold.

Towards the end of the fourth week he tentatively fished out his manuscript and began to read it—with pauses. He grew interested in it. He saw new possibilities in the story.—His life was getting back on to the rails again.

XI

Greater bodily peace and comfort than he found in that thick-set, creeper-covered, little cottage in the Rue Lucas, man might scarcely hope for. Anything more would have tended to luxury and made for restraint.

He was free as the wind to come and go as he listed, to roam the lonely lanes all night and watch the coming of the dawn—which he did; or to lie abed all day—which he did not; to do any mortal thing that pleased him, so long only as he gave his hostess full and fair warning of the state of his appetite and the times when it must be satisfied.

His quarters were not perhaps palatial, but what man, king of himself alone, would live in a palace?

He bumped his head with the utmost regularity against the lintel of the front door each time he entered, and only learned at last to bob by instinct. And the beams in the ceilings were so low that they claimed recognition somewhat after the manner of a boisterous acquaintance.

But doors and windows were always open, night and day, and his good friends the dogs came in to greet him by way of the windows quite as often as by the doors.

All through the black times those two were his close companions, and no better could he have had. They asked nothing of him—or almost nothing, and they gave him all they had. They were grateful from the bottom of their large hearts for any slightest sign of recognition. And they were proud of his company, which to others would have proved somewhat of a wet blanket. Without a doubt they assisted mightily in his cure, though neither he nor they knew it.

Every morning when he jumped up to see the weather, the first things that met him when he reached the open window, were four eager eyes full of welcome, and a grave intelligent brown face and hopeful swinging tail, and a dancing white face and little wriggling body.

Then he would pull up the blinds and they would enter with an easy bound and a scramble, and while he hastily flung on his things they would prowl about, now pushing investigating noses into an open drawer, and again taking a passing drink out of his water-jug by way of first breakfast.

Then, away through the gaps in the jewelled hedges, with the larks at their matins overhead, and the tethered cows nuzzling out the dainty morning grasses, and watching the intruders speculatively till they passed out of sight into the next field.

"Which way? Which way? Which way?" shrieked Scamp, as he tore to and fro down every possible road to show that all were absolutely alike to him. While Punch bounded lightly to the first dividing of the ways and waited there with slow-swinging tail to see which road Man would choose.

The Harbour—or Les Lâches—which? Every morning Scamp raced hopefully towards the sweet-smelling tunnel of hawthorn trees that led down to the other tunnel in the rock and the tiny harbour, because, for a very small dog, the granite slip was much easier to compass than the steep ledges of Les Lâches. And every morning Punch waited quietly at Colinette to see how Man would go.

And when the tide was low and the harbour empty, Punch knew it was Les Lâches almost before Man's face had turned that way, and off he went at a gallop, and Scamp came tearing back with expostulatory yelps, and got in Punch's way and was rolled head over heels, but always came right side up at the fourth turn and rushed on without even a remonstrance, for that was a very small price to pay for the exalted companionship of Punch and Man.

So, past La Peignerie and La Forge, with the thin blue smoke of gorse fires floating down from every dumpy chimney and adding a flavour to the sweetest air in the world,—with a morning greeting from everyone they met—over the heights and down the zigzag path to the sloping ledges, and in they went, all three, into the clearest and crispest water in the world, water that tingled and sparkled, full charged with life and energy.

Then shivers and shakes, and hasty play with a towel, and they were racing back across the heights to breakfast and the passing of another day, of which the greatest charm had passed already with that plunge into the life-giving sea.

If you are inclined to think that I enlarge too much on these two friends of his, let me remind you that a man is known by the company he keeps, and these two were Graeme's sole companions for many a day—those first dark days in the sunny little isle, when all human companionship would have been abhorrent to him.

In their company he found himself again. Their friendship weaned him by degrees from the jaundiced view of life which Margaret's dereliction had induced. They drew him, in time, from his brooding melancholy, and through the upbuilding of the body restored him to a quieter mind.

Let no man despise the help of a dog, for there are times when the friendship of a dog is more sufferable, and of more avail, and far more comforting, than that of any ordinary human being.

PART THE FOURTH

I

It was just two days before the end of Graeme's fourth week in Sark. His spirits were rising to the requirements of his work, and he was looking forward with quite novel enjoyment to a steady spell of writing, when his hostess startled him, as she cleared away his breakfast, by saying—

"It iss the day after to-morrow you will be going?"

"Eh? What? Going? No, I'm not going, Mrs. Carré. What made you think I was going? Why, I've only just come."

His landlady put down the dishes on the table again as a concrete expression of surprise, put her hands on her hips by way of taking grip of herself, and stared at him.

"You are not going? Noh? But it wass just for the month I thought you kem."

"Not at all. I may stop two months, three months,—all my life perhaps. Won't you let me live and die here if I want to?"

"Ach, then! It iss not to die we woult want you. But I thought my man said it wass just for the month you kem, and—my Good!—I haf let your roomss for the day after to-morrow," and her face had lost its usual smile and was full of distress and bewilderment.

"You've let my rooms? Oh, come now!—But now I think of it, I believe I did say something about a month or so, when I spoke to John Philip. Well now, what will you do? Put me out into the road? Or can you find me somewhere else?—though I'm quite sure you'll not be able to find me any place as comfortable as this."

"Whatt will we do?" she said, much disturbed, and gazed at him thoughtfully. Then, with sudden inspiration, "There iss the big house up the garden?" and looked at him hopefully.

"But it's empty."

"Everything iss there, and all ready for them to come any time they want to. It woult only mean making up a bed and you coult come here for your meals."

"That would do first-rate if you can arrange it."

"I will write to Mrs. Lee to-day and ask her to tell me by the telegraph. It will be all right."

"That's all right then. Who's the wretched person who is turning me out of here?"

"It is two leddies. They wrote to the Vicar, and he asked John Philip and he told my man."

"Two ladies! Then I can't possibly have my meals in here. You'd better let me join you in the kitchen,"—a consummation he had been striving after for some time past, in fact ever since his literary instincts had shaken off the thrall and got their heads above the mists,—with a view, of course, of turning a more intimate knowledge of his surroundings to profitable account.

But his hostess was jealous of her kitchen and would not hear of it.

"There iss no need. I will arrange it, and you will tek your meals in here just as usual. Which room woult you like in the big house?"

"I'll go up and have a look round. Does it make any difference to you which I choose? I'd like one with a balcony if it's all the same to you."

"It iss all the sem, and I will get it ready for you as soon ass I hear from Mrs. Lee. You will not be afraid, all alone by yourself up there?"

"Afraid? No. What is there to be afraid of?"

"Och, I do not know. Only—all alone—sometimes one iss afraid—"

"There aren't any ghosts about, are there?"

"Ghosts? Noh!"—with a ghost of a laugh. "I do not believe in ghosts or any such things, though some people does. There are some people"—very scornfully—"will not go by the churchyard at night, and"—lest so sceptical a mind should provoke reprisal—"I do not know that I woult myself. And down by the Coupée—But the house there iss too new to have anything like that." "Well, if I see any I'll try and catch one and bring it down to breakfast."

And so it was arranged that, if the permission of the owner of the Red House could be obtained, he should sleep there and come down to the cottage for his meals, Mrs. Carré undertaking that no inconvenience should thereby be caused to any of those concerned.

He strolled up the garden, with the dogs racing in front, to choose his bedroom, and came across his host unwillingly busy with hoe and spade in the potato patch. His whole aspect betokened such undisguised sufferance that Graeme could not repress a smile.

"Like it?" he asked.

"Noh!"

"Sooner be at the fishing?"

A nod and a brief smile, and Graeme left him to his unwelcome labours, and passed through the gap in the tall hedge to his new abode.

It was a well-built house, gray granite below and red tiles up above, with a wide verandah round the lower storey and white balconies to the upper one; the inside was all polished pitch pine, and the rooms were large and airy and suitably furnished for summer occupancy. It was left in Mrs. Carré's charge, and she and the sun and wind kept it always sweet and clean, and ready for use at an hour's notice.

With the assistance of his two friends, who displayed an active and intelligent interest in the matter, he chose the room with the largest balcony, and said to himself that the coming of the ladies was, after all, a blessing in disguise. He believed he would be even more comfortable there than he had been at the cottage. He would have been quite willing to move in at once if that had been possible.

Next morning, however, the permission duly arrived, and in many trips he gaily carried all his belongings up the garden and installed himself in the balcony room.

It was a very delightful room, with fine wide outlook—over towards the church in its dark embowerment of evergreen oaks, which some of the folk would not pass by night; over the long sweep of the land towards Little Sark; then, over to the left, a glimpse of the sea and a dark blue film on the horizon which he knew was Jersey.

This room and the balcony outside should be his workshop, he decided, and he looked forward, with an eagerness to which he had been stranger for weeks past, to burying himself in his work and finding in it solace and new strength.

II

Graeme possessed a lively imagination, else surely he had never taken to writing. But a lively imagination, sole occupant of a ten-roomed house in a strange land whose inhabitants believed firmly in ghosts and spirits and things that walked by night, and that house but a stone's-throw from the black churchyard where such discomforting things might naturally be supposed to congregate, was not nearly so enjoyable a possession at midnight as in the full light of day.

He lay awake for hours, hearing what seemed to him uncanny sounds about the house, inside and out. The night wind sighed through the heavy pale leaves of the eucalyptus trees, and set the roses and honeysuckle on the verandah posts whispering and tapping. In the stark silence, sounds came out of the other nine empty rooms as though they chose that quiet time for passing confidences. The stairs creaked as though invisible feet passed up and down. And once he could have sworn to stealthy footsteps along the verandah below his window.

He laughed at his own foolishness. Ghosts, he vowed, he did not believe in, and the Sark men were notably honest. All the same it was close on daylight before he slept.

When he pushed through the dewy hedge and went down to the cottage for breakfast, his hostess's eyes twinkled as she asked, "You did not see any ghosts—Noh?"

"Not a ghost, but all the same it did feel a bit lonesome. What would you say to my taking Punch with me to-night, just for company?"

"Yess indeed, tek him. He iss quiet. The other iss too lively."

"And when do your ladies arrive?"

"With the boat. When will you be pleased to have your dinner?"

"I'm off to Little Sark for the day. How would seven o'clock suit you and them?"

"I will mek it suit. They will haf dinner before or after. It will be quite all right."

He spent the day with the dogs, scrambling among the rugged bastions at the south end of the island, investigated the old silver mines, bathed, all three, in the great basin of Venus in the hollow under the southern cliffs, and came home after sunset, tired and ravenous.

"Well, have your ladies come?" he asked, as he sat down to his dinner.

"Oh yess, they are come. They are gone for a walk. One of them is Miss Hen and the other iss Miss Chum."

"Good Lord, what names! Two old maids, I presume,—curls and spectacles and that kind of thing!"

"They are not old, noh. And they are ferry nice to look at, especially Miss Chum."

"Well, well, so she ought to be to make up for her name."

"They were quite put out to think of having turned you out of your roomss—"

"Not half as much as I was, but you can assure them that I am delighted they came. It's as nice a house as one could wish for, and if you can arrange the meals all right I'll not trouble them in the least. How long are they going to stay?"

"They are like you. They do not know. It may be a month, it may be more."

"Oh well, I'll keep out of their way as much as possible. People who come to Sark come to be quiet, I expect. Don't trouble about coffee tonight, Mrs. Carré. I shall just have a smoke and then turn in. I'm tired but and I want a good night's rest."

"Ah yess. Well, you will tek Punch to-night, and then you will hear no ghosts."

The sky was still softly suffused with the clear rose and amber of the sunset when he leaned over the wall, as he filled his pipe, and looked out into the darkening road.

"Har-Héri! Qué-hou-hou!" croaked a hoarse little voice in the hedge opposite.

"Hello, Johnnie-boy! That you?"

"Where you bin te-day?"

"Where have I been? Down in Little Sark, prowling about the mines, stealing lumps of silver—"

"Godzamin! They an't any silver now."

"No? All right, my son. Then I'm telling you fibs."

"Show me."

"Ah, I don't carry it about with me."

"An't got any." And presently, as Graeme lit up, without deigning any answer,—"I seen a ghost las' night."

"Clever boy! What did you make out of it?"

"'Twas the ghost of old Tom Hamon's father. Was all white and dead-like."

"You're too previous, Johnnie. He's getting better."

"He's a-goin' to die."

"So are you sometime."

"No, I a'n't. Show me 'at silver."

"Sometime, perhaps, if you ask nicely. I'm going to bed now. Come along, Punch! Goodnight, Johnnie! Keep your eyes skinned for ghosts. Capital night for them, I should say," and he went off up the garden, with Punch stalking solemnly alongside.

And Johnnie Vautrin erected himself on his hands and haunches to see where he was going, while the vivacious Scamp, shut up in the wood-house and bereft of his bedfellow, and doubtless fearful of ghosts in every nerve of his quivering little body, rent the still night with his expostulations, as he heard them go past.

The scent of the pipe was lingering still in the forecourt when the ladies turned in out of the road, and they just caught a glimpse of the smoker disappearing through the gap in the hedge.

"Ah-ha! There goes the Bogey-Man!" said Miss Hen. "Does this dear little dog carry on this way all through the night, Mrs. Carré?"

"It iss becos the gentleman hass tekken Punch up to the house to kip away the ghosts," smiled Mrs. Carré.

"I should say this one would have been of more use."

"He will be quiet soon. Scamp, bad beast, be qui-et! A couche!"

"To keep away ghosts! What a muff he must be!" said Miss Hen. "Chum, what do you say to putting on white sheets and giving him a scare? If we did a skirly-whirly à la Loie Fuller, below his window, he'd probably have blue fits. Ghosts, indeed!"

"If that big brown Punch got out at you it's you would have the blue fits," said Miss Chum. "The Sark air is getting into your head, Hennie."

"Of course it is. That's what we came for, isn't it? You'll feel it yourself before you're two days older, my child. You're looking better than I've seen you for a month past."

"It's so delightful to feel free," said Miss Chum.

III

Thoroughly tired out, and with a guardian angel on the mat at his bedside, in the shape of a long brown body which sought fresh ease in an occasional sprawl, and flopped a responsive tail each time he dropped a friendly pat on to its head in the dark—Graeme looked confidently for a sound night's rest.

He fell asleep indeed at once, but woke with a start sometime in the night, with the impression of a sound in his ears. Had he really heard something? Or was it only the tail-end of a dream? Wood-lined houses talk in the night. Was it only the pitch pine whispering of the old free days in the scented woods? He could not be sure, so he lay still and listened.

And as he waited, it came again—a low, wailing cry, long-drawn and somewhat curdling to the blood.

Outside or inside? He could not be sure.

Cats? Cats can do wonders in the way of uncanny noises, but somehow this did not sound like cats. There was something human, or inhuman, in it, and his door suddenly shook as though something tried to get in.

He bethought him to feel for Punch. But his hand fell on space, and as he struck a match to see the time and what had become of his companion, the church bell tolled one dismal stroke, and he saw Punch standing like a bronze statue at the door, with his nose down at the crack, his tail on the droop, and every hair apparently on the bristle.

At the glow of the match the drooping tail gave one slow swing, but he did not look round.

Graeme struck another match, and lit his candle, and jumped into his shoes.

"What is it, old fellow?" And Punch scraped furiously at the door again, and so explained that part of the matter.

There came a sudden scuffling fall against the door. Punch rasped at it with his front feet in strenuous silence. If he had been able to give voice it would have been a relief to both of them. His mute anxiety added to the weirdness of the proceedings, and Graeme experienced a novel creeping about the nape of the neck.

Ghosts or no ghosts, however, it had to be looked into. He picked up a heavy boot, turned the key, and flung open the door. Punch went down the stairs in two long bounds, and a rush of cold air put out the candle. He laid it down and followed cautiously, ready to launch the boot at the first sign of uncanniness.

The rush of night air came through a small pantry opening off the hall. The window in it was wide open, and there was no sign of Punch. He and the ghost had evidently gone through that way. Graeme and the boot followed.

It was a dark night between moons. The velvet-black vault was brilliant with stars, but the earth was full of shadows. The fleshy leaves of the eucalyptus trees showed pale against the darkness. The night wind set them rustling eerily. From somewhere beyond them, past the dark hedge, there came a sound of subdued strife. Graeme clutched his boot and sped towards it, drenched with dew from every disturbed branch.

The sounds led him into the potato patch in the lower garden, and in the dimness he became aware that Punch was standing on something that struggled to get up and was held down by the great brown paws and body.

No ghost, evidently. Graeme dropped his boot and stooped and laid hold of the struggler, and knew in a moment, in spite of his own disturbance of mind, that this ghost at all events had materialised into the bodily form of Master Johnnie Vautrin, and he wondered how many more might have done the same if they had been followed up as closely.

He lifted the squirming small boy who had not spoken a word.

"So this is what Sark ghosts are made of, is it, Master Johnnie?" he asked, giving him a shake. "You little scamp! For once you shall have what you jolly well deserve," and he carried him, kicking and wriggling, back to the house, shoved him through the window, and held him with one hand while he got through himself. Punch followed with an easy bound, and they all went upstairs. Graeme found his candle, and lit it and looked at his prisoner.

Johnnie was covered with mould from the potato patch, but his black eyes gleamed through it as brightly as ever, and, as far as Graeme could distinguish through its masking, his face showed no sign of confusion.

"Do you know what we do with naughty little ghosts in England, Johnnie?"

Johnnie's eyes glittered like a snake's.

"We spank 'em, Johnnie. I'm going to spank you—hard."

Then Johnnie spoke.

"I'll put tha evil eye on you."

"Two if you like, my son,—or twenty if you've got 'em handy. Evil eyes rather tickle me. We'll see which makes most impression—my hand or your eye," and he laid the black-magic man across his knee, and gave him such a genuine motherly quilting as he had never experienced in his life before. Hot blows he was accustomed to, but this cool, relentless, tingling flagellation, all on the one spot, and continued till every particle of blood in his body seemed to leap to meet each stroke, was new to him, and it made a great and lasting impression.

He did not cry, but tried to bite and scratch the operator, and Punch stood looking on with a grave smile on his face and a slowly swinging tail expressive of the greatest satisfaction.

Discipline over, Graeme handed him out through the pantry window, bade him to go home to bed, and fastened the window behind him. The night passed without further disturbance, and Graeme awoke as the dawn glimmered golden on his wide-open window.

In ten minutes he was racing bareheaded past Colinette and La Forge towards Les Lâches, a towel round his neck and Punch bounding silently by his side. They had stolen out the back way through the top of the post-office fields, and had left Scamp still prisoner in the woodhouse, lest the hysterical joy of his release should disturb the ladies.

And presently they were racing back home, all aglow with the tingling kisses of the waves, and rough of hair with the salt and the wind.

The sun was up but not yet stripped for the long day's race to the west. The eastern skies still gleamed through a faery haze with the soft iridescence of a young ormer shell, the tender pinks and greens and golds of the new day's birth-chamber mellowing upwards into the glorious blue of a day of days.

'The year's at the spring,
The day's at the morn;
Morning's at seven;
The hillside's dew-pearled:
The lark's on the wing;
The snail's on the thorn;
God's in his heaven—
All's right with the world!'

The lilt of the joyous words had often been with him as he sped through the sleeping fields to his morning plunge.

This day of days, as though his soul forecasted what was coming, they sang in his heart and on his lips. His cure was surely near completion. The salt was regaining its savour. Life was worth living again.

And it was then, when he had come through the valley and was ready to climb again, that the glory came to him.

As the two friends sprang lightly over the turf wall into the garden of the Red House, they saw a sight which one of them will not forget as long as he lives.

In the gap of the tall hedge, where the path led down to the cottage,—ringed in its darkness like a lovely picture in a sombre frame, with a pale eucalyptus rising stately on either side; and behind it all, and gleaming softly through and round it all, the tender glories of the new day,—stood a girl in a dove-coloured dress, bareheaded, holding the dew-pearled branches apart with her two hands, and gazing at him with wide eyes, and parted lips, and startled face.

And the girl was Margaret Brandt.

IV

Graeme's first thought was that he was dreaming. He blinked his eyes to make sure they were not playing him false.

If she had disappeared at that moment, he would have sworn to hallucinations and the visibility of spirits to the day of his death.

But she did not disappear, and Punch proved her no spirit by stalking gravely up to give her welcome. Without taking her startled eyes off Graeme, she dropped one white hand on to the great brown head and the diamonds sprinkled her dove-coloured dress.

"Mr. Graeme!" she said, in a voice which very fully expressed her own doubts as to his reality also.

"Mar—Miss Brandt? ... Is it possible?"

They had both drawn nearer, he along the broad gravel walk, she along the narrow path between the eucalyptus trees.

"Are you quite sure you are real?" he asked breathlessly, and for answer she laughed and stretched a friendly hand towards him.

He took it with shining eyes, and then bent suddenly and kissed it gently, and his eyes were shining still more brightly as she drew it hastily away.

"But whatever brings you here?" she asked abruptly.

"We're just out of the sea,"—and the joy of the sea and the morning, and this greatest thing of all, was in his face.

"But why are you here? What are you doing here?"

"Doing? We're living here."

"Did you know I was here? How—?" she began, with a puzzled wrinkle of the fair white brow, and stopped.

"I did not know. I wish I had."

"If you did not know, how—why—?"

"If I had known perhaps I should not have dared to follow you. On the whole I'm glad I did not know."

"I don't understand.... How long have you been here?"

"Just four weeks," he said, with a smile at thought of the blackness of those four weeks now that he stood in the sunshine.

"Four weeks! Then you mean—you mean that I—that we—followed—"

"In the mere matter of time, yes!—and of place too," he laughed." For you turned me out of my rooms."

"Do you mean to say you are the Bogey-Man?"

"Well,—no one ever called me so to my face before, but I'm bound to say I've felt uncommonly like one for the past four or five weeks."

"Come with me," she said hastily. "I must put this right at once, or Hennie—" and she turned and went through the gap in the hedge.

"Put what right?" he asked, as he followed.

"Oh—you," she said hastily.

"I'm all right—now. And who is Hennie?"

"My friend Miss Penny—"

"I beg your pardon. I thought you said Hennie."

"Henrietta Penny. She was at school with me. We are taking care of one another."

They had come to the forecourt of the cottage.

"Hen!" cried Margaret. The window was wide open, but the blind was discreetly down.

"Hello, Chum!" came back in muffled tones. "What's up now? Been and got yourself lost again?"

"Come out, dear. I want you."

"Half a jiff, old girl. Give a fellow a chance with his back hair. You had first tub this morning, remember."
At which Graeme's eyes twinkled in unison with Margaret's.

"There's a gentleman waiting to see you, dear," said Margaret, to prevent any further revelations.

"A what?"—and there followed a clatter of falling implements as though a sudden start had sent them
flying. "Wretch!—to upset one like that! It's that big brown dog, I suppose. I know you, my child!"

Then the blind whirled up and a merry face, in a cloud of dishevelled hair, looked out, a pair of horrified
eyes rested momentarily on Graeme, and the blind rattled down again with something that sounded like
a muffled feminine objurgation.

And presently the inner door opened and Miss Penny came forth demurely, and bowed distantly in the
direction of Margaret and Graeme.

She was of average height but inclined to plumpness, and so looked smaller than Margaret; and she had
no great pretensions to beauty, Graeme thought—but then he was biassed for life and incapable of free
and impartial judgment—save such as might be found in a very frank face given to much laughter, a
rather wide mouth and nice white teeth, abundant dark hair and a pair of challenging brown eyes which
now, getting over their first confusion—and finding herself at all events fully dressed, wherein she had
the advantage of him—rested with much appreciation on the young man in front of her.

The salt water was still in his hair, and the discrepancies in his hasty attire were but partly hidden by the
damp towel round his neck. Nevertheless he was very good to look upon. His moustache showed crisp
against the healthy brown of his face; his hair, short as it was, had a natural ripple which sea-water
could not reduce; and his eyes were brimming with the new joy of life and repressed laughter. Miss
Penny liked the looks of him.

"Margaret Brandt, I will never forgive you as long as I live," said she emphatically.

"All right, dear! This is Mr. Bogey-man whose rooms we have appropriated. He wished to be introduced
to the other malefactor. Miss Henrietta Penny—Mr. John Graeme! Mr. Graeme and I have met before."

If Mr. John Graeme had had more experience of women, the flash that shot across from the brown eyes
to the dark blue ones might have told him stories—for instance, that his name and would-have-been
standing towards her friend were not entirely unknown to Miss Penny; that, for a brief half second, she
wondered—doubted—and instantly chid herself for such a thought in connection with Margaret Brandt.

But Margaret herself, being a woman, caught the momentary challenge and repelled it steadily.

"I am very pleased to meet you, Miss Penny—in such a place, and in such company. I have heard of you
from Miss Brandt," said Graeme.

"Never till five minutes ago," laughed Margaret.

"Yes, if you will pardon me—once before, at Lady Elspeth Gordon's. Unless I am mistaken, Miss Penny
had just been across to Dublin to take a degree which Cambridge ungallantly declined to confer upon
her."

"Quite right!" said Miss Penny. "M.A. They're misogynists at Cambridge."

"Will you oblige me by informing Miss Penny, Mr. Graeme, that this meeting is purely accidental? I caught a spark in her eye and I know what it means. Had you the very slightest idea that we were coming to Sark?"

"Not the remotest. When I saw you standing in the hedge there, with the morning glories all about you, I first doubted my eyes, then I thought you a vision—"

"And do you think it possible that I knew of you being here?"

"I am certain you did not. Nobody knows. I left no address, and I told no one where I was going. I have not had a letter since I left London. I have been buried alive in this heavenly little place."

"There now, Mademoiselle," said Margaret, with a bow. "Are you satisfied now?"

"I was satisfied before you opened your mouth, my dear. The possibility inevitably suggested itself, but it was stillborn. Has not our friendship passed its seventh birthday?"

"Thank you, dear. But the coincidence of our coming to bury ourselves in Sark, and Mr. Graeme's coming to bury himself in Sark, was almost unbelievable."

"Not at all," said Miss Penny. "If you could both trace back you would probably find the same original spring of action—a chance word from some common friend, or some article you have both read. Then, when circumstances loosed the spring, you both shot in the same direction. What was it loosed your spring, Mr. Graeme?"

"Well,—I wanted to get away out of things. I'm busy on a book, you see, and I'd heard of Sark—"

"Same here!" said Miss Penny—"less the book. We wanted to get away out of things—and people, and we'd heard of Sark, and here we are. Was it you suggested Sark, or I, Meg?"

"I'm sure I don't know, dear. You, I should think."

"I will take all the credit of it."

Just then Mrs. Carré, who had been down to John Philip's for bread, turned in out of the road with a loaf under each arm. At sight of all her guests fraternising, her face lit up with a broad smile, and Scamp, who had whirled in after her, twisted himself into hieroglyphics of delight and rent the air with his expression of it, and then launched himself at Punch and taxed him with perfidy in going off to bathe without him.

"Ah, you have med friends with the leddies," she said to Graeme. "Scamp! Bad beast, be qui-et! A couche!"

"I'm doing my best, Mrs. Carré."

"That iss very nice."

"Very nice, indeed!" And Miss Penny asserted afterwards that he was looking at Margaret all the time.

"I told them you were a nice quiet gentleman and wouldn't disturb them at all," said Mrs. Carré.

"I'll do my very best not to. So far the disturbance has been all on their side, but I'm standing it very well, you see. You'll let me show you the sights, won't you?" he said to Miss Brandt. "I've been here a month, you see, and I know it all like a book. I've done nothing but moon about since I came—"

"I thought you were busy on a book," said Miss Penny.

"Er—well, you see, you have to do a lot of thinking before you start writing. I've been thinking," and perhaps more than one of them had a fairly shrewd suspicion as to the line his thoughts had taken.

"Now, if I don't cut away and dress, and get my breakfast and clear out, I shall be in the way of the ladies, and Mrs. Carré will never forgive me," he said. "I do hope you will include me in your plans for the day."

His bow included them both, and he sped off up the path through the high hedge, with the two dogs racing alongside.

"Meg, my child, we will go for a little walk," said Miss Penny.

V

The salt Sark air is uplifting at all times. The sea-water has a crisp effervescence of its own which tones and braces mind and body alike. Add to these the wonder of Margaret's unexpected presence there and, if the gift of large imagination be yours, you may possibly arrive—within a hundred miles or so—of the state of John Graeme's feelings as he raced up that path and bounded up the stairs of the Red House four at a time.

He looked out of the wide-open window across the fields, while the dogs, as usual, took the opportunity of appeasing their thirst at his water-jug,—for water lies at the bottom of deep cool wells in Sark, and sensible dogs take their chances when they offer.

Was this the room he had left an hour ago in the fresh of the dawn—a man whose gray future was just beginning to lift its bruised head out of the shadows?

Were those gleaming emerald fields the dim wastes he had sped across with his dumb companion, feeling as friendly towards him as towards anything on earth?

Were those trees over there, with the glow of spring-gold in their tender green leaves, the gloomy guardians of the churchyard where ghosts walked of a night?

Was that streak of blue away beyond the uplands, with the purple film along its rim, only the sea and a hint of Jersey, or was it a glimpse of heaven?

Was he, in very truth, that John Graeme who, for thirty days past, had been striving with all his might to root the thought of Margaret Brandt out of his life—and succeeding not at all?

It was the face of a stranger—a stranger with new joy of life in his sparkling eyes—that looked back at him out of the glass, as he plied his brushes, and tied his neck-tie with a careful assiduity to which the John Graeme of the past thirty days had been a stranger indeed.

It was amazing. It was almost past belief. Yet this was himself, and there was the gap in the dark hedge—never dark again to him so long as one twig of it lived—the gap where he had come upon her standing like a goddess of the morning with the glories of the dawn all about her. And somewhere not far away, under this same heavenly blue sky, was Margaret. And there was no sign or hint of Jeremiah Pixley in her atmosphere—nor of Charles Svendt.

What could it possibly all mean?

Miss Penny—Hennie Penny! What a delightfully ludicrous name! And what a delightful creature she was!—Miss Penny, unless he had been dreaming, had said they had come to get away from things—and people! Now what did she mean by that—if she really had said it and he had not been dreaming?

Was it possible Margaret had come to get away from Jeremiah Pixley and Charles Svendt? On the face of it, it seemed not impossible, for Graeme's only wonder was that she could ever have borne with them so long.

His brain was in a whirl. The eyes of his understanding were as the eyes of one immured for thirty days in a dark cell and then dragged suddenly into the full blaze of the sun. If he had just drunk a magnum of champagne he could not have felt more elevated, and he would certainly have felt very different. For his eye was clear as a jewel, and his hand was steady as a rock, though his heart had not yet settled to its beat and the red blood danced in his veins like fire.

"Jock, my lad," he said to himself, as he got the knot of his tie to his liking at last,—"keep a grip of yourself and go steady. Such a thing is enough to throw any man a bit off the rails. Ca' canny, my lad, ca' canny!"

VI

"Meg, I rather like young men with rippled hair," said Miss Hennie Penny, as they passed the Carrefour and strolled between the dewy hedges towards La Tour, with larks by the dozen bursting their hearts in the freshness of the morning above them.

"Do you, dear? I thought you scorned young men?"

"As a class, yes!—Especially the Cambridge variety. But not in particular. I make an exception in this case."

"So good of you!" murmured Margaret in her best company manner.

"Why did you never tell me how nice he was?"

"Tell you how nice he was? I don't remember ever discussing him with you in any shape or form whatever."

"Not to say discussed exactly, but you can't deny that you've mentioned him occasionally."

"So I have William Shakespeare and Alfred Tennyson—"

"And Charles Pixley!"

"That's quite different—"

"You're right, my dear. This is a horse of quite another colour. An awfully decent colour too. I'm glad you appreciate it. He's as brown as a gipsy and not an ounce of flab about him. Charles Pixley is mostly flab—"

"Don't be rude, Hen. You don't know Charles. And do drop your school slang—"

"Can't, my child. It's part of my holiday, so none of your pi-jaw! If you want me to enjoy myself you must let me have my head. You can't imagine how awfully good it tastes when you've been doing your best to choke girls off it for a year or two. It's one of the outward and visible signs of emancipation. This is another!" and she sprang up the high turf bank of the orchard of La Tour and danced a breakdown on it, and then jumped back into the road with ballooning skirts, to the intense amazement of old Mrs. Hamon of Le Fort, who had just come round the corner to draw sweet water from the La Tour well.

"People will think you're crazy," remonstrated Margaret.

"So I am, and you're my keeper, though it's supposed to be the other way about. The air of Sark has got into my head. What a quaint bonnet that old lady has! I wonder what colour it was in its infancy. Good-morning, ma'am! Isn't this a glorious day?" And old Madame Hamon murmured a word and passed hastily on lest worse should befall.

"Hennie, be sensible for a minute or two. I want you to consider something seriously."

"Sensible, if you like, Chummie, for 'tis my nature to. Serious?—Never! How could one, with those larks bursting themselves in a sky like that? And did you ever see hedges like these in all your life? What's it all about?—Ripply-Hair?"

"Yes. Don't you see how awkward the whole matter is—"

"Awkward for Charles Pixley maybe. I don't see that anybody else need worry themselves thin about it."

"I'm not thinking of Mr. Pixley. It's—"

"Ripply-Hair? Well, that's all right! Jolly sight nicer to think about him. I like his eyes too. There's something in them that seems to invite one's confidence. Perhaps you haven't noticed it? If I had a father-confessor—which, thank's-be, I haven't, and a jolly good thing for him!—I should stipulate for him having eyes just like that. Ripply hair too, I think. Yes. I should insist on his having hair just like Mr. Graeme's."

They had strolled along past Le Fort till the road lost itself in a field above Banquette, and there they came to an involuntary stand and stood gazing.

Before them, the long, broken slopes of the Eperquerie swept down from the heights to the sea, one vast blaze of flaming gorse—a tumultuous torrent of solid sunshine stayed suddenly in its course. And, in below the sunshine of the gorse, where rough Mother Earth should have been, there lay instead a soft sunset cloud, the tender cream-yellow and green of myriads of primroses and the just uncurling fronds of the bracken—primroses in such unbroken sheets and masses as to give a weird effect of remoteness and impalpability to that which was solid and close at hand.

"Wonderful!" murmured Margaret.

"Glorious!" murmured Miss Penny. "Is it really old Mother Earth we're looking at?"

"No, dear! It's a bit of the sky fallen down there and the sun has rolled over it into the sea. See the bits of him in the wavelets! And did you ever in your life see a green like that water below the rocks?"

"Sky and sun above, sun and sky below!—with trimmings of liquid emerald and sapphire, shot with white and gold. Meg, my child, this is a long way from No. 1 Melgrave Square."

"A long, long way!" assented Margaret thoughtfully. And then, to take advantage of her companion's comparative soberness through the stirring of her feelings,—"Hennie, do you think we ought to stop?"

"Stop?" and Miss Penny fronted her squarely. "Stop? Why, we've only just come. What's disgruntling you, Chummie?"

"Can't you see how awkward it is?"

"Well,—that depends—"

"No one would believe it was all pure accident."

"Perhaps it isn't," said Miss Penny oracularly.

"Why, what do you mean?" said Margaret, bristling in her turn.

"Oh, I'm imputing no guile, my child. I'm miles away up past that kind of thing. What I mean is this— perhaps it was meant to be, and you couldn't help yourselves. Now if that should be the case, it would be flying in the face of Providence to go and upset it all. What are your feelings towards him?"

"Feelings? I have no feelings—"

"Oh yes, you have, my child. You're not made of marble, though you can look it when you try. Why, I have myself. I like him—the little I've seen of him—and in spite of the fact that he caught me doing my hair, which is enough to turn anyone against anyone. I shall probably like him still more the better I get to know him. What have you against him?"

"I've nothing whatever against him. I—"

"Then, my dear, we'll sit tight. If anyone should go it's he, since he's been here a month, and we've only been one day. But if he goes it will only be because you make him. You've no ill-will towards him?"

"I've no feeling at all about him, except that it's awkward his being here."

"Then we'll just put the blame on Providence, and sit tight, as I said before. I'll see you come to no harm, my child. I could make that young man, or any young man, fly to the other end of the island by simply looking at him."

"Think so, dear?" and Margaret, the issue being decided for her, came back to equanimity.

"Sure!" said Miss Penny.

VII

He was sitting on the low stone wall that shut off the cobble-paved forecourt from the road, with his back towards them, when they sauntered through the open door after breakfast. He was smoking the choice after-breakfast pipe of peace, legs dangling, back bent, hands loosely clasped between his knees. He was very beautifully dressed as regards tie and collar—for the rest, light tweeds and cap of the same, and shoes which struck Miss Penny as flat. But these things she only noticed later. At present all she saw was a square light-tweed back, and a curl of fragrant smoke rising over its left shoulder.

Below him in the dust were his two friends,—Punch, gravely observant of his every movement, and occasionally following the smoke with an interested eye; Scamp, no less watchful, but panting like a motor-car, and apparently exhausted with unrewarded scoutings up and down every possible route for the day's programme.

In the hedge, on the opposite side of the road, sat a very small boy bunched up into an odd little heap, out of which looked a long sharp little face and a pair of black eyes as sharp as gimlets and as bright as a rat's, and beside him sat a big black cat busy on its toilet, which it interrupted in order to eye the ladies keenly when they appeared.

"Now, see you here, my son," they heard from the other side of the broad tweed back, "if you don't make it fine for the next thirty days you and I will have words together. If you want it to rain, let it rain in the night. Not a drop after four A.M., you understand. If you turn it on after four in the morning there'll be another rupture of diplomatic relations between you and me, same as there was last night."

The small boy's beady eyes twinkled, and he squeaked a few words in Sarkese.

"You have the advantage of me, Johnnie. And I've told you before it's not polite to address a gentleman in a language he's not familiar with, when you're perfectly acquainted with his own. The only word I caught was 'Guyablle!' and that's not a word for young people like you and me, though it may suit Marielihou. I'm very much afraid I'll have to speak to the schoolmaster about you, after all, and to the Vicar too, maybe. What? A Wesleyan, are you? Very well then, it's Monsieur Bisson I must speak to."

Here the small boy, with his face crumpled up into a grin, pointed a thin grimy finger past the young man, and he turned and saw the ladies. He doffed his cap and jumped down and tapped out his pipe, and the dogs sprang up expectant;—Punch, grave as ever but light on his feet for instant start; Scamp twisting himself into figure-eights, and rending the air with such yelps of delight that not a word could they pass.

"Johnnie! Stop him!" shouted Graeme. The small boy in the hedge flung out his arm with a sudden threatening gesture, and the circling Scamp fled through the gateway and up the garden with a shriek of dismay, and remained there yelping as if he had been struck.

"Odd that, isn't it?" said Graeme. "Johnnie's the only person that can stop that small dog talking; and, what's more, he can do it a hundred yards away. If the dog can see him that's enough, and yet they're good enough friends as a rule. Look at Punch!"

The big brown fellow was standing eyeing the small boy with an odd expression, intent, expectant, doubtful, with just a touch of apprehension in it, and perhaps of latent anger.

"Can you do it with Punch?" asked Miss Penny.

The small boy shook his head. "Godzamin, he'd eat me if I tried," he said, and lifted his eyes from the dog's, and the dog walked quietly up to Margaret and pushed his great head under her hand.

"He's a fine fellow," she said, caressing him.

"A most gentlemanly dog," said Miss Penny. "His eyes are absolutely poetical,—charged with thoughts too deep for words."

"Yes, he's dumb," said Graeme, stooping to pull a long brown ear.

"Really?" asked Margaret, looking into his face to make sure he was not joking.

"We've been close friends for a month now, and I've never heard his voice even in a whisper, nor has anyone else. I've an idea Johnnie here has put a spell on him."

"Poor old fellow!" said Margaret, fondling the big brown head.

"Oh, he's quite happy—bold as a lion and graceful as a panther, and Scamp talks more than enough for the two of them."

"And what a fine big cat you have, Johnnie!" said Miss Penny, and stretched a friendly hand towards Marielihou. "What do you call it?"

"Marrlyou," growled Johnnie; and Marielihou bristled and spat at the advancing white hand, which retired rapidly.

"The nasty beast!" said Miss Penny, and Marielihou glared at her with eyes of scorching green fire.

"Marielihou is not good company for anyone but herself," said Graeme. "Now, where would you like to go?"

"We were up that way before breakfast," said Miss Penny, nodding due north.

"Been to the Coupée yet?"

"No, we've been nowhere except just along here. We were afraid of getting lost or tumbling over the edges."

"Then you must see the Coupée at once. And we'll call at John Philip's as we pass, to get you some shoes."

"Shoes?" and each stuck out a dainty brown boot and examined it critically for inadequacies, and then looked up at him enquiringly.

"Yes, I know. They're delicious, but in Sark you must wear Sark shoes—this kind of thing"—sticking up his own—"or you may come to a sudden end. And, seeing that you're in my charge—"

"Oh?" said Margaret.

"Come along to John Philip's," said Miss Penny. And as they turned down the road with Punch, the hedge opened and Scamp came wriggling through, with white-eyed glances for Johnnie Vautrin and Marielihou sitting in the bushes farther up.

VIII

Miss Penny and Graeme did most of the talking. Margaret was unusually silent, pondering, perhaps, her friend's utterances of the early morning, and still wondering at the strange turn of events that had so unexpectedly thrown herself and John Graeme into such close companionship that he could actually claim to be in charge of her, and had proved it beyond question by making her buy a pair of shoes which she considered anything but shapely.

Graeme understood and kept to his looking-glass promise.

His heart was dancing within him. It was impossible to keep the lilt of it entirely out of his eyes. They were radiant with this unlooked-for happiness.

It was Margaret's shadow that mingled with his own on the sunny road—when it wasn't Miss Penny's. It was Margaret's pleated blue skirt that swung beside him to a tune that set his pulses leaping. Miss Penny's skirt was there too, indeed, but a thousand of it flapping in a gale would not have quickened his pulse by half a beat.

And Miss Penny probably understood—some things, or parts of things—or thought she did, and was extremely happy in that which was vouchsafed to her. Oh, she knew, did Miss Penny! She had not, indeed, had much—if put into a corner and made to confess to bare and literal truth, not any—experience, that is personal and practical experience, of such matters,—if, indeed, such matters are capable of being brought to the test of such a word as practical. But she had read much about them—in search of truth, and right and fitting books to be admitted to the school library—and she knew all about it. And here, unless she, Henrietta Penny, was very much mistaken, was a veritable live love-affair budding and blossoming—at least she hoped it would blossom—before her very eyes. Budding it undoubtedly was, on one side at all events, and blossom it certainly should if she could help it on; for he had ripply hair, and deep attractive eyes, and a frank open face, and she liked him.

They were suddenly in the shade, threading a narrow cutting between high gorse-topped banks of crumbly yellow rock. Then, without any warning, the rock-walls fell away. They were out into the sunshine again, and in front stretched a wavering rock path, the narrow crown of a ridge whose sides sank sharply out of sight. From somewhere far away below came the surge and rush of many waters.

"This is the Coupée," said Graeme, as the dogs raced across. "Over there is Little Sark."

"It is grand!" said Margaret, gazing at the huge rock buttresses whose loins came up through the white foam three hundred feet below.

"It's awful!" said Miss Penny. "You're never going across, Mr. Graeme?" as he strolled on along the narrow ridge.

"Surely! Why not? It's perfectly safe. There was a wooden railing at this side, but it fell over about a fortnight ago, and at present the good folks of Little Sark and Big Sark are discussing who ought to put up a new one. I happened to be sitting over there when it fell. A party of visitors came down the cutting here, and one was just going to lean on the railing, to look down into the gulf there, when he had the sense to try it first with his foot and it went with a crash, and they got a scare and went back to the hotel to eat lobsters. It was really useless as protection, but it made one feel safer to have it there."

"It's horrible," said Miss Penny emphatically.

"Safe as London Bridge, if you'll only believe it. It's a good four feet wide. The school children used to trot over when it was not more than two and a half."

"And none of them fell over?"

"Never a one. Why should they?"

"Meg, my dear," said Miss Penny, with a sudden flash of incongruity," this is truly a very great change from Melgrave Square."

"It is," laughed Margaret. "Are you coming, Hennie?"

"I'll—I'll risk it if Mr. Graeme will personally conduct me. He's in charge of us, you know."

"Certainly!" and he held out his hand to her, and then looked at Margaret. "Will you please wait here till I come back for you?" And catching, as he thought, a sign of mutiny in her face,—"Although it's perfectly safe it's perhaps just as well to have company the first time you cross."

"Very well," she said, and Miss Penny clung convulsively to the strong unwavering hand while she gingerly trod the narrow way, and the dogs raced half-way to meet them.

"Go away!" she shrieked, and the dogs turned on their pivots and sped back.

"Now, you see!" he said, when she stood safe on the rounded shoulder of Little Sark. "Where was the trouble?"

"It's perfectly easy, Meg," cried Miss Penny, uplifted with her accomplishment.

He wondered whether she would vouchsafe him her hand or attempt the passage alone. But she put her hand into his without hesitation, and thenceforth and for ever the Coupée held for him a touch of sacred glamour. For the soft hand throbbed in his, and every throb thrilled right up into his heart and set it dancing to some such tune as that which sang in David when he danced before the Ark. But his hand was firm, and his head was steady, for that which he held in charge was the dearest thing in life to him.

Three hundred blessed feet was the span of the Coupée. How fervently he wished them three thousand—ay, three million! For every step accorded him a throb, and heart-throbs such as these are among the precious things of life.

Neither of them spoke one word. Common-places were very much out of place, and the things that were in his heart he might not speak—yet.

"Didn't I say so?" cried Miss Penny, as they stepped ashore on Little Sark. "It's as easy as winking."

"I never said it wasn't," said Margaret, with a deep breath. "But I doubt if you'd have come across alone, my child."

"It was certainly pleasanter to have something to hold on to," said Miss Penny.

And Graeme thought so too.

IX

Little Sark provides ample opportunity for the adventurous scrambler, and Graeme, having tested the novel sensation of those delicious heart-thrills, was eager for more.

They prowled round the old silver mines, and sat on the great rocks at Port Gorey which had in those olden times served for a jetty, while he told them how Peter Le Pelley had mortgaged the island to further his quest after the silver, and how a whole ship-load of it sank within a stone's throw of the place where they sat, and with it the Seigneur's hopes and fortunes.

They peered into the old houses and down the disused shafts, lined now with matted growth of ivy and clinging ferns,—the bottomless pits into which the Le Pelley heritage had disappeared. Then he took them for mild refection to Mrs. Mollet's cottage; and after a rest,—and with their gracious permission, a pipe,—he led them across to the wild south walls of the island, with their great chasms and fissures and tumbled strata, their massive pinnacles, and deep narrow inlets and tunnels where the waves champed and roared in everlasting darkness.

The dogs harried the rabbits untiringly, Punch in long lithe bounds that were a joy to behold; Scamp in panting hysterics which gave over-ample warning of his coming and precluded all possibilities of capture.

Graeme led them down the face of the cliff fronting L'Etac, the great rock island that was once a part of Little Sark itself.

"Once upon a time there was a Coupée across here," he said. "Some time our Coupée will disappear and Little Sark will be an island also."

"Not before we get back, I hope," said Miss Penny.

"Not before we get back, I hope," said Graeme, for would he not hold Margaret's hand again on the homeward journey?

Down the cliff, along white saw-teeth of upturned veins of quartz, with Margaret's hand in his, then back for Miss Penny, till they sat looking down into a deep dark basin, almost circular: lined with the most lovely pink and heliotrope corallines: studded with anemones, brown and red and green: every point and ledge decked with delicately-fronded sea-ferns and mosses: and the whole overhung with threatening masses of rock.

"Venus's Bath," he told them. "Those round stones at the bottom have churned about in there for hundreds of years, I suppose. The tide fills it each time, as you will see presently, but the stones cannot get out and they've helped to make their own prison-house,—wherein I perceive a moral. It's a delicious plunge from that rock."

"You bathe here?" asked Margaret.

"I and the dogs bathe here at times. There's one other thing you must see, and I think you may see it to-day. The tide is right, and the wind is right, and there's a good sea on."

They waited till the long waves came swirling up over the rocks and filled the basin and set the great round stones at the bottom grinding angrily. Then off again along the splintered face of the cliff, one by one, that is two by two over the difficult bits, till he had them seated among some ragged boulders with the waves foaming white below them, and swooking and plunking in hidden hollow places.

The wind was rising, and the crash of the seas on the rocks made speech impossible. He pointed suddenly along the cliff face, and not twenty yards away, with a hiss and a roar, a furious spout of water shot up into the air a rocket of white foam, a hundred feet high, and fell with a crash over the rocks and into the sea.

Twenty times they watched it roar up into the sky, and then they crawled back up the face of the cliff, wind-whipped and rosy-faced, and with the taste of salt in their mouths.

"That is a fine sight," said Margaret, with sparkling eyes and diamond drops in her wind-blown hair. He thought he had never seen her so absolutely lovely before. He had certainly never seen anyone to compare with her.

"That's the Souffleur—the blow-hole. There's a bigger one still in Saignie Bay, we'll look it up if the wind gets round to the north-west. I'm glad you've seen this one. It was just a chance."

"I'm blow-holed all to rags, and, Meg, your hair is absolutely disgraceful," said Miss Penny. So differently may different eyes regard the same object, especially when the heart has a say in it. He would have given all he was worth for an offered lock of that wind-blown hair.

As Margaret turned she caught his eye, perhaps caught something of what was in it.

"Am I as bad as all that?" she laughed in rosy confusion.

"You're"—he began impetuously, but caught himself in time.—"You're all right. When you go to see the Souffleur you must expect to get a bit blown."

"It's worth it," she said. "And I'm sure we're much obliged to you for taking us. We could never have got there alone."

"We'd never have got to Little Sark, to say nothing of the Souffleur," said Miss Penny very emphatically.

"And now perhaps you'll forgive me for making you buy those shoes."

"My, yes! They're great," said Miss Penny, looking critically at her feet. "But decidedly they're not beautiful."

X

They loitered homewards, chatting discursively of many things, in a way that made for intimacy. Miss Penny and Graeme, indeed, still did most of the actual speaking, as he remembered afterwards, but Margaret was in no way outside their talk, and if she did not say much it is probable that she listened and thought none the less.

The Coupée afforded Graeme another all-too-short span of delight, while Margaret's hand throbbed in his and she entrusted herself to his protection.

He took them home by the Windmill, and through the fields and hedge-gaps into the grounds of the Red House, and in his heart's eye saw Margaret standing once more in the opening of the tall hedge with the morning glory all about her—just as he would remember her all his life.

"Time?" demanded Miss Penny, as they passed along the verandah.

"Half-past seven."

"Then you are half an hour late for your dinner. I propose that we ask Mrs. Carré to serve us all together to-night," said Miss Penny, "or we may all fare the worse."

"I shall be delighted," began Graeme exuberantly, "unless—" and he snapped a glance at Miss Brandt.

"We shall be glad if you will join us," she said quickly.

"I will be there in two minutes," he said, and sped up the Red House stairs to make ready.

"I hope to goodness he won't," said Miss Penny, as they passed through the hedge. "Now don't you say a word to me, Margaret Brandt. It was you invited him"

"Oh!"

"'We shall be glad if you will join us.' If that isn't an invitation I'd like to know what it is. And I heard you say it with my own two ears,—moi qui vous parle, as we say here."

"You know perfectly well that I could not possibly do anything else, Hennie. I believe you just did it on purpose. I don't know what's come over you."

"John Graeme. I like him. And after all he'd done for us—that Coupée, and Venus's Bath, and the Souffleur, and he like to lose his dinner over it all! What could a kind motherly person like me do but suggest—simply suggest, in the vaguest manner possible—"

"Yes?—" as she stopped in a challenging way.

"I merely threw out the suggestion, I say, in the vaguest possible way, that as we were nearly dying of hunger he should allow us to ask Mrs. Carré to let us have our dinner half an hour earlier than usual—"

"Oh!"

"And then you struck in, in your usual lordly fashion, and begged him to join us. And I'm bound to say he took it very well, not to say jumped at it."

"Hennie, you're a—"

"Yes, I know. And if I live I'll be a be-a, and perhaps more besides,"—with a cryptic nod.

"Now, what do you mean by that?"

"Wait patiently, my child, and you'll see."

"I believe the Sark air is affecting your—whatever you've got inside that giddy head of yours."

"Of course it is. That's what I came for, and to keep you out of mischief, you infantile law-breaker."

Graeme's two minutes were each set with considerably more than the regulation sixty seconds—diamond seconds of glowing anticipation, every one of them. And, to his credit, be it recorded that he allotted several of them to the invocation of most fervent blessings on Miss Penny, who, at the moment, was vigorously disclaiming any pretension thereto.

But, quite soon enough for his hosts, as he considered them,—his guests, according to Miss Penny,—he appeared at the cottage, bodily and mentally prepared for the feast, and showing both in manner and attire due sense of the honour conferred upon him.

It was a festive, and for one of them at all events, a never-to-be-forgotten meal. The strong Sark air had got into all their heads, and whatever prudish notions might have been working in Margaret, she had bidden them to heel and took her pleasure as it came.

Her mood, however, for the moment was receptive rather than expressive. Miss Penny and Graeme still did most of the talking, and Margaret sat and listened and laughed, not a little astonished at finding herself in that galley.

"What is the penalty for aiding and abetting a criminal in an evasion of the law, Mr. Graeme?" chirped Miss Penny one time, and took Margaret's energetic below-table expostulation without a wince.

"It would depend, I should say, on the particular dye of criminal. What has your friend been up to, Miss Penny? Is he a particularly black specimen?"

"In the first place he's a she, and in the next place her complexion has a decided tendency towards blonde. As to dye—I am in a position to state on oath that she does not."

For a moment he was mystified, then his eye fell on Margaret's face, full of glorious confusion at this base betrayal by her bosom friend.

"The Sark air does get into people's heads like that at times," he said diplomatically. "It's just in the first few days. But you soon get used to it. I felt just the same myself—losing faith in things and thinking ill of my friends, and so on. You'll be quite all right in a day or two, Miss Penny,"—with a touch of sympathetic commiseration in his voice.

"Oh, I'm quite all right now," said Miss Penny enjoyably. "I thought it only right and proper to let you know where you stand. At the present moment you are as likely as not aiding and abetting a breaker of the British laws and her accomplice. You may become involved in serious complications, you see."

"If that means that I can be of any service in the matter I shall be only too delighted,—if you will not look upon me as an intruder." He spoke to Miss Penny but looked at Margaret.

"Ah-ha! Qualms of conscience—"

"Hennie is a little raised, Mr. Graeme," broke in Margaret. "Please excuse her. A good night's rest will make her all right."

"Never felt better in my life," sparkled Miss Penny. "But seriously, Mr. Graeme, it is only right you should understand, for we don't quite know where we are ourselves, and I'm going to tell you even though Margaret kicks all the skin off my leg in the process. In a word,—we've bolted."

"Bolted?" he echoed, all aglow with hopeful interest.

"Yes—from Mr. Pixley and all his works. And as he had been threatening to make us a Ward of Court, you see—well, there you are, don't you know."

"I see," he said, and there was a new light in his eyes as he looked at Margaret, and his soul danced within him again as David's before the Ark.

"For reasons which seemed adequate to myself, Mr. Graeme,"—began Margaret, in more sober explanation.

"They were, they were. I am sure of it," sang his heart. And his brain asked eagerly, "Had Charles Svendt anything to do with it, I wonder?"

"—I thought it well to remove myself from the care of my guardian Mr. Pixley—"

"Splendid girl! Splendid girl!" sang his heart.

"—And as I have still some of my time to serve—"

"How long, O Lord, how long?" chaunted his heart, with no sense of impropriety, for it was sounding pæans of joyful hope.

"—You see—" said Margaret.

"I see."

"Do you think they could make me go back to him?" she asked anxiously.

"To Mr. Pixley? Certainly not—that is if your reasons for leaving him seemed adequate to the Court, as I am sure they would."

She offered no explanation on this point. All that she left unsaid, and that he would have given much to hear, seemed dancing just inside Miss Penny's sparkling eyes, and as like as not to come dancing out at any moment.

"You see," said Graeme, "I happen to have been making some enquiries from a legal friend on that very point—"

"Oh!" said Margaret, and Miss Penny's eyes danced carmagnoles.

"In connection with a story, you know. One likes to get one's legal points all right. In any case, as I was just about to tell Miss Penny for the benefit of her criminal friend, there would be lots of red tape to unwind before they could do anything, and this little isle of Sark is the quaintest place in the world in the matter of its own old observances and their integrity, and the rejection of new ideas. Mr. Pixley does not know you are here, of course?"

"Not much, or he'd have been over by special boat long since," said Miss Penny. "We managed it splendidly."

"And how long?" began Graeme, in pursuance of his train of thought, but stopped short at sound of the words, since they bore distant resemblance to a curiosity which seemed to himself impertinent.

But Miss Penny knew no such compunctions. She did not want to miss one jot or tittle of her enjoyment of the situation.

"About six months," said she quickly.

"Well, I should think we"—how delightful to him that "we," and how Miss Penny rejoiced in it!—"could hold them at bay for that length of time. The machinery of the law is slow and cumbersome at best, and in this case, I imagine, it would not be difficult to put a few additional spokes in its wheels."

If his face was anything to go by there were many more questions he would have liked to put—judicial questions, you understand, for a fuller comprehension of the case. But he would not venture them yet. He had got ample food for reflection for the moment, and his hopes stood high.

Never for him had there been a dinner equal to that one. Better ones he had partaken of in plenty. But the full board and the quality of the faring are not the only things, nor by any means the chief things, that go to the making of a feast.

The nearest approach to it had been that dinner with the Whitefriars, at which he first met Margaret Brandt, and that did not come within measurable distance of this one.

XII

"Will you be pleased to tek your dinner with the leddies again to-night?" asked Mrs. Carré, as she gave Graeme his breakfast next morning.

"I would be delighted," he said doubtfully. "But are you quite sure they would wish it, Mrs. Carré."

"But you did get on all right with them," she said, eyeing him wonderingly. "They are very nice leddies, I am sure."

"Oh, we got on first rate. We didn't quarrel over the food or fall out in any way. But—"

"Well then?"

"Will it be any easier for you?" he asked thoughtfully.

"Well, of course, it will be once setting instead of twice, and that iss easier—"

"Then suppose you put it to them on that ground, Mrs. Carré, solely on that ground, you understand. And if they are agreeable, I—well, I shall not raise any objections."

And so, presently, Mrs. Carré said to the ladies, "You did get on all right with the gentleman last night, yes?"

"Oh, quite, Mrs. Carré," sparkled Miss Penny.

"I wass wondering if it would please you to dine all at once together again each night. You see, it would save me the trouble of setting twice. I did ask him and he said he didn't mind if you didn't. He iss a very nice quiet gentleman, I am sure."

"I'm sure it's very good of him," said Miss Penny. "By all means serve us all at once together, Mrs. Carré. I guess we can stand it if he can."

"That iss all right then," said Mrs. Carré, and the common evening meal became an institution—to Graeme's vast enjoyment.

XIII

When the girls went into their room after breakfast to put on their hats and scrambling shoes, they saw Graeme sitting on the low stone wall, as usual, smoking his after-breakfast pipe, and they caught a part of the conversation in progress between him and Johnny Vautrin.

"I see five crows 's mawnin'," they heard in Johnnie's sepulchral voice.

"Really, now! Catch any?"

"There wuss five crows."

"Ah—five? That's an odd number! And what special ill-luck do you infer from five crows, Johnnie?"

"Someone's goan to be sick," said Johnnie, with joyous anticipation.

"Dear me! That's what five crows mean, is it?"

"Ouaie!"

"They didn't go into particulars, I suppose,—as to who it is likely to be, for instance, and the exact nature of the seizure?"

"They flew over to church there and settled in black trees."

"Vicar, maybe, since they went that way."

"Mebbe!"—hopefully.

"Well, well! Perhaps if we gave him a hint he might take some precautions."

"Couldn' tek nauthen 'd be any use 'gainst crows. Go'zamin, they knows!"

"You're just a confirmed old croaker, Johnnie."

"A'n't!" said Johnnie.

"Where's our old friend Marielihou?"

"She's a-busy," said Johnnie, wriggling uncomfortably.

"Ah,—killing something, I presume. Is it going to keep fine for the next three or four weeks?"

"I don' think."

"You don't, you little rascal?"

"You might do your best for us, Johnnie," said Miss Penny, as they came through the gap in the wall. "And if it keeps fine all the time I'll give you—let me see, I'll give you a shilling when we go away."

Johnnie's avidious little claw reached out eagerly.

"Godzamin!" said he. "Gimme it now, an' I'll do my best."

"Earn it, my child," said Miss Penny, and they went on up the road, leaving Johnnie scowling in the hedge.

"Well, where would you like to go to-day?" asked Graeme. "Will you leave yourselves in my hands again?"

"I'm sure we can't do better," said Miss Penny heartily. "Yesterday was a day of days. What do you say, Meg?"

"It looks as though we were going to occupy a great deal of Mr. Graeme's time," said Meg non-committally.

"It could not possibly be better occupied," he said exuberantly.

"And how about your story, Mr. Graeme? Is it at a standstill?" asked Miss Penny.

"Not at all. It's getting on capitally."

"Why, when do you work at it?"

"Oh,—between times, and when the spirit moves me and I've got nothing better to do."

"Is that how one writes books?"

"Sometimes. How do you feel about caves?"

"Ripping! If there's one thing we revel in it's caves, principally because we know nothing about them."

"Then we'll break you in on Grève de la Ville. They're comparatively easy, and another day we'll do the Boutiques and the Gouliots. Then we can get a whole day full of caves by going round the island in a boat—red caves and green caves and black caves and barking-dog caves—all sorts and conditions of caves—caves studded all round with anemones, and caves bristling with tiny jewelled sponges. Sark is just a honeycomb of caves."

"Spiffing!" said Miss Penny. "If Mr. Pixley gets on our track we'll play hide-and-seek in them with him."

"Then we ought to spend a day on Brecqhou—"

"A day on Brecqhou without a doubt!"

"And if we can get the boat from Guernsey to call for us at the Eperquerie, and can get a boat there to put us aboard, we might manage Alderney."

"Sounds a bit if-fy, but tempting thereby. Margaret, my dear, our work is cut out for us."

"And Mr. Graeme's cut out from him, I'm afraid."

"Oh, not at all, I assure you. It's going ahead like steam," and they began to descend into Grève de la Ville, the dogs as usual ranging the cliff-sides after rabbits, disappearing altogether at times and then flashing suddenly into view half a mile away among the gorse and bracken.

Sark scrambling requires caution and constant asistance from the practised to the unpractised hand, and Graeme omitted none of the necessary precautions. Whereby Margaret's throbbing hand was much in his,—so, indeed, was Miss Penny's, but that was quite another matter,—and every convulsive grip of the little hand, though it was caused by nothing more than the uncertainties of the way, set his heart dancing and riveted the golden chains still more firmly round it.

There are difficult bits in those caves in the Grève de la Ville,—steep ascents, and black drops in sheer faith into unknown depths, and tight squeezes past sloping shelves which seem on the point of closing and cracking one like a nut; and when they crawled out at last into a boulder-strewn plateau, open to the sea on one side only, they sighed gratefully at the ample height and breadth of things, and sank down on the shingle to breathe the free air and sunshine.

He amused them by telling them how, the last time he was there, he found an elderly gentleman sitting with his head in his hands, on that exact spot. And how, at sight of the new-comer, he had come running to him and fallen sobbing on his neck. He had been there for over an hour seeking the way out, and not being able to find it, had got into a panic.

"I wonder if you could find the place we came in, now?" said Graeme. "Scamp, lie down, sir, and don't give me away!"

"Why, certainly, it's just there," said Miss Penny, jumping up energetically and marching across, while the dogs grinned open-mouthed at her lack of perception. For it wasn't there at all, and she searched without avail, and at last sat down again saying, "Well, I sympathise with your old gentleman, Mr. Graeme. If I was all alone here, and unable to find that hole, I should go into hysterics, though it's not a thing I'm given to. I suppose we did get in somehow."

"Obviously! And that's where the advantage of a guide comes in, you see."

"I, for one, appreciate him highly, I can assure you. Where is that wretched hole?"

"Here it is, you see. It's a tricky place. I shall never forget the look of relief on that old fellow's face at sight of me. I believe he thinks to this day that I saved his life. He stuck to me like a leech all the way through the further caves and till we got back to the entrance."

"We're not through them yet then?"

"Through? Bless me no, we're only just starting, but there's no use hurrying. Tide's right, and we have plenty of time."

"I feel as if I'd been lost and found again," said Miss Penny. "If Mr. Pixley comes along we'll induce him in here and leave him to find his way out."

"It would take more than you to get Mr. Pixley in here, Hennie," said Margaret quietly. "He'd never venture off the roads, even if he risked his life in reaching Sark. He's much too careful of himself."

"He thinks a good deal more of himself than I do," said Miss Penny. "With all deference to you, Meg, since he's a relative, I consider him a jolly old humbug."

XIV

The days were packed with enjoyment for Graeme; not less for Miss Penny; nor—illuminated and titillated with a conposed expectancy as to whither all this might be leading her—for Margaret herself.

Graeme took the joyful burden of their proper entertainment entirely on his own shoulders. He reaped in full now the harvest of his lonely wanderings, and compared those former gloomy days with these golden ones with a heart so jubilant that the light of it shone in his eyes and in his face, and made him fairly radiant.

"That young man grows handsomer every day," was Miss Penny's appreciative comment, in the privacy of hair-brushing.

Margaret expressed no opinion.

"I thought him uncommonly good-looking as soon as I set eyes on him, but he's growing upon me. I do hope, for his sake, that I shan't fall in love with him."

And at that a tiny gleam of a smile hovered for a moment in the curves of Margaret's lips, behind the silken screen of her hair.

No trouble was too great for him if it added to their pleasure. He provisioned their expeditions with lavish discrimination. He forgot nothing,—not even the salt. He carried burdens and kindled fires for the boiling of kettles, and saw to their comfort and more, in every possible way. He assisted them up and down steep places, and Margaret's hand grew accustomed to the steady strength of his. She came to look for the helping hand whenever the ways grew difficult. At times she—yes, actually, she caught herself grudging Hennie-Penny what seemed to her too long an appropriation of it.

Never surely were the beauties of Sark seen under happier auspices, or through eyes attuned to more lively appreciation. For love-lit eyes see all things lovely, and no more perfect loveliness of sea and rock and flower and sky may be found than such as go to the making of this little isle of Sark.

He guided their more active energies through the anemone-studded and sponge-fringed caves under the Gouliots; through the long rough-polished, sea-scoured passages of the Boutiques; down the seamed cliffs at Les Fontaines and Grande Grève; along the precarious tracks and iron rings into Derrible; with the assistance of a rope, into Le Pot. And for rest-times they spent long delightful afternoons sitting among the blazing gorse cushions of the Eperquerie, and on that great rock that elbows Tintageu into the waves, and looks down on the one side on Port du Moulin and the Autelets, and on the other into Pegane Bay and Port á la Jument.

This high perch had a peculiar fascination for Margaret. She could have sat there day after day with perfect enjoyment. She never tired of it all—the crisp green waters below, with their dazzling fringe of foam round every gray rock and headland; the gold-tipped pinnacles of the Autelets, with their fluttering halos of gulls and sea-pies and cormorants, and their ridi-fringe of tawny seaweed and foamy lace; the rounded slopes of the Eperquerie; the bold cliffs behind, with their sprawling gray feet in the emerald sea, and their green and gold shoulders humping up into the blue sky; beyond them the black Gouliot rocks and foaming Race, and the long soft bulk of Brecqhou with its seamy sides and black-mouthed caves.

And here one day they had a novel experience, and Margaret learned something—got fullest proof, at all events, of something her heart had already told her.

They were sitting in the sea-ward cleft of this great rock behind Tintageu, one afternoon, and Graeme had just succeeded in getting the kettle to boil by means of an armful of old gorse bushes, when, straightening up for a rest, he said suddenly,—"Hello! Look at that now!" and pointed out towards Guernsey.

And there they saw a low white cloud, lying on the sea as though it had just dropped solidly out of the sky. Sea and sky were vivid vital blue, the sun shone brilliantly, Guernsey, Jethou, and Herm gleamed like jewels, and the white cloud lay between the upper and the nether blue like the white ghost of a new-born island not yet invested with the attributes of earth.

And, as they watched, it crept quickly along the blue-enamelled plain. It swallowed up the southern cliffs of Guernsey. Its creeping nose was level with the tall Doyle column. It crept on and on, till Castle Cornet disappeared and Peter Port was lost to sight. On and on—Jethou was gone, and bit by bit the long green and gold slopes of Herm were conquered, and its long white spear of sand ran out of the low white cloud. And still on, till all the outlying rocks and islands vanished, and where had been the glow and colour of life was nothing now but that strange pall-like cloud.

The blue of the sea in front had whitened, and suddenly the sentinel rocks at the tail of Brecqhou disappeared, and the white cloud came sweeping towards the watchers on the rock by Tintageu.

"We're in for it too," said Graeme, hastily emptying his kettle and packing up the tea-things. "Seems to me we'd better get ashore."

But the cloud was on them, soft films of gauzy mist with the sun still bright overhead. Then quickly-rolling folds of dense white cloud blotted out everything but the path on which they stood. The gorse and blue-bells and sea-pinks at their feet drooped suddenly wan and colourless, as though stricken with mortal sickness, and wept sad tears. They stood bewildered, while the pallid folds grew thicker and thicker, lit from above with a strange spectral glare, and coiling about them like the trailing garments of an army of ghosts. From the unseen abysses all round came the growl and wash of wave on rock and shingle, from the cliff above Pegane came the frightened bleat of a lamb, and an invisible gull went squawking over their heads on his way inland.

With an instinct for safer quarters, Miss Penny had started off towards the path which led precariously across the narrow neck to the mainland. The neck itself, with white clouds of mist billowing on either side, and streaming raggedly across the path, looked fearsome enough. She gave a startled cry and stood still.

"Stay here!" said Graeme to Margaret. "Don't move an inch!" and he felt his way, foot by foot, towards the causeway.

And Margaret, who had been regarding it all simply as a curious experience, felt suddenly very lonely and not very safe.

She heard him speak to Miss Penny, but she could not see two feet in front of her.

Then, after what seemed a long time, she heard above her—

"Miss Brandt? Margaret? Oh, good God!"—and there was in his voice a note that was new to her. Sharp and strident with keenest anxiety, it set a sudden fire in her heart, for it was for her.

"I am here, Mr. Graeme," she cried, and he came plunging down to her through the dripping gorse and bracken.

"Thank God!" he said fervently. "Why ever did you move?"

"I have not stirred."

"I must have got wrong. It is blinding. It will be safest to wait here, I think. Will you hold on to my arm?"

And as she slipped her hand through it she felt it trembling—the arm that had always been so strong and steadfast in her service—and she knew that this too was for her.

"Where is Hennie?" she asked.

"She's all right. I made her sit down among the bushes and told her she'd surely get smashed if she moved."

It was a good half-hour before the cloud drew off and they saw Guernsey, Herm, and Jethou sparkling in the sun once more.

Then they crossed the narrow path over the neck, and Margaret was glad they had not attempted it in the fog.

They picked up Miss Penny, damp but cheerful, and went home. For everything was dripping, and the pleasures of camping out were over for that day, but there were fires about that all the fogs that ever had been could not begin to extinguish.

XV

As the girls sat basking in the window-seat for a few minutes after breakfast one morning, they surprised a private conversation between their cavalier and Master Johnnie Vautrin. Graeme, with his back to them, sat smoking on the low stone wall. Johnnie was, as usual, bunched up in the hedge opposite.

"Well, Johnnie?" they heard. "Seen any crows this morning?"

"Ouaie!"

"How many then, you wretched little croaker?"

"J'annéveu deu et j'annéveu troy."

"Ah now, it's not polite—as I've told you before—to talk to an uneducated foreigner, in a language he does not understand. How many, in such English as you have attained to, and what did they mean according to your wizardry?"

"Pergui, you, too, are not polite! Your words are like this"—measuring off an expanding half yard in the air,—"they are all wind."

"Smart boy! How many crows did you see this morning?"

"First I saw two and then I saw three."

"Two and three make five. Croaker! Five crows mean someone's going to be sick. And which way did they go this time?"

"Noh, noh! First it wass two, and when they had gone then it wass three more."

"I see. And two black crows—what might they mean now?"

"Two crows they mean good luck."

"Clever boy! Continue! Three black crows mean—?"

"Three crows—they mean a marrying,—ouaie, Dame!"

"Ah, a marrying! That's better! That is very much better. It strikes me, Johnnie, that two lucky crows are worth twopence, and three marrying crows are worth threepence. And as luck would have it I've got exactly five pennies in my pocket. Catch, bearer of good tidings! Here you are—one, two, three, four, five! Well caught! Is it going to keep fine?" and Marielihou stopped licking herself to look at Graeme, and then went on again with an air of,—"I could tell you things if I would, but it's not worth while,"—in her ugly green eyes.

"I don' think," said Johnnie, jumping at the chance of ill news.

"You don't, you little rascal? Here, give me back my hard-earned pence! You're a little humbug."

"What's Johnnie been up to now?" asked Miss Penny, as she came out into the open.

"He's giving me lessons in necromancy and the black art of crows. He declines to pledge his honour on the continued brightness of the day."

"Oh, Johnnie! And we're going to Brecqhou!"

"I cann'd help."

"But you might send us on our way rejoicing."

"Gimme six pennies an' I will say it will be fine."

"I'm beginning to think you're of a grasping disposition, Johnnie. If you don't take care you'll die rich."

"Go'zamin, I wu'n't mind."

Then Graeme came out again, with the hamper he had had packed in the kitchen under his own supervision, and their cloaks, which, thanks to Johnnie, he had picked off the nails in the passage, and they set off for Havre Gosselin and Brecqhou.

XVI

"You'll not forget to come back for us about eight," Graeme shouted to the boatmen, as they pushed off from the fretted black rock on which their passengers had just made precarious landing.

"Nossir!" and they pulled away to their fishing.

"If it should be a fine sunset," he explained to the ladies, "the view of the Sark cliffs from Belême there, opposite the Gouliots, is one of the finest sights in the island."

The place they had landed was a rough ledge on the south side just under the Pente-à-Fouaille, some distance past the Pirates' Cave, and the ascent, though steep, was not so difficult as it looked. Graeme, however, in his capacity of chaperon, insisted on convoying them separately to the top—whereby he got holding Margaret's hand for the space of sixty pulse-beats—and then went down again for the cloaks and provisions.

Brecqhou, at the moment, was uninhabited. Its late occupant had thrown up his post suddenly, and gone to live on Sark with his wife, and a new caretaker had not yet been appointed. So they went straight to the house, deposited their belongings in the sitting-room, and then started out for a long ramble round the island.

First they struck west to Le Nesté, and scrambled among the rough rocks of the Point, stepping cautiously over the gulls' nests which lay thick all about, some with eggs and some with young.

The wonders of the sea-gardens in the rock-pools of Moie Batarde, and the entrancing views of Herm and Jethou and Guernsey, gleaming across the sapphire sea, with a magnificent range of snowy cloud-mountain breasting slowly up the deep blue of the sky behind, and looking solid enough to sit on, as Miss Penny said, absorbed them till midday.

Then they returned to the house, lit a fire of dried gorse, filled their kettle at the well and set it to boil, and carried out a table and chairs, for eating indoors was out of the question with such beneficence of sunshine inviting them to the open.

All the afternoon was occupied with the wonders of the Creux-à-Vaches, with its bold scarps and rounded slopes draped with ferns and enamelled with flowers, and the crannies and indentations of the northern side of the island. They sat for a time on Belême cliff entranced with the wonderful view of the bold western headlands of Sark, unrolled before them like a gigantic panorama from Bec-du-Nez to the Moie de Bretagne,—a sight the like of which one might travel many thousand miles and still not equal. And they promised themselves a still finer view when the setting sun washed every cliff and crag and cranny with living gold.

But as they turned to tramp through the ragwort and bracken towards the house, intent on cups of tea, the sight of the western sky gave them sudden start. The solid range of snow-white cloud-mountains had climbed the heavens half-way to the zenith, and was stretching thin white streamers still further afield. And its base in the west had grown dark and threatening, with pallid wisps of cloud scudding up it like flying scouts bearing ill tidings.

"Wind, I'm afraid," said Graeme, "and maybe thunder—"

And as he spoke a zigzag flash ripped open the dark screen, and a crackling peal came rattling over the lead-coloured sea and bellowed past them in long-drawn reverberations.

"Johnnie was right after all, the little monkey."

"I'm sorry now I didn't give him that sixpence," said Miss Penny.

"I don't suppose it would have made much difference—except to Johnnie. However, I hope it will soon blow over. Good thing we've got a shelter, and we can enjoy our tea while the elements settle matters among themselves outside."

The storm broke over them before the kettle boiled. The rain thrashed the house fiercely under the impulse of a wild south-west wind, which grew wilder every minute, and the thunder bellowed about them as though the very heavens were cracking.

"This is a trifle rough on inoffensive pilgrims," said Graeme. "I'm really sorry to have got you into it."

"You didn't do it on purpose, did you, Mr. Graeme?" asked Miss Penny, with pointed emphasis.

"I did not. I devoutly wish you were both safe home in the Rue Lucas."

"All in good time. Meanwhile, we might be worse off, and this tea is going to be excellent. Margaret, my child, do you know that tea under these conditions is infinitely preferable to tea in Melgrave Square, under any conditions whatsoever?"

"It is certainly a change," said Margaret.

"And a very decided improvement. It's what some of my young friends would call 'just awfully jolly decent,'" said Miss Penny.

"We're not out of the wood—that is to say, the island—yet," suggested Graeme.

"Or we shouldn't be here enjoying ourselves like this. Brecqhou is sheer delight."

"On a fine day," said Margaret quietly.

"Or in a thunderstorm," asserted Miss Penny militantly. But Margaret would not fight lest it should seem like casting reflections on their present estate.

The thunder rolled over the wide waters with a majesty of utterance novel to their unaccustomed city ears, the rain drew a storm-gray veil over everything past the well, the wind waxed into hysterical fury, tore at the roof and gables, and went shrieking on over Sark. And above the rush of wind and rain, in the short pauses between the thunder-peals, the hoarse roar of the waves along the black bastions of Brecqhou grew louder and louder in their ears.

Graeme's face grew somewhat anxious, as he stood at the window and peered westward as far as he could see, and found nothing but fury and blackness there. He had a dim recollection of hearing of outer islands such as this being cut off from the mainland for days at a time. He could imagine what the sea must be like among the tumbled rocks below. And he had seen the Race of the Gouliot in storm time once before, and doubted much if any boat would face the whirl and rush of its piled-up waters.

What on earth were they to do if the men could not get across for them?

Suppose they had to pass the night there?

Good Heavens! Suppose they could not get across for days? What were they to live on?—to come at once to the lowest but most pressing necessity of the situation?

They had weather-proof shelter. Firing they could procure from the interior woodwork of the house and outbuildings. And they had a small amount of tea and sugar, and half a tin of condensed milk, and rather more than half of the day's provisions, since they had contemplated high tea before embarking again. He determined that, if the storm showed no signs of abating, the high tea must be a low one, since its constituents might possibly have to serve for to-morrow's breakfast as well.

Both girls, their own perceptions strung tight by the electric state of matters outside, noticed the touch of anxiety in his face as he turned from the window, but both declined to show it.

"How's her head, Captain?" asked Miss Penny jovially.

"Dead on to a lee shore," he answered in her own humour. "But the anchorage is good and we're not likely to drift."

"Come! That's something to be thankful for, under the circumstances. Brecqhou banging broadside on to that big black Gouliot rock would be a most unpleasant experience. How about the sunset cliffs of Sark?"

"They're very much under a cloud. I'm afraid we must pass them for this time and choose a better. The cliffs indeed are there, but the sun is much a-wanting."

"Hamlet without the ghost of a father or even a sun."

"Truly!" And looking at Margaret, he said earnestly, "I can't tell you how sorry I am it has turned out this way."

"But it is no fault of yours, Mr. Graeme. No one could possibly have foreseen such a breakdown in the weather, with such a glorious morning as we had."

"After all, I'm not at all sure it isn't all Mr. Graeme's fault," said Miss Penny musingly.

"As how?" he asked.

"Didn't you stop me giving Johnnie Vautrin six demanded pennies to keep it fine all day?"

"I discouraged the imposition, certainly. But I don't suppose Johnnie could have done much—except with your sixpence."

"He's a queer clever boy, is Johnnie. He certainly said it wasn't going to keep fine."

"Little humbug!"

"Yet you gave him fivepence for seeing—or saying he saw—two crows and three crows, because two crows mean good luck and three crows mean—"

"You talk as if you believed his nonsense, Hennie," broke in Margaret.

"Perhaps I do—to some extent. He certainly declined to pledge himself to a fine day, and it remains to be seen if the rest of his—"

"—Humbug," suggested Graeme.

"We'll say predictions, since we're in a superstitious land,—come true. I shouldn't be a bit surprised. Thunderstorms are not, as a rule, deadly, and it is conceivable that they may, at times, even be means of grace. Would you mind piling some more gorse on that fire, Mr. Graeme? A counter-illumination is cheerful when the heavens without are all black and blazing. What a joke it would be if we had to stop here all night!"—she said it with intention, and Graeme understood and blessed her.

"We'll hope it won't come to that," he said, as lightly as he could make it. "But, if it should, we could make ourselves fairly comfortable. Robinson Crusoes up to date!"

"No—Swiss Family Robinsons!" was Margaret's quota to the lightening of gloom. "The way everything turned up just when that interesting family required it struck me as marvellous even when I was a child."

"You always were of an acutely enquiring—not to say doubting—disposition, my dear, ever since I knew you," said Miss Penny.

"I always liked to get at the true truth of things, and humbug always annoyed me."

"No wonder you found Mr. Pixley a trial, dear," said Miss Penny.

"You don't mean to cast stones of doubt at that shining pillar of the law and society, Miss Penny?" said Graeme, tempted to enlarge on so congenial a subject.

"Mr. Pixley does not appeal to me—nor I to him. I like him just as much as he likes me. And that's just that much,"—with a snap of the fingers.

"I'm afraid you and I are in the same boat," said Graeme enjoyably.

"I shouldn't be a bit surprised,—and for the same reason. We both like—"

"What shall we do for provisions, Mr. Graeme, if the storm continues?" asked Margaret, and Miss Penny smiled knowingly.

"I suggest husbanding those we have. It can't surely last long."

"Mrs. Carré was telling us the other night that once no steamer could get to Sark from Guernsey for three weeks," chirped Miss Penny. "If a steamer couldn't get to Sark, how should a small boat get to Brecqhou—Q.E.D.?"

"Gracious!" cried Margaret in dismay.

"Mr. Graeme would have to catch rabbits for us—and fish. And I believe there are potatoes growing outside there. Our clothing will be in rags, Meg. Mr. Graeme will be a wild man of the woods, and all our portraits will appear in the illustrated papers. The Outcasts of Brecqhou. Marooned on an Uninhabited Island. Three Weeks Alone."

"I'm off for a look round," said Graeme. "If that boat should be waiting for us, somewhere down below, it would be too stupid for us to be waiting for it up here," and he turned up his coat collar and pulled his cap over his brows.

"You'll get soaked," said Margaret. "Please take this, it will help a little," and she jumped up and thrust her golfing cloak into his hands. He seemed about to refuse, then thanked her hastily, and threw it over his shoulders and went out.

The wind caught him and whirled him along towards Belême cliffs. He tacked to the south and made a slant for the place where they had landed. As soon as he was out of sight of the house he drew the hood of the cloak over his head and rejoiced in it.

To be wearing her cloak brought Margaret appreciably nearer. Possibly that hood had even been over her head, had touched her shining hair, her fair soft cheek. He pressed it to his face, to his lips, and the hot blood danced in his veins at his temerity. The gale bellowed outside and drove him staggering, but inside the hood was the uplifting warmth and glow of personal contact with the beloved. Her very mantle was sacred to him. He fancied he could detect in it a subtle intimation of herself. He hugged it close, and leaned back upon the gale, and drifted towards the southern cliffs.

One glance at the black rocks below,—now hidden by the rushing fury of the surges, now outstanding gaunt and grim, with creamy cascades pouring back into the roaring welter below,—showed him how impossible it would have been for any boat to approach there.

He plunged on through the masses of dripping ragwort towards the eastern cliff, and stood absorbed by the grim fury of the Gouliot Race. The driven waves split on the western point of Brecqhou and came rocketing along the ragged black rocks on either side in wild bursts of foam. The Gouliot Passage was roaring with the noise of many waters, and boiling and seething like a gigantic pot. The sea was white with beaten spume for half a mile each way, and up through the tumbling marbled surface great black coils of water came writhing and bubbling from their tribulation on the hidden rocks below. The black fangs of the Gouliots were grimmer than ever. The long line of scoured granite cliffs on either side looked like great bald-headed eagles peering out hungrily for their prey.

There were no boats at the anchorage in Havre Gosselin. He learned afterwards that they had all run to the shelter of Creux Harbour on the other side of the island. He breasted the gale and headed for the house.

"I'm very much afraid we're stuck for the night," he said, as they looked up enquiringly on his entrance. "There's not a sign of a boat, and I'm quite sure no boat could face that sea. Sark looks like an outcast island—the very end of the world."

"Then we'll make ourselves comfortable here," said Miss Penny. "We began to fear you'd been blown over the cliffs. Is there plenty of wood in the house?"

"I'll go and get some more," and he came back with a great armful of broken driftwood, and went again for as much gorse as he could carry in a rude wooden fork he found near the stack.

"You must be soaked through and through," said Margaret.

"Bit damp, but your cloak was a great help," and he piled gorse and chunks of wood on the fire till its roaring almost drowned the noise of the storm outside.

XVII

"Well, I call this absolutely ripping," said Miss Penny exuberantly, as they sat by the fire of many-coloured flames, after a slender cup of tea and as hearty a meal as Graeme would allow them in view of possible contingencies. "Do please smoke, Mr. Graeme. It just needs a whiff of tobacco to complete our enjoyment."

"Sark," she added, leaning back with her hands clasped behind her head, "when no one knows you're there, is just heavenly. No letters, no telegrams, no intrusion of the commonplace outside world! Those are distinctly heavenly attributes, you know—"

It was truly extraordinary how, with nothing more than a very general intention thereto, she played into his hands at times. Here now was a very simple question he had been wanting to put to Miss Brandt for days past. For the answer to it might shed light in several directions. But he had been loth to force matters, and had quietly waited such opportunity as might arise in a natural way without undue obtrusion of the doubt that was in his mind.

"'Peace—perfect peace!' as Adam Black used to sigh," he said. "And by the way"—turning to Margaret—"speaking of letters, I have often wondered at times if you ever received two that I sent you concerning Lady Elspeth—just about the time she was called away to Scotland?"

She looked back at him with surprise, and his question was answered and his doubt solved before ever she opened her lips.

"About Lady Elspeth? No,—I certainly never got them."

"H'm!" he nodded thoughtfully. "The first I feared might have gone astray through some stupidity of the post-office. But the second I dropped into your letter-box myself. Moreover—"

"I never got them,"—with a charming touch of colour.

"Moreover—?" said Miss Penny expectantly, with a dancing light in her eyes.

"Well," he said, after a pause, "to tell you the whole story, Mr. Pixley assured me that you had had them and had handed them on to him."

"Mr. Pixley said that?" and Margaret sat up, with very much more than a touch of colour in her face now. In fact it was militantly red and vastly indignant.

"Yes. I—well, I called upon him at his office just to find out if—well, if you were ill or anything like that, you know. And among other interesting information he told me that, and cut off my head with his glasses and threw my remains out into the street;" at which Margaret smiled through her indignation.

"Mr. Pixley," said Miss Penny emphatically, "is a—a Johnnie Vautrin on a larger scale. Had he any other interesting items of information for you, Mr. Graeme?"

"Well—yes, he had. But I can estimate them now at their proper value, and it can rest there."

"It was Mr. Black's enthusiasm for Sark at that Whitefriars' dinner that put it into my head when—when we were wondering where to go. I remember now," said Margaret.

"It was Black's enthusiasm for Sark that put it into my head when I was wondering where to go," said Graeme.

"There you are, you see," said Miss Penny. "I knew you must have had some common inspiration."

"I am greatly indebted to Black. He's one of the finest fellows I know. He's done me more than one good turn, but I shall always count Sark his chiefest achievement," said Graeme heartily.

XVIII

The wind howled round the house, and whuffled in the chimney, and sent spurts of sweet-scented smoke to mingle with the fuller flavour of Graeme's tobacco. The walls were bare plaster, discoloured with age and careless usage. The chairs were common kitchen chairs, and the table a plain deal one. But the driftwood burned with flames whose forked tongues sang silently but eloquently of wanderings under many skies, of rainbow isles in sunny seas, of vivid golden days and the black wonders of tropic nights, of storms and calms, and all the untold mysteries of the pitiless sea.

But to two at least of the party—and perhaps even to three—that bare room was radiant beyond any they had ever known.

Orange and amber lightening into sunshine, purple into heliotrope, tender greens and lucent blues, burning crimson and fiery red, were the flames of the driftwood, and in these surely the imagination may find its happiest auguries. For if the dancing flames, out of their chastened knowledge, sang only of the past, in the minds of their watchers they were singing of futures brighter and more glowing than anything the past had ever known. And so, to two at least of them,—and perhaps to three,—never surely was there room so radiant as that bare room in that empty house on Brecqhou.

Miss Penny had the high endowment of a large heart, a wide imagination, and sentiment sufficient for a high-class girls' boarding-school.

She found herself for the moment out of place, yet she could not remove herself without too obvious an intention. She did the next best thing. She settled herself on her chair in a corner, slipped off her shoes, sat on her feet, and went to sleep.

Margaret, indeed, glanced at her suspiciously once or twice, without moving her head by so much as a hair's-breadth. But she seemed really and truly asleep, and for a moment Margaret was amazed that anyone could think of sleep in that enchanted room. But then she remembered that it was different— Hennie was Hennie, and she was she, and it was for her that the crystal ball of life had opened of a sudden and shown the radiance within.

How long they sat in silence before the rainbow fire she never knew.

Hennie was snoring gently—purring as one might say—in the most genuinely ingenuous fashion.

Graeme, in the riot of happy possibilities evoked by the disclosure of Mr. Pixley's perfidy, would have been content to sit there for ever, since Margaret was at his side. It was enough to know that she was there. He did not need to turn his head to enjoy the sight of her with gross material vision. Every tight-strung fibre of his being told him of her nearness, in ways compared with which sight and sound and touch are gross and feeble travesties of communication. Their spirits surely reached out and touched in that silent communion before the rainbow fire.

There were many things he wanted to ask her now. But they could wait, they could wait. The Doubting Castles he had built in his despair had had no foundations. He was building anew already, and now with rosy hope and golden faith, and the topstones of his building mingled with the stars.

He woke of a sudden to a sense of lack of consideration for her in his own enjoyment. Doubtless she was tired out, and was only kept from following Miss Penny's example by his cross stupidity in sitting there in that stolid fashion.

"Pray forgive me!" he said, as he rose quietly. "You must be tired, too. I will take the other room and you can join Miss Penny."

"I'm not the least tired. I never felt more awake in my life. Surely the wind has fallen."

He went to the door and opened it and looked out.

"It is only a lull. It will probably blow up again stronger than ever," and as he turned he found her at his elbow.

"Let us go outside," she said, and he could have taken her into his arms. Instead, he tiptoed across the room and got her cloak, and placed it on her shoulders with a new, vast sense of proprietorship.

He knew just how she felt. Even that room of rare delights was not large enough just then for her and for him. The whole wide world, and the illimitable heights of the heavens, could scarce contain that which was in them. Their hearts were full, and that which was in them was that of which God is the ultimate perfection. And in their ears, in the gaps of the storm, was the roaring thunder of the great white waves as they tore along the black sides of Brecqhou.

"Tell me more about those letters," she said briefly. "What did you write?"

"I wrote, nominally, to inform you of Lady Elspeth's sudden call to Scotland, but actually to tell you how sorely I regretted the sudden break in our acquaintance which had become to me so very great a delight."

"And when you got no answer?"

"I waited and waited, and then I had a sudden fear that you might be ill. And to satisfy myself I called on Mr. Pixley at his office. He told me you were quite well, that you had had my letters, and had handed them to him."

"Anything more?"

"Yes,—he said you were shortly to marry his son."

"That is what he wished,—and that is why I am here."

"Thank God! Then I may tell you, Margaret. I had been building castles and you were mistress of them all and of my whole heart. When Mr. Pixley knocked them into dust I came here to fight it out by myself, and a black time I had. Then God, in His goodness, put it into your heart to come too. Will you marry me, Margaret?"

"Yes, Jock."

And there, in the lull of the gale, in the lee of the lonely house on Brecqhou, they plighted their troth with no more need of feeble words, for their hearts had gone out to one another.

And all along the gaunt black rocks the great waves, which a moment before had been growling in dull agony, roared a mighty chorus of delight, and rolled it up the sloping seams of Longue Pointe, and flashed it on in thunderous bursts of foam from Bec-du-Nez to L'Etac.

And Miss Henrietta Penny, awakening about this time, and finding herself alone, laughed happily to herself, and sighed just once, and said from her heart, "God bless them!"—and did not go to sleep again, though to look at her you would never have known it, save for the fact that she no longer purred in her sleep,—for the woman has yet to be born who ever pleaded guilty to actual snoring.

XIX

Graeme slept that night just as much as might have been expected under the circumstances, and that was not one wink. Nevertheless, when morning came, he felt as strong and joyous as a young god. New life had come to him in the night, and he felt equal to the conquering of worlds. For love is life, and the strength and the joy of it.

He was out with the dawn, to a gray rushing morning full of the sounds of sea and wind. He drew a canful of water from the well, and had such a wash as no soap and a handkerchief would permit of. Then he drew another canful and left it outside the door of the ladies' room, and strode off to Belême to see if the boats had got back to their anchorage. But the little bay was a scene of storm and strife, a wild confusion of raging seas and stubborn rocks, the fruits of the conflict flying up the cliffs in spongy gouts of spume, and dappling the waters far and wide with fantasies of troubled marbling,—and there was not a boat to be seen.

But the sight of the great white seas roaring up the Sark headlands, as far as he could see on either hand, was one never to be forgotten. It was worth the price they had paid, even though it spelt a further term of captivity, and he turned back to his duties with that new glad glow in his heart which was no longer simply hope but the full and gracious assurance of loftiest attainment.

He had seen potatoes growing in a plot near the house. So, after lighting a fire in the kitchen and setting the kettle to boil, he rooted about till he found the remains of a spade and set himself to unaccustomed labours.

When Miss Penny came out of her room, freshfaced and comely coiffured, she found a ring of potatoes roasting in the ashes and the kettle boiling, and Graeme came in, bright-eyed and wind-whipped, wiping his hands on a very damp handkerchief.

"I am so glad, Mr. Graeme," she said, with sparkling eyes and face, and hearty outstretched hand.

"Margaret has told you?"

"Of course Margaret has told me. Am I not her keeper, and haven't I been hoping for this since ever I saw you?"

"That is very good of you. I thought, perhaps—"

"Thought it might take me by surprise, I suppose—and perhaps that I might take it badly? Not a bit! It fulfils my very highest hopes. And I can assure you you have got a prize. There are not many girls like Margaret Brandt."

"Don't I know it? I have known it from the very first time I met her—at that blessed Whitefriars' dinner."

"I think you will make her very happy."

"I promise you I will do my very best."

And then Margaret came into the kitchen and knew what was toward.

She looked like a queen and a princess and a goddess all in one, with a flood of happy colour in her face and a glad glow in her eyes, and no more hint of maidenly shyness about her than was right and natural. And Miss Penny's eyes were misty of a sudden, as Graeme went quickly up to her friend, and feasted his hungry eyes on her face for a moment, and then bent and gallantly kissed her hand. For in both their faces was the great glad light that is the very light of life, and Miss Penny was wondering if, in some distant future time, it might perchance be vouchsafed to her also to attain thereto.

"I hope you both slept well," he said gaily. "I've done my best in the provisioning line. I know we've got plenty of salt, for one generally forgets it and so I always put in two packets."

"You've done splendidly," said Miss Penny, tying up tea in a piece of muslin and dropping it into the kettle.

"I'd have tried for a rabbit, but I wasn't sure if either of you could skin it—"

"Ugh! Don't mention it!"

"And I knew I couldn't, so we'll have to put up with roasted potatoes and imagine the rabbit. I've been told they do that in some parts of Ireland,—hang up a bit of bacon in a corner and point at it with the potato and so imagine the flavour."

"Potatoes are excellent faring—when there's nothing better to be had," said Miss Penny, rooting in the basket. "However, here are three of yesterday's sandwiches, slightly faded, and some biscuits—in good condition, thanks to the tin. Come, we shan't absolutely starve!"

And they enjoyed that meal—two of them, at all events, and perhaps three—as they had never enjoyed a meal before.

"And the weather?" asked Margaret.

"The blessed weather is just as it was; perhaps even a bit more so,—the most glorious weather that ever was on land or sea!"

"But—" said Margaret, smiling at his effervescence.

"No, I'm afraid it can't last very much longer, and potatoes and salt I know would begin to pall in time. After breakfast you shall see the grandest sight of your lives,—and for the rest, we will live in hope."

XX

And, after all, they saw what they had specially come to see—a sunset from Belême cliff.

For the day remained gray and boisterous until late in the afternoon. They had lunched—with less exuberance than they had breakfasted—on potatoes and salt and a thin medicinal-tasting decoction made from breakfast's tea-leaves; they were looking forward with no undue eagerness to potato dinner without even the palliative of medicinal tea; and even Miss Penny acknowledged that, choice being offered her, she would give the preference to some other vegetable for a week to come;—when, of a sudden, the gray veil of the west opened slowly, like the lifting of an iron curtain, and let the light behind shine through.

And the light was as they could imagine the light of heaven—a pure lucent yellow as of the early primrose, but diaphanous and almost transparent, as though this, which seemed to them light, was itself in reality but an outer veil hiding the still greater glory behind. The curtain lifted but a span, and the lower rim of it curved in a gentle arch from the middle of Guernsey to the filmy line of Alderney. All below the sharp-cut rim was the sea of heavenly primrose, with here and there a floating purple island edged with gold. All above was sombre plum-colour flushed with rose, the edges fraying in the wind, and floating in thin rosy streamers up the dark sky above.

The sun, larger than they had ever seen him in their lives, dropped gently like a great brass shield from behind the dark curtain into the sea of primrose light, and the primrose flushed with crimson over Guernsey and with tender green and blue over Alderney.

They hastened away to Belême cliff, and then they saw what they had hoped to see, and more;—the mighty granite frontlets of Sark all washed with living gold—- shining from their long conflict with the waves, and gleaming, every one, like a jewel,—from Bec-du-Nez to Moie de Bretagne. And, out in the dimness, behind which lay Jersey, there suddenly appeared the perfect circle of a rainbow such as none of them had ever dreamed of—a perfect orb of the living colours of the Promise—resting bodily on the dark sea like a gigantic iridescent soap-bubble, glowing and pulsing and throbbing under the level beams of the setting sun.

"Wonderful!" murmured Margaret.

"I never saw more than half a bow before," whispered Miss Penny.

"Nor I," said Graeme. "But then, you see, nothing ever was as it is now. Things happened last night."

At which Miss Penny smiled and murmured, "Of course! That accounts for everything. The whole world is changed."

And they watched and watched, in breathless admiration, first the cliffs, and then the bow, and then the sun, and then the cliffs and bow again, till the last tiny rim of the sun sank behind the dark line of Herm, and the bow went out with a snap, and the cliffs in front grew gray and sank back into their sleep, as the shadows crept up out of the sea.

And, presently, the primrose sea in the clouds lost its transparent softness and flushed with rose and carmine. The tender greens and blues in the north deepened, and the sky above glowed crimson right into the far east. And the sea below was like a ripe plum with a rippling bloom upon it, and then it answered to the glow "above and became like burnished copper. And over it, from the south end of Sark, came a dancing white sail, at sight of which Graeme leaped to his feet.

"The show is over," he cried, "and here comes your highnesses' carriage."

"I wouldn't have missed it for anything," said Margaret softly, with a rapt face still.

"It was worth living on potatoes for a month for," said Miss Penny. "All the same, I hope Mrs. Carré will have some dinner for us when we get home."

The boat was heading for the Pente-à-Fouaille where they had landed the day before, and they hurried to meet it, Graeme full of misgivings as to the embarkation, for the waves were still roaring up the rocks in bursts of foam, though the wind had fallen somewhat.

But the boatmen knew their business, and had brought an extra hand for its safe accomplishment. They dropped the sail and pulled round a corner of the black rock. Then, while two of them kept the boat from destruction, the other stood and Graeme dropped the girls one by one into his arms, and was a very thankful man when he tumbled in himself, all in a heap, and wiped the big drops of sweat from his brow.

A stroke or two with the oars and they were plunging back through the hissing white caps, but not, as he had expected, to Havre Gosselin.

"Where to?" he shouted to the blue-guernseyed stalwart nearest him.

"Grande Grève. We couldn' beach in Havre Gosselin, and mebbe the leddies wouldn' like to climb the ladders," with a grin at the leddies.

"Not much!" said Miss Penny. "Margaret, my dear, prepare yourself! I'm going to be sick if this goes on much longer."

But before she had time to be sick they had rounded the shoulder of Port-és-Saies, and their boat's nose ran up the soft sand of a low tide in Grande Grève, and the green waves came curling exultantly in over the stern. The men leaped out and hauled bravely, and in a moment the girls were ashore.

"Couldn' get back nohow last night, sir. 'Twould a bin as much as our lives were worth. Hope ye didn' starve," said the spokesman with another genial grin.

"No, we didn't expect you. We dug potatoes and cooked them. Here you are, and thanks for coming as soon as you could," and, from their smiling faces, their reward without doubt covered not only that which they had actually done but that also which they had unwittingly helped to do.

The boat shoved off and made for its own anchorage, and Graeme led the girls up the toilsome path to the Coupée.

It was after nine when they reached the cottage, and the first thing they saw was Johnnie Vautrin sitting in the hedge opposite, with Marielihou licking her lips alongside.

"I just seen seven crows," cried Johnnie gleefully.

"Little rascal! You dream crows," said Graeme, whose desires at the moment ran to something more palatable and satisfying.

"And what do seven crows mean, Johnnie?" asked Margaret.

"Seven crows means everything's oll right!"

"Clever boy! You see just what you want to see," said Graeme, and then Mrs. Carré appeared at the door of the cottage.

"Ah then, here you are!" she said, with a large welcoming smile. "And the dinner I haf been keeping for you for an hour an' more."

"You're a good angel, Mrs. Carré," said Graeme gratefully. "We are a bit late, aren't we? I hope you've put yesterday's dinner and to-day's together. We've had nothing to eat to speak of for a month. What did you think when we never turned up last night?"

"Oh, but I knew you would be all right. There iss a house on Brecqhou, and there iss watter, and you had things to eat, and it was better on Brecqhou last night than on the watter."

"It was," said Graeme heartily, and sped off up the garden for a much-needed wash and brush-up.

"Now what would I like myself if I was in their place?" asked Miss Penny of herself, while she rectified the omissions of the last two days in the matter of Nature's cravings for a more varied diet than Brecqhou afforded.

"Why, to be alone and free from the observation of Miss Hennie Penny," she promptly answered herself, and as promptly acted on it.

"Meg, my dear, I am aweary. I am not accustomed to playing Swiss Family Robinson. By your leave, Monsieur and Mademoiselle, I will wish you good-night and pleasant dreams," and she went off into the bedroom.

"May she have as tactful a chaperone when her own time comes," said Graeme, with a smile. "Do you think you would sleep better if you went to bed at once or if you had a little walk first?"

"I am not the least bit sleepy," said Margaret.

"Then a stroll will do you good," and they went out into the night. And Miss Penny, as she heard their feet on the cobbles, smiled to herself a little wistfully.

Such a night of stars! The gale had swept the heavens and thinned the upper air till the Milky Way was a wide white track strewn thick with jewels, and the greater lights shone large and close. As they sauntered in silence towards La Tour, their faces towards the stars among which their full hearts were ranging in glorious companionship, one of the lesser lights silently loosed its hold and dropped slowly from zenith to horizon, in a fiery groove that momentarily eclipsed all else.

And while Graeme was still pressing to his heart the soft arm that lay in his, in silent enjoyment of the sight and at their sharing it, another star swung loose, and another, and another, till the glittering vault seemed laced with fiery trails and they stood in rapt admiration.

"What a sight!" said Margaret softly. "I have never seen anything like that before."

"Nor I. The very stars rejoice with us.... You have made me the happiest man in all the world this day, Margaret. I can hardly believe it is real ..."

"I am real," she said, with a low warm little laugh. "And I am happy. Kiss me, Jock!" and he kissed her there under the falling stars, and she him, in a way that left no doubt as to what was in them, and the evening incense of the honeysuckle and hawthorn wafted fragrance all about them.

There was still a tender touch of colour in the sky over the western sea as they came out on the Eperquerie.

"When are you free, Margaret?" he asked,—the first word since they kissed in the lane.

"I am twenty-one on New Year's Day."

"Six whole months! How can we possibly wait all that time?"

"Why should we?" she asked delightfully.

"Undoubtedly—why should we?" he said, on fire with her charming readiness. "You are probably by this time ringed with legal pains and penalties, but they are all less than nothing."

"What could they do?"

"I believe they clap the male malefactor into prison—"

"I will go with you."

"I'm not sure if there are any married cells."

"And how long would they keep us there?"

"Till, in their opinion, I had purged my contempt, I believe."

"And how long would that be?"

"I've no idea. It probably depends on circumstances. Do you know that, until Lady Elspeth told me, I had rib idea that you had any money. It was rather a blow to me."

"I don't see why."

"But I told our old friend that if—well, if, you understand—I should insist on everything you had being settled on yourself."

"You and Lady Elspeth seem to have discussed matters pretty freely," she said, with a laugh.

"She's the dearest old lady in the world, and delights in mothering me. She got me in a corner that afternoon, and taxed me with coming to her house for reasons other than simply to see herself—"

"And you—?"

"I had to own up, of course, and then she crushed me by telling me that you were an heiress, and that Mr. Pixley probably had views of his own concerning you."

"Which he had, but they happened not to coincide with mine, and so I came to Sark."

"Happy day! I see you yet, standing in the hedge by the Red House, and I believing you a vision."

"I could hardly believe my eyes either. You seemed to come jumping right out of the sky."

"I jumped right into heaven—the highest jump that ever was made."

"I was a bit put out at first, you know—"

"I know you were."

"I thought you had learned we were coming, and had followed us here."

"Whereas—" he laughed.

"Exactly!"

I

"But yes, I can marry you in the church," said the Vicar, blowing out smoke, and laughing enjoyably across at Graeme, who sat in another garden chair under the big trees in front of the Vicarage.

"In spite of the fact that we are aliens?"

"Oh, it is not so bad as that. We ab-sorbed you by conquest and so you are really a part of us. We are all one family now."

"And such a marriage would be perfectly legal and unassailable?"

"I shall marry you more firmly than if you were married in Cant-er-bury Cath-edral," laughed the Vicar.

"That should suffice. But why more firmly? How improve on perfection?"

"I will tell you," said the Vicar, with increased enjoyment, as he leaned forward and tapped Graeme's knee. "It is this way.—If you are married in Cant-er-bury Cath-edral you can be divorced,—n'est-ce pas? Oui! Eh bien!—If you are married in my church of Sark you can never be divorced. C'est ça! It is the old Norman law."

"We will be married in your church of Sark," said Graeme, with conviction.

"That is right. I shall marry you so that you shall never be able to get away from one another."

"Please God, we'll never want to!"

"Ah yes! Of course. C'est ça!"

II

"We have never had a case of the kind, as far as I know. Certainly not in my time," said the Seigneur, smiling quizzically across the tea-table at Graeme. "But you gentlemen of the pen are allowed a certain amount of license in such matters, are you not?"

"We sometimes take it, anyhow. But one likes to stick as close to fact as possible."

They were sitting in the shady corner in front of the Seigneurie, with four dogs basking in the sun beyond, and beyond them the shaven lawns and motionless trees, the leafy green tunnel that led to the lane, and a lovely glimpse into the enclosed gardens through the ancient gateway whose stones had known the saints of old.

Graeme had put a certain proposition to the Lord of the Island, nominally in connection with the story he was busy upon, but in reality of vital concern to the larger story in which Margaret and he were writing the history of their lives.

"Sark, you know, is a portion of the British Empire, or perhaps I should say the British Empire belongs to Sark, but we are not under British law. We are a law unto ourselves here," said the Seigneur.

"And the authority of a British Court would carry no weight with you? In the case I have put to you, if the Court of Chancery ordered you to surrender the young lady, you would refuse to do so?"

"I could refuse to do so. What I actually would do might depend on circumstances."

"I see," said Graeme musingly, and decided that the Seigneur's goodwill was worthy of every possible cultivation both by himself and Margaret. For he did not look like one who would help a friend into trouble.

III

"I've been thinking a good deal about it, and I really don't see any reason why we should wait,"—said Graeme, looking at Margaret.

And Miss Penny said "Hear! Hear!" so energetically that Margaret laughed merrily.

"We are both of one mind in the matter, an life is all too short at its longest, and most especially when it offers you all its very best with both hands—"

"Hear! Hear!" said Miss Penny.

"And time is fleeting," concluded the orator.

"And that kettle is boiling over again," and Miss Penny jumped up and ran to the rescue.

They were spending a long day in Grande Grève—the spot that had special claims upon their liking since their landing there after that memorable trip to Brecqhou. They had brought a full day's rations, prepared with solicitous discrimination by Graeme himself, and a kettle, and a great round tin can of fresh water from the well at Dixcart, and a smaller one of milk.

So high were their spirits that they had even scoffed at Johnnie Vautrin's intimation that he had seen a magpie that morning, and it had flown over their house. But magpie or no magpie they were bent on enjoyment, and they left Johnnie and Marielihou muttering black spells into the hawthorn hedge, and went off with the dogs down the scented lanes, through the valley where the blue-bells draped the hillsides in such masses that they walked as it were between a blue heaven and a blue earth, and so by the meadow-paths to the Coupée.

Their descent of the rough path down the side of the Coupée with all this impedimenta had not been without incident, but eventually every thing and person had been got to the bottom in safety.

Then, while the dogs raced in the lip of the tide and Scamp filled the bay with his barkings, the girls had disappeared among the tumbled rocks under the cliff, and Graeme had sought seclusion at the other end of the bay. And presently they had met again on the gleaming stretch of sand; he in orthodox tight-fitting dark-blue elastic web which set off his long limbs and broad shoulders to great advantage; Hennie Penny in pale blue, her somewhat plump figure redeemed by the merry face which recognised all its owner's deficiencies and more than made up for them all; Margaret, tall, slim, shapely, revealing fresh graces with every movement,—a sea-goddess in pale pink—a sight to set the heart of a marble statue plunging with delight.

Hennie Penny persisted in wearing an unbecoming cap like a sponge-bag, which subjected her to comment.

Margaret's crowning glory was coiled in thick plaits on top of her head, and if it got wet it got wet and she heeded it not.

Both girls had draped themselves in long towels for the walk down to the water, and Graeme's heart sang with joy at the surpassing beauty of this radiant girl who had given her heart and herself and her life into his keeping.

Dainty clothing counts for much in a girl's appearance. Not every girl shows to advantage in bathing costume. But when she does, she knows it, and the hearts of men are her stepping-stones.

Hennie Penny was a cautious swimmer. She preferred depths soundable at any moment by the dropping of a foot, and if the foot did not instantly touch bottom she fell into a panic and screamed, which added not a little to the hilarity of their bathes.

Margaret and Graeme, however, were both at home in the water. They delighted to set their faces to the open and breast steadily out to sea, rejoicing in the conquest of the waves. But he always watched over her with solicitous care, for there are currents, and cross-currents, and treacherous undertows round those coasts, and the wary swimmer is the wiser man.

And the dogs always swam with them, Punch lunging boldly ahead with the ease and grace of a seal, looking round now and again to see if they were coming, and turning the moment they turned. While Scamp, away in the rear, thrashed along spasmodically, with a yelp for every stroke, but would not be left out of it. The sight of his anxious little face and twisting nose more than once set Margaret laughing, so that she had to turn on her back and float till she got over it, greatly to the small dog's satisfaction.

Full of life and the mighty joy of it, they found the going unusually easy that day. The water was like the kiss of new life, crisp, tonic, vitalising. There was no more than a breath of wind, no more than a ruffle on the backs of the long blue rollers that came sweeping slowly in out of the West.

Graeme, as he glanced round in his long side-strokes at the lovely eager face gemmed with sparkling water-jewels, took full deep breaths of delight and gratitude to the All-Goodness that had vouchsafed him such a prize.

The kiss of the life-giving water had induced a tender flush of colour in the soft white neck, as though the pink of her bathing-suit had spread upwards. He could see the pulsing blue veins in neck and temple as she rose to her stroke. A tiny tendril of water-darkened hair lifted and fell on her neck like a filament of seaweed on a polished rock. Her eyes were very bright, and seemed larger than usual with the strenuous joy of it all. The wonder of her beauty absorbed him. He could hardly turn his face from it. He would have been content to go on swimming so for ever.

But, glancing past the sweet face one time, he saw that they had gone farther than he knew, and Scamp had turned long since and was yelping towards the shore.

"Better turn now," he said quietly, and she floated for a moment's rest, then turned and they headed for the shore, and Punch passed them noiselessly.

They ploughed along in good cheer for a time, and then, of a sudden, it seemed to him that they were making but poor progress.

He fixed his eyes on a rock on the shore and swam steadily on.

They had been opposite it. Twenty strokes, and the rock, instead of facing them, had swung slowly to the north. They were making less than no progress. They were drifting. They were in the grip of a current that was carrying them towards the black fangs of Pointe la Joue.

A cold sweat broke out among the sea-drops on his brow. Pointe la Joue is an ill place to land, even if they could make it, and the chances were that the current would carry them past.

How to tell her without undue upsetting? A panic might bring disaster.

He looked round at her. The bright face was high and resolute. She was not aware of the danger, but from that look on her face he did not think she would go to pieces when he told her.

The rock he had been watching stood now at an angle to their course.

"Are you tired, Meg?" he asked.

"I'm all right."

"Turn on your back and float for a minute or two," and he set the example, and Punch saw and came slipping back to them.

"We're in a cross current," he said quietly. "And we're making no way—"

"I know. I was watching a rock on the shore. What's the best thing to do?"

"We'll rest for a few minutes and then go with the tide round Pointe la Joue. We can land in Vermandés. You're not cold, are you?"

"Not a bit."

When he lifted his head the Coupée was shortened to a span, and the southern headland folded over it as he looked. They were drifting as fast as a man could walk at his fastest. They were abreast the black rocks of La Joue.

"Now, dearest, a little spurt and we shall be in the slack. If you get tired, tell me," and they struck out vigorously on a shoreward slant in the direction they were going.

There should have been a backwater round the corner of Vermandés. He had counted on it. And there was one, but so swift was the rush of the tide round the out-jutting rocks of La Joue, that for some minutes, as they battled with the rough edge of it, it was touch and go with them.

At a word from her his arm would be at her service. But she fought bravely on, and could admire Punch's graceful action even then. The waves smacked her rudely in the face. Great writhing coils came belching up from below and burst under her chin and almost swamped her. One, as strong as a snake, rose suddenly under her, flung her off her stroke, rolled her over, made her for a moment feel utterly helpless.

"Jock!"

He had been watching her closely. His arm flashed out in front of her.

"Grip!" and she hung on to it and it felt like a bar of steel.

"Now!"—when she had recovered herself somewhat. "Grip the top of my suit."—She hooked her fingers into it and he struck out through the turmoil.

It was a tough little fight. She struck out vigorously behind to help him. And, though the losing of the fight might mean tragedy and two white bodies ragging forlornly along the black teeth of Little Sark, she still had time to notice the mighty play of muscles in his back and arms, and the swelling veins in his sunburnt neck, and the crisp rippled hair above, and she rejoiced mightily in him. And—while possible deaths lurked all about them—her soul grew large within her at thought of the brave heart in front, and the strenuous will, and the shapely body, and the powerful muscles—all battling for her—all hers—and she theirs. What matter if they were beaten, if they but went out together! What matter Death so long as he did not divide them! So uplifted was she with the joy of him.

And then, with a final wrestle, they were in slack water, and she loosed her hold and struck out alongside him.

And presently he was helping her carefully up a seamed black rock, and the hand she gripped was shaking now, and she knew it was not for himself.

"Thank God!" said Graeme fervently, as he sank down heavily beside her, and panted while the water ran out of them, and Punch scrambled up and lay quietly alongside. "Meg,—we were in peril."

"Jock," she said jerkily, for her heart was going now quicker than usual, "I do not believe I would have minded—if we'd gone together."

"Ay—together, but, God be thanked, it did not come to that!"

They sat in silence for a time, finding themselves, while the green seas swelled up to their feet, and sank out of sight below, and their rock was laced with cascades of creamy foam.

"How shall we get back?" asked Margaret at last. "Hennie will be in desperation. She will think we are drowned."

"We can climb the head and round into Grande Grève, but it would be pretty rough on the feet. Or we can wait till the tide turns and swim in again—"

"When will it turn?"

"It's full at noon," he said, studying the waters in front. "But how that affects matters here none but a Sarkman could say. Tides here are a law unto themselves, like the people."

"How would that do?" asked Margaret, as a black boat came slowly round the rocks from Les Fontaines, sculled by an elderly fisherman.

"It is old Billy Mollet after his lobster-pots," and he stood up and coo-eed to the new-comer, and waved his arms till Billy saw them and stared hard and then turned leisurely their way.

"Guyablle!" said the old man, as he drew in. "What you doin' there now?"

"Got carried out of Grande Grève by a current, Mr. Mollet. Will you take us back in your boat?"

"Ay, ay!" and he brought the boat as near to the rock as he dared, and his weather-stained old eyes settled hypnotically on the fairest burden his old tub had ever carried, as Graeme handed her carefully down and helped her to spring into the dancing craft, and then sprang in himself with bleeding feet and shins, while Punch leaped lightly after him and crawled under a thwart.

"Ye must ha' been well out for tide to catch ye," said Billy, with no eyes for anything but the vision in clinging pink.

"Yes, we were too far out and couldn't get back."

"Tide runs round them rocks."

He dropped his oar into the rowlock and Graeme took the other, and in five minutes they were speeding across the sands of Grande Grève—Margaret to cover, Graeme to his pocket for Billy's reward.

Miss Penny had a driftwood fire roaring among the rocks, and the kettle was boiling.

"Where on earth have you two been?" she cried, at sight of Margaret skipping over the stones to her dressing-room, and got only the wave of a white arm in reply.

And presently Graeme came along in easy piratical costume of shirt and trousers and red sash, and sat down and lit a pipe.

"We went a bit farther than we intended," he explained, but did not tell her how nearly they had gone out of bounds altogether.

"You'll enjoy a cup of tea. You look as if you'd been working hard."

"There is a bit of a current round that point."

"Ah, you should follow a good example and keep within touch of the bottom. Here you are, Meg—fresh made for every customer. Help yourself, Mr. Graeme. I've had mine, I couldn't wait. Tea never tastes so good as when you're half full of salt-water, and I got right out of my depth once and swallowed tons. I screamed to you two to come and save me, but you never paid the slightest attention, and for all you cared I might have been drowned five times over."

"One would have been quite once too many," said Graeme, holding out his cup. "For then you couldn't have lighted that fire and made this tea. And I'm half inclined to think we wouldn't be enjoying it a quarter so much if a little blue corpse lay out there on the shining sand, and we'd had to turn to and make it ourselves."

"Horrible!" said Miss Penny, with a little shiver. "With your little blue corpses! It's all very well to joke about it, but I assure you, for a minute or so, I thought I was done for. The bottom seemed to have sunk, and I was just going after it when my foot came on a rock and that helped me to kick ashore."

"A narrow escape," said Graeme, with a sympathetic wag of the head. "You've no right to risk your life that way. We still need you. What do you say to being bridesmaid at a Sark wedding?"

"It is the hope of my life," said Miss Penny, sparkling like Mars in a clear evening sky.

"I really don't see any reason why we should wait"—said Graeme, looking very earnestly at Margaret, and behind the look was the thought, born of what they had just come through together, that life spills many a full cup before the thirsty lips have tasted it. "What do you say, Margaret?"

And she, knowing well what was in him, and being of the same mind, said, "I am ready, Jock. When you will."

"I'll call on the Vicar to-morrow," he said joyfully. "It would be such a pity to disappoint the hope of Miss Penny's life,"—as that young person came back with the merry kettle.

"I am indebted to you," said Hennie Penny. "What about dresses, Meg?"

IV

It was that same night, as they were sauntering home from a starlight ramble, that they came on Johnnie Vautrin crouched in the hedge with Marielihou, and Marielihou had her hind leg bound up in a piece of white rag.

"Hello, Johnnie! What's the matter with Marielihou?" asked Graeme. And Marielihou turned her malevolent yellow-green eyes on him and looked curses.

"Goderabetin! She've got hurt."

"Oh! How was that?"

"I d'n know. Wisht I knowed who done it;" and just then, as luck would have it, old Tom Hamon came sauntering along in the gloaming, smoking a contemplative pipe with long slow puffs.

And at sight of him Marielihou ruffled and swelled to twice her size, and raked up most horrible and blood-curdling oaths from away down in her inside into her black throat, and spat them out at him, as he came up, in a fusillade that sounded like ripraps, and her eyes flamed baleful fires.

"Cuss away, y'ould witch!" said old Tom, with a grin through his pipe-stem. "How's the leg?" and Marielihou with a final volley disappeared among the bushes, and Johnnie crawled after her.

"What on earth does he mean?" whispered Meg.

"Mr. Hamon has an idea that Marielihou and old Mme. Vautrin have something in common. In fact I believe he goes so far as to say that they are one and the same. Black magic, you know,—witchcraft, and all that kind of thing."

"How horrid!"

"B'en!" chuckled old Tom again. "You find out how 'tis with th' old witch. We know how 'tis with Marrlyou. 'Twere the silver bullet did it. If sh' 'adn't jumped 'twould ha' gone through 'er 'ead," and he went off chuckling through his pipe-stem.

And the next evening, as they were sauntering slowly through the darkening lanes to the windmill, to see the life-lights flash out all round the horizon, it happened that they met the doctor just turning out of his gate.

"Hello, doctor! How's old Mme. Vautrin to-day?" asked Graeme.

"She's going on all right," said the doctor, with a touch of surprise. "There seems a quite unusual amount of interest in that old lady all of a sudden. How is it?"

"What is it's wrong with her?"

And the doctor eyed him curiously for a moment, and then said, "Well, she says she hurt her leg ormering, slipped on a rock and got the hook in it. But—Well, it's a bad leg anyway, and she won't go ormering or anything else for a good long time to come."

Which matter, in the light of old Tom Hamon's silver bullets and evident knowledge of Marielihou's injury, left them all very much puzzled, though, as Graeme acknowledged, there might be nothing in it after all.

V

It was just after the second lesson, the following Sunday, that the Vicar stood up, tall and stately, his youthful face below the gray hair all alight with the enjoyment of this unusual break in the even tenour of his way, and soared into unaccustomed and very carefully enunciated English.

"I pub-lish thee Banns of Marrr-i-ache between John Cor-rie Graeme of Lonn-donn and Mar-garet Brandt of Lonn-donn. If any of you know cause, or just im-ped-i-ment, why these two pair-sons should not be joined to-gether in holy matri-mony, ye are to de-clare it. This is thee first time of as-king."

Margaret and Miss Penny and Graeme heard it from their back seat among the school-children, and found it good.

There were not very many visitors there. Such as there were felt a momentary surprise at two English people choosing to get married in Sark, though, if it had been put to them, they must have confessed that there was no lovelier place in the world to be married in. They also wondered what kind of people they were.

Some few of the habitants knew them and turned and grinned encouragingly, though even they were not quite certain in their own minds as to which of the two ladies was the one who was to be married. The children all smiled as a matter of course and of nature.

And Margaret felt no shadow of regret at thought of the gauds and fripperies of a fashionable wedding which would not be hers. In John Graeme's true love she had the kernel. The rest was of small account to her.

And that little church of Sark, plain walled and bare of ornament, always exerted upon her a most profoundly deepening and uplifting influence. It epitomised the life of the remote little island. Here its people were baptized, confirmed, married, buried.

And here and there, on the otherwise naked walls, was a white marble tablet to the memory of some who had gone down to the sea and never returned. And these she had studied and mused upon with emotion the first time she went there, for surely none could read them without being deeply touched.

"A la memoire de John William Falle, âgé de 37 ans, et de son fils William Slowley Falle, âgé de 17 ans, Fils et petit fils de William Falle, Ecr. de Beau Regard, Sercq. Qui furent noyés 20'eme jour d'Avril 1903, durant la traversée de Guernsey a Sercq. 'Ta voie a été par la mer et tes sentiers dans les grosses eaux.'"

"A la memoire de Pierre Le Pelley, Ecuyer, Seigneur de Serk, noyé près la Pointe du Nez, dans une Tempête, le 13 Mars, 1839, âgé de 40 ans. Son corps n'a pas été retrouvé; mais la mer rendra ses morts."

"In memory of Eugène Grut Victor Cachemaille, second son of the Revd. J.L.V. Cachemaille, Vicar of Sark. Born Jan. 14, 1840, and lost at sea in command of the Ariel, which left London for Sydney, Feby. 1872, and was heard of no more. 'He was not, for God took him.'"

Yes, she would sooner be married in that solemn little church than in Westminster Abbey, for there there would be mighty distractions, while here there would be nought to come between her and God and the true man to whom she was giving herself with a full heart.

VI

"This is the second time of asking."

"This is the third time of asking."

And so far none had discovered any just cause or impediment why John Corrie Graeme and Margaret Brandt should not in due course be joined together in holy matrimony.

On the occasion of the third asking, however, one in the congregation, a casual visitor and in no way personally concerned in the matter, found it of sufficient interest to make mention of it in a letter home, and so unwittingly played his little part in the story.

Meanwhile, the glorious summer days between the askings were golden days of ever-increasing delight to Graeme and Margaret, and of rich enjoyment to Miss Penny.

Never was there more complaisant chaperone than Hennie Penny. For, you see, she took no little credit to herself for having helped to bring about their happiness, and the very least she could do was to further it in every way in her power.

In her own quaint way she enjoyed their "lovering," as she called it, almost as much as they did themselves. And that being so, they would have felt it selfish on their part to deprive her of any portion of her rightful share in it.

And that was how Miss Hennie Penny became so very knowing in such matters, and also why she lived in a state of perpetual amazement at the change that had come over her friend.

For Margaret, affianced to the man who had her whole heart, was a very different being from Margaret harassed and worried by Mr. Pixley and his schemes for her possession and possessions.

Charming and beautiful as she had always been, this new Margaret was to the old as a radiant butterfly to its chrysalis,—as the glory of the opening flower to the promise of the bud. And Hennie Penny's quickened intelligence, projecting itself into the future, could fathom heights and depths and greater glories still to come.

But even now, when they went along the lanes festooned as for a wedding with honeysuckle and wild roses, the faces of those they met lighted up at sight of them, and few but turned to look after them when they had passed, and Miss Penny's truthful soul took none of the silent homage to herself.

Margaret was supremely happy. She could not have hidden it if she had tried. She made no attempt to do so. She gave herself up to the rapturous enjoyment of their "lovering" with all the naïve abandon of a delighted child. The little ties and tapes and conventions, which trammel more or less all but the very simplest lives, fell from her, snapped by the expansion of her love-exalted soul. She was back to the simple elementals. She loved Jock, Jock loved her. They were happy as the day was long. Why on earth should they not show it? If she had had her way she would have had every soul in all the world as happy as they two were.

"I feel like an elderly nurse with two very young children," said Miss Penny to the pair of exuberants.

"O Wise Nurse! We shall never be so young again," laughed Graeme.

"But we are never going to grow any older inside," laughed Margaret.

"Never!" said Graeme, with the conviction of absolute knowledge, and carolled softly—

"O it's good to be young in the days of one's youth!
Yes, in truth and in truth,
It's the very best thing in the world to be young,
To be young, to be young in one's youth."

"Very apropos!" said Miss Penny. "Did you make it on the spot?"

"In anticipation," he laughed. "It's the opening song in a very charming comic opera I once committed. But it was too good for the present frivolous age, and so I have to perform it myself."

"I would like to give all the children on the island—" began Margaret.

"All the other children—" corrected Graeme.

"All the children—including Hennie and you and me—the jolliest feast they've ever had in their lives, the day we are married."

"Of course we will, and the doctor shall get in an extra supply of palliatives. They shall look back in after years and say—'Do you remember that feast we had when the loveliest of all the angels came down from heaven and was married to that delightful Englishman?'—Briton, I ought to say! I do wish our dear old Lady Elspeth could be here. How she would enjoy it!—'That feast,' they will say, 'when we were all ill for a month after and the doctor died of overwork.' They will date back to it as ancient peoples did to the Flood. It will be a Great White Stone Day to generations to come. Let us hope there will be no new white stones over yonder"—nodding in the direction of the churchyard—"in commemoration of that great day."

"We will draw the line short of that," said Margaret seriously.

"We'll give them all the gâche they can eat—home-made, and such as their constitutions are accustomed to,—and fruit and frivolities from Guernsey. I'll go across the Saturday before—"

"We will go across," said Margaret.

"Of course we will. We older children will go, and we'll take Nurse with us,"—with a bow towards Hennie Penny,—"and we'll make a day of it, and have ices again at that place in the Arcade, and then we'll go round the shops and clear them out for the benefit of Sark."

"Ripping!" said Miss Penny.

VII

They had already made one trip to Guernsey, crossing by the early Saturday boat and returning the same evening.

But that was a strictly business affair.

"We're feeling frightfully fossilised at having bought nothing, except what we absolutely needed, for nearly a month," said Miss Penny. "From that point of view I should imagine the Garden of Eden may have been just a trifle slow—"

"Ah, you see, Mother Eve hadn't had the advantages of a superior education," said Graeme.

"And there are some fripperies we simply must have," said Miss Penny, "even for a runaway wedding like this. You see, when we decided to come here we had no idea how much farther we were going, and so we couldn't possibly provide. Of course if we had known you were here—"

At which Margaret laughed.

"You would have provided accordingly," said Graeme. "Well, you must put all the blame on to Mr. Pixley. I wonder what he would say if he knew all about it."

"He would use language unadapted to prayer-meetings and public platforms," said Miss Penny. "He can, you know, when he tries hard."

"I imagined so. It will be rather amusing to see what he'll do when he finds out."

"He'll do the very nastiest thing that is open to him, whatever that is, and poor Mrs. Pixley will have an exceedingly bad time. And he'll probably have a fit on his own account."

"Oh, we can hardly expect him to be so kind as all that—"

"The only one I'm sorry for is Charles Svendt. He's really not half a bad sort, in his way, you know," said Miss Penny.

"I'm sorry, but I'm afraid, under the circumstances, I can't squeeze out any sympathy even for Charles Svendt."

Arrived at St. Peter Port, the ladies permitted him to attend them to the door of the largest drapery establishment they could find, and then told him he was at liberty to go and enjoy himself for a couple of hours.

"Two hours? Good Heavens! What can you want in there for two hours?"

"Usual thing!" sparkled Miss Penny. "Tablecloths!"—with which cryptic utterance he had to be satisfied.

"And where do we meet again—if ever?"

"Hauteville House—Victor Hugo's. It's part of your honeymoon—a bit on account."

"And whereabouts is it?"

"No idea. If we can find it, you can. Au revoir!"

He went first to get his hair cut, since the practice of the tonsorial art in Sark is still in the bowl-and-scissors stage.

Then he sought out a lawyer of repute, whose name he had got from the Vicar, and gave him instructions for the drawing of a brief but comprehensive deed of settlement of all Margaret's portion on herself absolutely and entirely. While this important document was being engrossed, he sought out the Rector of St. Peter Port, in George Place, and in a short but pleasant interview was accepted as tenant of the whole of the Red House in Sark for the month of July, with the option of a longer stay if he chose.

Then back to the lawyer's, where he signed his deed, paid the fees, and took it away with him.

After that, to fill in the time occupied elsewhere by the purchase of mythical tablecloths, he rambled up and down the quaint foreign-flavoured streets till he found a jeweller's shop of size, in the Arcade, and decided, after careful inspection from the outside, that it would answer all requirements.

For he had a ring and half a ring to buy for Margaret, and he thought he would buy one also for Hennie Penny, as a pleasant reminder of their good days in Sark.

So utterly unconventional had their proceedings been, so thoroughly had the spirit of the remote little island possessed them, and so all-sufficient had they been to one another, that the thought of an engagement ring had troubled his mind as little as the lack of it had troubled Margaret's. But the absolute necessity of a wedding ring had reminded him of his lapse, and now he would repair it on a scale remotely commensurate with his feelings. Remotely, because, if his pocket had borne any relation to his feelings, he would have bought up the whole shop and lavished its contents upon her, though he knew that the simple golden circlet would far outweigh all else in her mind.

He was waiting placidly for them in the shade of the dark trees of Hauteville, when they came panting up the steep way, flushed with victory and the joys of purchase after long abstinence.

"Well, has the proprietor of that big shop retired with a competence?" he asked, as he threw away the end of his cigar.

"Can you lend us our boat-fares home?" gasped Miss Penny.

"So bad as all that? I can't say yet. I've not begun my own purchases. We'll see when I'm through. If I'm cleaned out too we'll offer to work our passages."

"You can pawn your watch. Meg and I haven't got one between us. We left them at home on purpose."

"Thoughtful of you. Now let us into the treasure-house."

They enjoyed the wonders of Hauteville immensely,—objectively, the wonderful carved work and the tapestries, the china and the furniture,—the odd little bedroom with the bed on the floor, so that the Master could roll out to his work at any moment of inspiration, and the huge balconies, and the glass eyrie on the roof whence he surveyed his wide horizons, and where, above the world, he worked;—and subjectively, the whole quaint flavour and austere literary atmosphere of the place.

"No wonder he produced masterpieces," said Graeme, delighting in it all. "The view alone is an inspiration."

Then he took them up to Old Government House for lunch and a rest in the garden, and then away to the Arcade to the jeweller's shop, which proved adequate to all his demands;—for Margaret, a half-hoop of diamonds which the jeweller, with an air of sincerity, assured them were as fine stones as he had ever seen in the course of a long and prosperous career. Which ring Margaret would thenceforth value before all her others, though in the simple matter of intrinsic worth her jewel-case could beat it hollow.—And a plain gold circlet which, when she got it, would be more precious to her than all the rest put together.—And for Miss Penny, in spite of her protestations, a handsome signet ring which, when cornered, she chose in preference to a more feminine jewel, and which was left to be engraved with her family crest and motto.

"I have never adopted the habit of rings," she said, as they drifted towards the ice-shop. "Chiefly, perhaps, because I never had any worth wearing. But I've always thought I would like to wear a crest signet. I shall prize this, Mr. Graeme, as the very greatest treasure I have—"

"Until someone gives you a plain gold one, Hennie, and that will put all the rest into the shade," said Margaret.

"Ah!" said Miss Penny.

VIII

Their journey home—that is, to Sark—that day was not entirely without incident. For when they got down to the quay, Sark had disappeared completely, and Herm and Jethou were no more than wan ghosts of their natural selves, in a dense white mist.

"Ah-ha! Here is our old friend of Tintageu," said Graeme jovially. "Well, I must confess to bearing him no ill-feeling—if he doesn't land us on a rock this time. Going, captain?"

"Oh yess, we go. I think it will lift," said Captain Bichard.

"Don't run us on a rock anyway."

"I won'd run you on no rock. I coult smell my way across;" and they started, feeling their way cautiously past Castle Cornet, into the open, where black jaws lined with white teeth lie in wait for the unwary.

And just as they got to the south of Jethou they saw a sight the like of which none of them had ever seen before, nor, from the exclamations about them, had any of the rest.

The mist in front was like a soft white curtain, and upon it, straight ahead of their bows, appeared suddenly a mighty silver bow, not a rainbow, because there was no rain and so there were no colours. But, like the bow they had seen from Belême Cliff, this also was a perfect circle, all but a tiny segment where it appeared to rest upon the sea, and its only colour was a dazzling silvery sheen which waxed as they watched it in breathless silence. Then it waned, bit by bit, till at last it was gone, and only the white mist curtain remained.

"How very lovely!" murmured Margaret.

"A good omen for certain," said Miss Penny. "Even Johnnie Vautrin couldn't make any ill news out of that. It was your wedding arch, Meg."

"Well, that's the first time I ever saw a white rainbow," said Graeme to the captain.

"First time I ever saw one myself, sir."

"Not very common then."

"Never heard of one before."

"We're evidently in luck."

"Mebbe, but we won't crow till we've made the Creux. Kip your eyes skinned, lads!"

"Ay, ay, zur!" and the crew lined the bulwarks on their knees, with their chins on the rail, their eyes peering into the puzzling veil in front, and their ears alert for the wash of wave on rock.

They were going slow, hardly moving in fact at times, waiting to pick up their course as any possible mark should come into view, with muttered comments from the puzzled lookouts, and an occasional growl of dissent from views propounded by the younger members, while the passengers all stood in silent discomfort as though ready for contingencies.

For the tides and currents in those seas are strange and gruesome. Even as they lay, apparently motionless, with the sea as smooth as oil all round them, there came a sudden turmoil, and they were in a wild race of waters, with bubbling coils and swirls and frothing gouts of foam from rocks that lay fathoms deep below.

"La Grune," growled one of the keen-eyed watchers, and was discounted at once by doubtful growls from the rest.

Then a black ledge loomed through the mist and faded again before they had more than a glimpse of it.

"Les Dents," ventured one.

"Hautes Boues,"—so divergent were their views.

A sound of waters and another dark loom of rock.

"Sercul," said one.

"L'Etac," said another.

Then the engine bell tanged sharply, and they went ahead. The captain had seen more than the rest and knew where he was, and they all breathed more freely. And presently, with a wide berth to the dangers of the south-east coast, they nosed slowly in again, picked up La Conchée without dissentients, and so into Creux Harbour in a way that seemed to Graeme little short of marvellous.

"Fogs at sea are beastly—there is no other word for it—but all the same I'm glad we saw the Wedding-Bow," said Miss Penny.

IX

They had fixed on the Wednesday following the last time of asking, for their wedding-day. But when they came to discuss the matter with Mrs. Carré, it was found that an alteration would be necessary.

"Ah, but that will not do," said their landlady, who was in high feather at so unique an event taking place in her cottage, so to speak, though, as a matter of fact, the festivities were to be carried out within the ampler precincts of the Red House. "You see, old Mr. Hamon he iss died very sudden—"

"Not old Tom surely?" asked Graeme.

"He iss old Tom's father, and they will bury him on Wednesday, and you would not like to be married the sem day—"

"No, indeed," said Margaret. "We will wait."

"And, you see, all them that would be coming to the wedding would be at the funeral, for efferybody belongs to efferybody else here."

"Must be a bit awkward at times," suggested Graeme.

"Oh noh!" with a touch of airy aloofness. "I haf been at a wedding and a funeral and a baptism all in one week all among the sem people. And I was at one young man's wedding one day last year and at his funeral the same day the next week after."

"That was dreadful," said Margaret. "Do you think it would be safe to fix it for the following Wednesday, Mrs. Carré?"

"Oh yes, I think! There iss no one very sick. Mr. Hamon he wass a very old man and he died very sudden. He wass just knocking a nail in the pigsty and he drop down and died."

"Poor old man!"

"He wass very old and he wass a good man. No one ever said any harm of old Mr. Hamon."

"Then if no one else dies we'll say the following Wednesday," said Graeme. "And if—well, if anything happens to prevent it, then we must go across to Guernsey and get Mr. Lee to marry us."

"Oh, but that woult not do. We will keep them all alive till you are married. It woult neffer do to disappoint them all when we are all looking forward to it here."

"Very well then, see you all keep alive."

"And you will come to old Mr. Hamon's funeral?"

"H'm! I don't know. We'll see, Mrs. Carré. We'd sooner be at our own wedding, you know, than at anybody else's funeral."

"They woult like it iff you woult. And he was a goot old man. They tell me to ask if you woult be pleased to come."

"If they would like us to come we will come, Mrs. Carré," said Margaret.

And so it came about that instead of kneeling before the altar that Wednesday they stood by the graveside.

X

The Red House and the cottage were centres—nay, whirlpools—of mighty activities for days beforehand.

Mrs. Carré insisted on cleaning down the Red House from top to bottom for the home-coming of the bride, though, to Graeme's masculine perceptions, its panelling of polished pitch pine from floor to ceiling, in which you could see yourself as in a mirror, had always appeared the very acme of cleanliness and comfort, with the additional merit of a tendency towards churchwardly thoughts.

But when he ventured on a mild remonstrance anent the necessity for so gigantic an upsetting, Mrs. Carré laughingly said, "Ach, you are only a man. You woult neffer see"—and whirled her broom to the endangerment of his head.

For Margaret's honeymoon—that, is, such of it as she had not enjoyed before her marriage—was to consist of a change of residence from the cottage, and a walk up the garden and through the hedge of gracious Memories, to the wider—ah, how much wider!—as much wider and larger and more beautiful as wifehood at its best is wider and larger and more beautiful than maidenhood at its best—to the wider accommodation of the Red House. And Mrs. Carré was determined that it should be speckless and sweet, and fit in every way for the coming of so beautiful a bride.

She had found them a young girl, Betsy Lefevre, a niece of her own, to serve as handmaid during their occupancy of the house, but insisted herself on acting as cook and general housekeeper. Miss Penny was to reside at the cottage for a week after the wedding, but was to go up the garden to her meals, and at the end of that time she was to join them at the Red House as an honoured guest.

And the kitchen at the cottage, and the kitchen at the House, and several other kitchens in the neighbourhood, were baking gâche enough apparently to feed a regiment, and as the day approached, roasts of beef and mutton, and hams and other substantial fare, were much in evidence. And the kitchens were thronged with ladies in sun-bonnets, which had originally been black but were now somewhat off-colour with age and weather, and all the ladies' faces were as full of importance as if they had been Cabinet ministers in the throes of a crisis.

Among these concentric energies, Margaret and Miss Penny completed their own simple preparations, and Graeme busied himself with the details of the children's feast which was to take place in an adjacent field.

He went down to the harbour to meet the Tuesday morning's boat which was to bring over the fruit and frivolities ordered from Guernsey—strawberries enough to start a jam factory, grapes enough to stock a greengrocer's shop, chocolates, sweets, Christmas crackers and fancy biscuits, in what he hoped would prove sufficiency, but had his doubts at times when he saw the eager expectancy with which he was regarded by every youngster he met.

He was just starting out when Johnnie Vautrin hailed him from his lair in the hedge.

"Heh, Mist' Graeme! I seen—"

"Better not, Johnnie!" he said, with a warning finger. "If it's anything uncomfortable I'll come right over and jump on you and Marrlyou."

"Goderabetin, you dassen't!"

"Oh, dassen't I? If you don't see everything good for this week, and fine weather too, you little imp, I'll—"

"Qué-hou-hou!" croaked Johnnie, and Marielihou yawned and made a futile attempt to wash behind her ears but found it discomforting to a sore hind-leg, so gave it up and spat at him instead.

"And, moreover, I won't have you at my party."

"Hou-hou! I'm coming. Ma'm'zelle she ask me."

"I'll tell her to send you back-word."

"She wun't, she wun't. Where you goin'?"

"To the harbour, to see if all the good things have come for the other little boys and girls."

"Oh la-la! Good things and bad things come by the boat. Sometime it'll sink and drown 'em all."

"Little rascal!" and he waved his hand and went on.

"Late, isn't she, Carré?" he asked, as he leaned over the sea-wall with the rest.

"She's late, sir."

"I hope nothing's happened to her. I'll never forgive her if she's made an end of my sweet things for the kiddies."

"She'll come."

And she came. With a shrill peal she came round the Burons and made for the harbour.

And Graeme, wedged into the corner of the iron railing where it looks out to sea, to make sure at the earliest possible moment that that which he had come to meet was there, met of a sudden more than he had looked for.

"Well ... I'll be hanged!" he jerked to himself, and then began to laugh internally.

For, standing on the upper deck of the small steamer, and looking, somehow, very much out of place there, was a tall but portly young gentleman, in a bowler hat and travelling coat and a monocle, whose face showed none of the usual symptoms of the Sark lover. To judge from his expression, the little island impressed him anything but favourably. It offered him none of the relaxations and amusements to which he was accustomed. It looked, on the face of it, an uncivilised kind of a place, out of which a man might be ejected without ceremony if he chose to make himself objectionable.

Graeme kept out of sight among the other crowders of the quay till the bowler hat came bobbing up the gangway. Then he smote its owner so jovially on the shoulder that his monocle shot the full length of its cord and the hat came within an ace of tumbling overboard.

"Hello, Pixley! This is good of you. You're just in time to give us your blessing."

"Aw! Hello!" said Charles Svendt, agape at the too friendly greeting. "That you, Graeme?"

"The worst half of me, my boy. Margaret's up at the house. You'll be quite a surprise to her."

"Aw!" said Charles Svendt thoughtfully, as he readjusted his eyeglass. "Demned queer place, this!" and he gazed round lugubriously.

"It is that, my boy. Queerer than you think, and queerer people."

"Aw! Is there any—aw—place to stop at?"

"Thinking of stopping over night? Oh yes, several very decent hotels."

"Aw! Which are you at yourself now?"

"I? Oh, I'm a resident. I've got a house here."

"Dooce you have! Well, now, where would you stop if you were me?"

"Well, if I were you I should stop at the Old Government House—"

"Right! Whereabouts is it?"

"It's over in Guernsey. Boat returns at five sharp."

"Aw! Quite so! Very good! But I've got—er—business here, don't you know."

"Oh? Thinking of opening a branch here? Well, there's Stock's—but I doubt if you'd fit in there—"

"Fit? Why not fit? Stocks are my line."

"I think I'd try the Bel-Air if I were you—"

"Which is nearest?" asked Charles Svendt, looking round depreciatively.

"Bel-Air. Just along the tunnel there—"

"Good Lord! Along the tunnel—"

"Excuse me for a moment. I've got some things coming by this boat. I must see to them," and Graeme sped away to attend to his frivolities.

XI

"And what special business brings you to Sark, Pixley?" asked Graeme, as they passed through the tunnel of rock and climbed the steep way of the Creux—its high banks masses of ferns, its hedges ablaze with honeysuckle and roses, its trees interwoven into a thick canopy overhead,—a living green tunnel shot with quivering sunbeams. All of which was lost on Charles Svendt, whose chest was going like a steam-pump and whose legs were quivering with the unusual strain. Graeme regretted that he had not been landed on the ladders at Havre Gosselin, where he himself came ashore. He would dearly have liked to follow the portly one up those ladders and heard his comments.

In reply to Graeme's question he shook his head mutely and staggered on—past the upper reaches, where the corded roots of the overhanging trees came thrusting through the banks like twisting serpents; past the wells of sweet water that lay dark and still below, and ran over into the road, and trickled away down the sides in little streams; out into the sunshine and the quickening of the breeze;—till he dropped exhausted into a chair outside the door of the Bel-Air.

He sat there panting for close on five minutes, with unaccustomed perspiration streaming down his red face, and then he said "Demn!" and proceeded to mop himself up with his handkerchief.

Then he held up a finger to a distant waiter in the dining-room, and when he came, murmured, "Whisky—soda—two," and fanned himself vigorously till they came.

"Better?" asked Graeme, as they nodded and drank.

"Heap better! What a demnable place to get into!"

"There are one or two other entrances—"

"Better?"

"No, worse."

"Demn!"

"Now," he said presently, when his heart had got back to normal and he had lit a cigarette. "Let's talk business. Am I in time?"

"For the wedding? Just in time. It's tomorrow."

"Aw—er—you know what I've come for, I suppose?"

"I can imagine, but you may as well save yourself useless trouble. You can't do anything."

"Think not?"

"Sure. English—I should say, British—law doesn't run here, and you've no locus standi if it did."

"She's under age and her guardian objects. I represent him."

"He can object all he wants to, and you can represent him all you want to. It won't make the slightest difference."

"I can appear at the ceremony and show cause why it should not proceed."

"What cause?"

"Her guardian objects. The parson would hardly proceed in face of my objection."

"I think you'll find he would. However, we'll go and ask him presently. We'll pay a visit to the Seigneur also."

"Who's the Seigneur?"

"Lord Paramount of the island. His word goes. If he chooses, as he probably will, to tell you to go also, you'll have to go."

"Demn'd if I will!"

"He'll see to that. He'll put the Sénéchal and the Greffier and the Prévôt and the two constables and the Vingténier on to you, and bundle you out like a sack of potatoes."

"Oh, come, Graeme! This is the twentieth century!"

"That's another of your little mistakes, my friend. I can't tell you just exactly what year it is here, but it's somewhere between 1066 and, say, 1200 A.D."

"Afraid I don't quite catch on."

"Exactly! That's why you'll be off in this scene. We're under feudal law here, with a mixture of Home Rule. We don't care twopence for your English courts, and as for English lawyers, they're not much liked here, I believe."

"Rum hole!" mused Charles Svendt.

"Rum hole to make yourself a nuisance in. Jolly place to be happy in."

"H'm!" And presently he asked, "Where are you stopping?"

"I'll go along and tell the girls you're here—"

"Girls?"

"Miss Penny came with Margaret—"

"Aw—Miss Penny!"

"You'd better have your lunch here. They'll give you lobsters fresh from the kettle, and I'll stroll round later on and we'll get this matter settled up. So long!" and he went away up the Avenue and across the fields home.

And he went thoughtfully. It was annoying this man cropping up like this at the eleventh hour. Nothing, he felt sure, would come of his interference, but it might disturb Margaret and the general harmony of to-morrow's proceedings.

Her wedding-day is a somewhat nervous time for a girl, under the best of circumstances, he supposed. And though Margaret was as little given to nerves as anyone he had ever met, the possibility of a public attempt to stop her wedding might be fairly calculated to upset her.

Feudal as were the laws of the island, he could hardly knock Pixley on the head, as would have happened in less anachronistic times. And so he went thoughtfully.

XII

Margaret and Miss Penny were lying in long chairs on the verandah when he came over the green wall into the Red House garden, by the same gap as he had used that first morning when he came upon Margaret standing in the hedge.

They were resting from labours, joyful, but none the less tiring.

"Jock, we were just wanting you!" said Margaret, sitting up. "Have all the things come all right?"

"All come all right," and he wondered how she would take his next announcement. "In fact more came than we expected."

"I guess we can use it all," said Miss Penny. "You've no idea of the capacity of children. I know something about it, and these children are more expansible even than school-girls."

"I was surprised to meet a gentleman down there who says he has come across on purpose for the wedding."

"A gentleman—come for the wedding?" and both girls eyed him as pictured terriers greet the word "Rats!"

"I'll give you three guesses."

"Mr. Pixley," said Miss Penny.

"Bull's-eye first shot! Clever girl!"

"Not really, Jock!" said Margaret, with a suspicion of dismay in her voice.

"Well, Charles Svendt anyway—as representing the old man, he says."

"But what has he come for, and how did he get to know?"

"I didn't ask him. It was quite enough to see him there. He says he's going to stop it,"—and Margaret's cheeks flamed,—"but I've assured him that he can't, and I'll take jolly good care that he doesn't, if I have to knock him on the head and drop him off the Coupée."

"It would be shameful of him if he tried," cried Miss Penny. "Just let me have a talk with him, Mr. Graeme, and I'll make him wish he'd never been born. He's really not such a bad sort, you know. Where is he?"

"I left him at the Bel-Air about to tackle lobsters. My idea is to take him to the Vicar, then to the Seigneur. They both understand the whole matter. I explained it fully when I told them we intended getting married here. When they understand that this is the gentleman who would like to occupy my place, and that he has no legal grounds for interfering, I think they will open his eyes—"

"I do hope he won't make any trouble in the church," said Margaret, with a little flutter.

"I'll promise you he won't."

"I'm sure he won't, if you can make it quite clear that it could not possibly accomplish what, I suppose, his father sent him to try to do," said Miss Penny. "Charles Pixley is no fool, though he has his little peculiarities."

"It would be a wonder if he hadn't some, after his daddie," said Graeme lightly. "I'm sorry he's come, Meg, but I'm certain you don't need to worry about him. If I could have knocked him on the head and dropped him in the sea and said nothing to nobody—"

"Don't be absurd, Jock," said Margaret, and her voice showed that the matter was troubling her in spite of his assurances.

"After lunch I shall call for him and take him for a little walk. If you'd seen him when he got to the Bel-Air after toiling up the Creux Road! He was nearly in pieces. I'll trot him round to the Vicarage, and then to the Seigneurie, and then I'll bring him here and turn him over to you and Hennie Penny. He'll be as limp as a rag by that time, and as wax in your hands."

Nevertheless, Margaret could not quite get rid of the feeling of discomfort which the news of Charles Pixley's arrival had cast over her, and Graeme anathematised that young man most fervently each time he glanced at her face.

XIII

After lunch Graeme went back to the hotel, and found Pixley lolling on the seat outside, in a much more contented frame of mind than on his first arrival.

"You were right as to their lobsters, anyhow, Graeme," he said. "They're almost worth coming all the way for."

"All right. Now if you're rested we'll go for a stroll, and I'll set your mind at rest as to to-morrow. Then you'll be able to enjoy your dinner in a proper frame of mind."

"How far is it?"

"Just up there and round the corner. We'll see the Vicar first and you can try your hand on him."

The Vicar received them with jovial bonhomie.

"Ah-ha! The bridegroom cometh out of his chamber! And your friend? He is the best man—no?"

"He's not quite made up his mind yet, Vicar. Perhaps you can persuade him to it."

"But it is an honour—n'est-ce pas? To attend so beautiful a bride to the altar—"

"Well, you see, the fact is—Mr. Pixley would have preferred reversing the positions. He would like to have been bridegroom and me to be best man."

"Ah—so! Well, it is not surprising—"

"Moreover, he would like to stop the wedding now if he could—"

"Ach, non! That is not possible," said the Vicar wrathfully, the southern blood blazing in his face. "What would you do, my good sir, and why?"

"Miss Brandt is my father's ward," said Pixley sturdily. "My father objects to this marriage. He has sent me over to stop it."

"I understand," said the Vicar. "He wished his ward to marry you, but Miss Brandt made her own choice, which she had a perfect right to do, and, ma foi—" leaning back in his chair and regarding the two faces in front of him, he did not finish his sentence in words, but contented himself with cryptic nods whose meaning, we may hope, was lost upon Charles Svendt's amour propre.

"And what would you do?" asked the Vicar presently.

"Well, if necessary, I can get up in the church and state that there is just cause for stopping the marriage—"

"What just cause, I should ask you?"

"I have told you. My father—"

"I would not listen. I would order them to put you out—to carry you out, if necessary, for making dis-turb-ance in my church. I would tell them to sit on you in the churchyard till the wedding was over. What good would you do? Ach, non! Be advised, my good sir, and re-linquish any such in-tention. It will ac-complish nothing and only lead to your own con-fusion."

"My father is applying to have Miss Brandt made a ward in Chancery—"

"By that time she will be Mrs. Graeme, and I am sure very happy," shrugged the Vicar. "Non—you can do nothing, and, if you will be guided, you will not try."

And Charles Svendt lapsed into thoughtfulness.

XIV

"This is the Seigneurie," said Graeme, as they turned off the road, through the latched gate, into the deep-shaded avenue.

The Seigneur came to them in the Long Drawing-Room, where once upon a time the peacocks danced on the Queen's luncheon.

"Your time is getting short, Mr. Graeme," he said, with a quiet smile. "I hear of great doings in preparation at St. Magloire"—which was the official title of the Red House. "Have you given the doctor fair warning?"

"Oh, we'll try to keep them within bounds, Seigneur. My friend, Mr. Pixley here,"—the Seigneur made Mr. Pixley a seigneurial bow,—"has it in his mind to stop the proceedings if he can—"

"Oh?" said the Seigneur, with a glower of surprise. "And why?"

"Well, you see," said Pixley, "Miss Brandt is under age. She is my father's ward and he has other views for her—"

"Which obviously do not agree with Miss Brandt's."

"That is as it may be. But she is acting absolutely in opposition to his expressed wishes in this matter, and until she is of age she is under his authority."

"Just as far as he is in position to exert it, I presume."

"He is now applying to have her made a ward in Chancery, when, of course, she will be under the jurisdiction of the court."

"If you come to me, Mr. Pixley, when Miss Brandt is a ward of court, I will tell you now what my answer would be. I should tell you that your English court has no jurisdiction here. Miss Brandt is out of bounds and is quite free to do as she pleases. I have had the pleasure of making her acquaintance and Mr. Graeme's, and I should be sorry—for you—if you did anything to annoy them. In fact—" and he looked so fixedly at Charles Svendt, while evidently revolving some extreme idea in his mind, that that young gentleman's assurance fell several degrees, and he found himself thinking of dungeons and deportation.

It was to Graeme, however, that the Seigneur turned.

"If you have any reason to fear annoyance in this matter, Mr. Graeme, perhaps you will let me know as early as possible, and I will take measures—"

"Thousand thanks, Seigneur! Mr. Pixley will, I hope, think better of it. If not—well, I will send you word."

XV

Pixley was very silent as they walked back along the road to the Red House.

The ladies had tea ready on the verandah.

"Well, Charles," said Margaret, as he bowed before them, and Graeme nodded and smiled reassuringly at her over his back, "I won't pretend that I'm glad to see you. Why did you undertake so foolish an errand?"

"Perhaps Mr. Pixley could hardly help himself," said Miss Penny, sympathising somewhat with the awkwardness of his position.

"That is so," he said, with a grateful glance at her. "You see, the governor is crazy wild over this matter. It was only Sunday night he heard of it. A friend of young Greatorex wrote him that he'd heard your banns put up, and Greatorex congratulated the governor after church, and the governor nearly had a fit. He came over to my place like a whirlwind and practically ordered me to come across instanter and stop it. I may say," he said, looking at Margaret, "I tried to reason with him. I told him he must know that if you'd gone that length I was out of it, and nothing he could do would alter matters. But he would not hear a word. He simply raved until I promised to come over by first boat and see what could be done."

"You've only done your duty, Mr. Pixley," said Miss Penny. "But you simply can't stop it, so is it any good making any trouble? Put it on the highest grounds. You have had warmer feelings for Meg than she could reciprocate. You can possibly make some disturbance at her wedding, which would be painful to her and utterly useless to yourself. Is it worth while?"

"No, I'm dem—er—hanged if it is! I see I can do no good, and I'll be hammered if I'll play dog in the manger, even to oblige the governor. It's a disappointment to me, you know,"—he was looking at Miss Penny's bright face, surcharged with deepest sympathy.

"Of course it is," she said gently. "But a strong man bears his disappointments without wincing. I think you're acting nobly."

"Say, Graeme, will you have me as best man?"

"Delighted, my dear fellow. Miss Penny has been breaking her heart at thought of having no partner at the ceremony."

"Right! Then we'll say no more about it. How did you all come to meet here? Put-up job?"

"Not a bit of it," said Graeme. "Pure coincidence—or Providence, we'll say. You remember that Whitefriars' dinner, when Adam Black sat opposite to us? He was just back from Sark, and he said, 'If ever you want relief from your fellows—try Sark.' Well, later on, I had no reason to believe there was anything between you and Margaret, and I called on your father at his office. He sliced me into scraps with his eye-glass and flung the bits out into Lincoln's Inn,"—at which Charles Svendt grinned amusedly, as though he were familiar with the process.—"I wanted to get away somewhere to piece up again. Sark came into my head, and I came. A month later my landlady told me she had let my rooms to two ladies, as she had understood I was only stopping for a month, and I had to turn out and come up here. And, to my vast amazement, the two ladies proved to be Margaret and Miss Penny. How is that for coincidence?"

"I was standing in the hedge there," said Margaret, "early in the morning of the day after we got here, and Jock came leaping over the dyke there with a great brown dog, and stopped as if he'd been shot—"

"I thought you were a ghost, you see."

"And I couldn't believe my eyes. Then I asked him what he meant by following us here, and it turned out that it was we who had followed him, and turned him out of his cottage moreover."

"Deuced odd!" said Charles Svendt, screwing in his eye-glass and regarding them comprehensively. "Almost makes one believe in—er—"

"Telepathy and that kind of thing," said Miss Penny.

"Er—exactly—just so, don't you know!" and his glance rested on her with appreciation as upon a kindred soul.

XVI

Charles Svendt dined with them that evening, and in the process developed heights and depths of genial common-sense which quite surprised some among them.

They took him for a stroll up to the Eperquerie in the cool of the gloaming, and showed him more shooting stars than ever he had seen in his life, and a silver sickle of a moon, and a western sky still smouldering with the afterglow of a crimson and amber sunset, and he acknowledged that, from some points of view, Sark had advantages over Throgmorton Street.

In the natural course of things, Margaret and Graeme walked together, and since they could not go four abreast among the gorse cushions, Charles Svendt and Miss Penny had to put up with one another, and seemed to get on remarkably well. More than once Graeme squeezed Margaret's arm within his own and chuckled, as he heard the animated talk and laughter from the pair behind.

"I'm very glad he's taken a sensible view of the matter," said Margaret.

"Oh, Charles Svendt is no fool, and he certainly would have been if he'd done anything but what he has done. He saw that he could do no good and might get into trouble. The Seigneur scowled dungeons and gibbets at him, and he looked decidedly uncomfortable."

"I will tender the Seigneur my very best thanks the first time I see him."

When the men had seen the ladies home, they strolled up the garden to the Red House for a final smoke.

"Say, Graeme, I've been wondering what you'd have done if I'd played mule and persisted in kicking up my heels in church. I asked Miss Penny—and, by Jove, I tell you, that's about as sensible a girl as I've met for a long time—"

"Miss Penny is an extremely clever girl and an exceptionally fine character. Good family too. Her father was the Brigadier-General Penny who was killed in Afghanistan."

"So?"

"She's an M.A., and she's worked like a slave to educate her brothers and sisters, and they're all turning out well. I don't know any girl, except Meg, of whom I think so highly as Hennie Penny."

"Henrietta?"

Graeme nodded.

"Well now," said Pixley presently. "As a matter of information, what was in your mind to do if I'd gone on?"

"You'd never have got as far as the church, my boy."

"No? Why?"

"If the Seigneur hadn't stopped you, I would. But I'm inclined to think he'd have seen to you all right."

"By Jove, he looked it! What would he have done?"

"Confined you as a harmless lunatic till the ceremony was over, I should say, and then sent you home with the proverbial insect in your ear."

"And if he hadn't?"

"Then I should have taken matters into my own hands and bottled you up till you couldn't do any mischief. You could have hauled me before the court here, and I'd probably have been fined one and eightpence. It would have been worth the money, and cheap at the price, simply to see the proceedings."

"It's an extraordinary place this."

"It's without exception the most delightful little place in the world."

"Jolly nice house you've got here too. Think of stopping long?"

"Some months probably. The curious thing about Sark is that the longer you stop the longer you want to stop. It grows on you. First week I was here it seemed to me very small—felt afraid of walking fast lest I should step over the edge, and all that kind of thing. Now that I've been here a couple of months it is growing bigger every day. I'm not sure that one could know Sark under a lifetime. We'll take you round in a boat and show it you from the outside."

"I'll have to get back, I'm sorry to say. You see, I started at a moment's notice. Things are duller than a ditch in the City, but I'd no chance to make any arrangements for a stay. But I'll tell you what. If you're stopping on here and like to send me an invitation for a week or two, I'd come like a shot. I'll take a carriage up that road from the harbour, though, next time. Jove! I felt like a convict on the treadmill."

"You have the invitation now, my boy, and we'll be delighted to see you whenever it suits you to come."

"That's very good of you. Miss Penny be stopping on with you?"

"As long as she will. She'd got a bit run down and it's done her a heap of good."

"Well, if you'll show me how to go, I'll toddle off home now. I haven't the remotest idea where my digs are."

And Graeme led him through the back fields among the tethered cows, who stopped their slow chewing as they passed, and lay gazing after them in blank astonishment, into the Avenue and so to the Bel-Air.

"I'll come round then a bit before eleven and we'll all go along together," was Charles Svendt's parting word.

"Right! Au revoir!" and Graeme went home across the fields smiling happily to himself.

XVII

When Graeme came swinging over the green dyke in the early morning, with his towel round his neck and his two dogs racing in front, he found the Seigneur sitting in a long chair in the verandah, with four aristocratic dogs wandering about, who proceeded to intimate to Punch and Scamp that they were rather low fisher-dogs and not of seigneurial rank.

"Well, what about your would-be breaker of the peace?" asked the Seigneur, with a smile.

"He's come to his senses. I was going to bring you word as soon as I thought you'd be up. He's promised to be best man, and I'm hoping to get him to play heavy father also and give the bride away."

"Capital!"

"He was very anxious last night to know what would have happened if, as he put it, he'd persisted in playing mule and kicking up his heels in church."

"We'd have tied his heels so that he couldn't kick much," said the Seigneur, with his deep quizzical smile.

"That's what I told him. He seemed to think Sark a decidedly odd kind of place. But he's getting to like it, and I've invited him to come and visit us later on."

"That's all right as long as he behaves himself."

"Oh, he's a very decent chap. The only thing I had against him was that he wanted to marry my wife."

"Then all the ways are smooth now?"

"All smooth now, thanks to your assistance!"

"Well, all happiness to you both!" said the Seigneur as he rose. "My wife sends all good wishes"—for the Lady of the Manor lay sick in the great house among the trees and he would not leave her.

XVIII

As Graeme proposed, they talk still of that wedding in Sark.

Everything went smoothly. The Vicar had coached himself, by wifely tuition and much private repetition, into a certain familiarity with the Wedding Service in English, but would still have been more at home with it in French.

The church was more crowded than it had been within the memory of woman. Margaret looked charming, and Miss Penny absolutely pretty. Charles Svendt could hardly take his eyes off her, and caught himself wondering what the dooce she had done to herself since last night. For, by Jove! she's as pretty almost as Margaret herself—he said to himself.

And if Jeremiah Pixley could have seen his son, in fatherly fashion give away the bride that should have been his, he would without doubt have had fits—if the first one had not been of such a character as to obviate the necessity for any additional ones.

The habitants, old and young, had made holiday, donned their best as if it were Sunday, and crowded the church as if it were all the Sundays of the year rolled into one.

The Vicar had serious thoughts of improving so unique an occasion, but wisely decided to confine himself to the intricacies of the English language as displayed in The Form of the Solemnisation of Matrimony.

Mrs. Vicar presided at the harmonium, which had been specially tuned for the occasion, and the choir enjoyed to the full their privileges of position and observation and made ample use of them.

And when his friends knelt before the chancel rail,—to the exceeding scandal of the Vicar and Mrs. Vicar and the choir and all who saw, and to the vast enjoyment of Miss Penny and Charles Svendt and all the other youngsters in the place,—Punch walked solemnly up the aisle and stood behind them, with slow-swinging tail and a look of anticipation on his gravely interested face, while outside, Scamp, in the hands of some enterprising stickler for forms and ceremonies, rent the air with sharp cries of disappointment.

But John Graeme's soul, uplifted mightily within him at this glorious consummation of his hopes, and ranging high among the stars, saw none of these things. He held Margaret's hand in his, and looked into her radiant and blushing face, and vowed mighty vows for her happiness, and thanked God fervently for bringing this great thing to pass.

And Margaret's eye caught the marble slab, placed in the side wall of the chancel by the late Seigneur who built it, and prayed in her heart that the temple of their two lives might equally be builded—"to the Glory of God and with much care."

XIX

The small girls from the school, all specially arrayed in fancy white pinafores with knots of pink ribbon, burst out of the church like a merry bombshell while the less picturesque final ceremonies were being completed. When Graeme and Margaret came smiling down the aisle, the busy little maids were still vociferously strewing the path outside with green rushes and wild iris, and as they passed, those who had emptied their baskets ran back and picked up hasty armfuls of the scattered flowers, and ran on in front and strewed them again, so that for quite a long way their progress was one of gradually diminishing splendour.

But past the gap in the road, which led across country to the Red House, no flower-strewers came. For there the excited chatterers broke and whirled through like a flight of sea-pies, and made straight for the field of more substantial delights lest the boys should secure all the best places.

The wedding-party, however, having disdained the use of carriages for so short a distance, strolled quietly along the scented lanes, past the Boys' School, and by the Carrefour, with no apprehension of the feast beginning until they arrived, or of being relegated to back seats if they were late.

The cottage and the Red House had been buzzing hives since dawn, Mrs. Carré handling her forces and volunteers and supernumeraries with the skill of a veteran, and with encouragement so shrill and animated that it sounded like scolding, but was in reality only emphatic patois.

She had, indeed, left matters in the hands of certain tried elders while she sped across the fields to the church for a few minutes, just to see that everything there was done properly and in order. But she was back in the thick of things before the wedding-party reached home, and everything was ready and in apple-pie order for a merry-making such as Sark had not seen for many a day.

First, the children were settled at their long tables in the field behind the house, with good things enough in front of them, and active assistants enough behind them, to keep them quiet for a good long time to come.

Graeme and Margaret went round bidding them all enjoy themselves to their fullest, which they cheerfully promised to do, and the eager youngsters gave them back wish for wish, with one eye for them and one for the unusual dainties on the tables.

"Hello, Johnnie!" said Graeme to that young man, gorging stolidly, with a palpable interval between him and his neighbour on either hand, but with no other visible signs of wizardry about him. "Getting on all right?"

But there was no room for speech in Johnnie's mouth just then. He winked one black eye solemnly and devoted himself to the business in hand.

And Punch and Scamp, accepted favourites of the host and hostess, tore to and fro in vain attempt to keep pace with all the attentions lavished upon them by the guests as soon as their own desires had been satisfied. They devoured everything that was offered and attainable before it was withdrawn, and had no need to ask for more unless in the matter of storage-room.

Everybody was very happy and very excited, for no such feast had been in Sark within the memory of the oldest child present. And if Charles Svendt's Stock-Exchange friends could have seen him—merrily circling the tables and exhorting already distent youngsters to still greater and greater exertions; poking them in the ribs to prove, against their own better judgment, but in accordance with their inclinations, that there was assuredly still room for more; bidding them "Mangez! Mangez!" in the one word of French he could recall as specially applicable at the moment—it is certain they would not have known him.

And Miss Penny, too, looked as if she had never enjoyed herself so much in her life, and backed him up in all his endeavours right heartily. And now and again, when Charles Svendt looked at her, he said to himself, "By Jove, she's as good-looking a girl as I know, and as clever as they make 'em!"

For there is no greater beautifier in the world than happiness, and Hennie Penny was completely and quite unusually happy.

To the actual wedding-feast, Graeme had asked the Vicar and his wife, and such of the neighbours as he had come to know personally, especially not forgetting his very first friend in the island, whom he still always called Count Tolstoi, and Mrs. De Carteret. For the rest, he had given Mrs. Carré carte-blanche to invite whom she deemed well among her friends, and she had exercised her privilege with judgment and enjoyment.

The Sénéchal was there, and the Greffier, and the Prévôt and the members of the Court, ex officio, so to speak, and the Wesleyan minister who was on excellent terms with the Vicar, and the Post-Master and his jovial white-haired father, who built the boats and coffins for the community, and had supplied the tables for the feast; and many more—a right goodly company of stalwart, weather-browned men and pleasant-faced women, all vastly happy to be assisting at so unusual an event as an English wedding.

They drank the health of the bride and bridegroom in the special mulled wine thereto ordained by custom and prepared according to the laws of the Medes and Persians. And Graeme, on behalf of himself and his wife, assured them that there was no place in the world like Sark, and that they had never enjoyed a wedding so much in all their lives, and that if they had to be married a hundred times they could wish no happier wedding than Sark had given them.

And of all that company, none beamed more brightly, nor enjoyed himself more, than Charles Pixley, who, having come to curse, had, in most approved fashion, stayed to bless, and had even beaten the prophet's record by giving away to another the treasure he had desired for himself.

In the usual course of things, after the feasting would have come games and songs until dark. But that had been adjudged too much of an ordeal by the ladies, and the onus of it was laid upon the youngsters outside. While Margaret and Miss Penny rested from their labours, and Mrs. Carré and her helpers cleared the rooms for the festivities of the evening, and prepared the milder and more intermittent refections necessary thereto, Graeme and Pixley and the Vicar and others set the children to games and races, for which indeed their previous exertions at the tables had not best fitted them, but which nevertheless, or perhaps on that very account, were provocative of much laughter and merriment.

Then, when it grew dark, and the reluctant youngsters had been cajoled and dragged and packed off to bed, the hitherto-unprovided-for section—the young men and maidens, all in their best and a trifle shy to begin with—came flocking in for their share in the festivities, and Orpheus and Terpsichore held the floor for the rest of the night.

And they did dance! Margaret and Miss Penny and Graeme and Pixley thought they had seen dancing before, but dancing such as this it had never been theirs to witness.

If it lacked anything in grace—and far be it from me to say so—it more than made up for all by its inexhaustible energy and tireless enjoyment. The men had brought their own music in the shape of a concertina, which passed from hand to hand and with which they all seemed on equally friendly terms.

Jokes, laughter, round dances, refreshments, interludes of smokings and gigglings in the darkness of the verandah, occasional more intellectual flights in the shape of songs and recitations,—mostly of a somewhat lugubrious tendency, to judge by the faces of the auditors, but being mostly in patois they were unintelligible to the British foreigners,—more dances,—coats off now, to reduce the temperature of the performers,—more refreshments, more dances,—dances with broomsticks held between the partners, over which they slipped and skipped to the tune of caustic comments by the onlookers,—

dances between caps laid on the floor and which must on no account be touched by the dancers. And always the cry to the musician of the moment was,—"Faster! Faster!"—and the race between Orpheus and Terpsichore—between the music and the flying feet, grew still more fast and furious.

Now Charles Svendt, as we know, did not look like a dancing man, but dancing was one of the superficial accomplishments in which he excelled.

Miss Penny, also, through much experience with girls, was lighter of foot than she looked.

They stood for a time watching, and presently both their feet were tapping to the quickstep of the rest.

"Let's have a shot at it," said Charles. "Will you?" and he looked down at her.

"I'd love to," and in a moment they were whirling in the circle with the rest, but with a grace that none there could rival,—gallant dancers as the Sark boys and girls are.

"Delightful!" murmured Charles Svendt. "You dance like an angel, and we fit splendidly," and Hennie Penny found a man's arm about her decidedly and delightfully more inspiriting than all the arms of all the schoolgirls in the world, and danced as she had never danced before.

So swift and light and smooth and graceful was their flight that before long the rest tailed off and all stood propped against the walls to watch them.

"We've got the floor all to ourselves," murmured Miss Penny at last, as she woke to the fact.

"We've licked them into fits on their own ground," he laughed in her ear. "You can dance and no mistake. It's a treat to dance with a really good dancer."

"I think we ought to stop. We're stopping their fun," said Hennie Penny, and when he led her to a seat the rest of the room all clapped their enjoyment.

Graeme and Margaret danced a round or two to endorse the festivities, but they were not in it with Pixley and Hennie Penny, and they soon dropped out and clapped heartily with the rest.

When Charles Svendt, later on, suggested another dance, Miss Penny bade him go and dance with one of the Sark girls.

"But I don't want to dance with any of them. Besides, I don't know any of 'em, and I couldn't talk to her if I did."

"Oh yes, you can. They all speak English."

"Do they now? It don't sound like it. Come on, Miss Penny. They wouldn't enjoy it and I wouldn't enjoy it, and I never enjoyed anything so much in my life as that last round."

So Hennie took pity on him, and they danced many times amid great applause.

"Awfully good of you!" said Charles Svendt, as the dawn came peeping in through the east windows and the open front door; and Mrs. Carré, as Mistress of the Ceremonies, and a very tired one at that, bluffly informed the company that it was time to go home.

"I've enjoyed it immensely," said Hennie Penny, and if her face was any index to her feelings, there was no mistake about it.

XX

None of them will ever forget that great day.

Still less is any of them likely to forget the day that followed.

As dancing only ceased when the sun was about rising, before-breakfast bathing was declared off for that day, and they arranged to meet later on and stroll quietly down to Dixcart Bay during the morning and all bathe together there. Charles Svendt laughingly prepared them for an exhibition of incompetence by stating that his swimming wasn't a patch on his dancing, but that he could get along. Miss Penny gaily gave him points as to her own peculiar methods of swimming, which, as we know, demanded instant and easy touch of sand or stone at any moment of the halting progression. He confessed to a like prejudice in favour of something solid within reach of his sinking capacity, and they agreed to help one another.

They called for him at the hotel about eleven o'clock, and went joking through the sunny lanes of Petit Dixcart, crossed the brook that runs out of Hart's-Tongue Valley, and followed it by the winding path along the side of the cliff, among the gorse and ferns, down into the bay.

They had a right merry bathe with no grave casualties. Miss Penny, indeed, got out of her depth twice, to the extent of quite two inches, and shrieked for help, which Charles Svendt gallantly hastened to render; while Graeme and Margaret swam across from head to head, watched enviously by the paddlers in shallow waters.

They went home by the climbing path up the hillside, rested on The Quarter-deck while Charles Svendt got his breath back, and so, by the old Dixcart hotel, and the new one nestling among its flowers and trees, and up the Valley, to the Vicarage.

The Vicar was basking in the shade of the trees in front of the house.

"Ah-ha—Mr. and Mrs. Graeme! Good-morning! You are none the worse for being married? Non?" as he shook hands joyously all round, with both hands at once.

"Not a bit," laughed Graeme. "We're all as happy as sandboys."

"Comment donc—sandboys? What is that?"

"Happy little boys who dispense with clothes and paddle all day in the sand and water."

"Ah—you have been bathing! What energie! And you danced till—?"

"About four o'clock, I suppose. The sun was just thinking of rising as we were thinking of retiring."

"But it is marvellous! And you are not tired?"

"The bathe has freshened us all up," said Margaret.

Then Mrs. Vicar came out at sound of their voices, and felicitated them, and begged them to rest a while in the shade. But they were all hungry, and Charles Svendt laughingly asserted that he had swallowed so much salt-water, in rescuing Miss Penny from a watery grave, that his constitution absolutely needed a tiny tot of whisky, or the consequences might be serious.

So they went laughingly on their way, and Charles tried his best to get Miss Penny to go and show him the way to the Bel-Air, pleading absolute confusion still as to the points of the compass and the lie of the land.

He was to lunch with them at the Red House, but insisted on going home first to straighten up and make himself presentable. So they led him to the Avenue, and set his face straight down it, and bade him follow his nose and turn neither to the right hand nor to the left, and then they turned off through the fields by their own short-cut, and went merrily home.

I

Graeme was just finishing a beautiful knot in his tie, when he heard hasty feet crossing the verandah to the open front door. There was some unknown quantity in them that gave him sudden start.

"Graeme!" sharp, hoarse,—a voice he did not recognise.

He ran hastily out of the east bedroom, which he was using as a dressing-room.

"Hello there!" as he sprang down the stairs, "Why—Pixley? What's wrong, man?"

For Charles Pixley was standing there, leaning in at the doorway, looking as though he would fall headlong but for the supporting jamb. He had a brown envelope in his hand and a crumpled pink telegram. His face was white, and drawn, and haggard. His very figure seemed to have shrunk in these few minutes. Never had Graeme seen so ghastly a change in a man in so short a time.

Before Pixley could speak Miss Penny came hurrying along the path with a face full of sympathetic anxiety.

"What is it?" she asked. "I saw Mr. Pixley pass, and his face frightened me. Oh, what is wrong?"

Pixley glanced at her out of his woeful eyes, and at Margaret, who had just come running down the stairs. He seemed to hesitate for a moment. Then he groaned—

"You will have to know," and motioned them all into the dining-room and shut the door.

"This "—jerking out the telegram—"was waiting for me," and he handed it to Graeme, who smoothed it out and read, while Pixley dropped into a chair.

"Pixley. Bel-Air. Sark.

"Zizel, Amadou, Zebu, Zeta. Eno."

"Code," said Pixley briefly. "Meanings underneath," and dropped his head into his hands.

"Zizel," read Graeme slowly—"There is bad news. Amadou—your father. Zebu—has bolted. Zeta—we fear the smash will be a bad one. Eno—?"

"My partner's initials—they certify the wire," said Pixley hoarsely.

And they looked soberly at one another and very pitifully at the broken man before them.

"Don't take it too hard, Pixley," said Graeme quietly, laying a friendly hand on the other's shoulder. "It may not be as bad as this puts it. Codes are brutally bald things, you know"

The bowed head shook pitifully. He raised his white face and looked round at them with a shocked shrinking in his eyes.

"God forgive him!" he jerked. "And God forgive me, for I have doubted him at times! He was so—so—so demned good"—and Graeme's lips twitched in spite of himself, so closely was the expression in accord with his own feelings. But Pixley did not see the twitch, for he was looking at Margaret and Hennie Penny, and he was saying with vehemence—

"Will you believe me that I knew absolutely nothing of this? He never discussed his affairs with me nor I mine with him, and we had no business together except on purely business lines. If he had to buy or sell he sent it my way, of course,—nothing more. You will believe me, Graeme—"

"Every word, my boy—"

"We all believe it, Mr. Pixley," said Hennie Penny warmly.

"And I know it, Charles," said Margaret.

"It is very good of you all," he groaned. "I must get back at once, Graeme. How soon is there a boat?"

"Five o'clock. You'll have to stop a night in Guernsey, which is a nuisance."

Charles Svendt shook his head in dumb misery. It was crushing to be so far away—thirty hours at least, and he gnashing within to be on the spot and at work, learning the worst, seeing what could be done.

Then, with a preliminary knock on the door, Mrs. Carré came in with brilliant lobsters and crisp lettuces for lunch, and, hungry as they all were, their souls loathed the thought of eating.

"They are just out of the pot," beamed she, "and the lettuces were growing not five min'ts ago. Ech!"—at sight of Pixley—"is he ill?"

"Mr. Pixley has just had bad news from home, Mrs. Carré," said Graeme. "He will have to go by to-day's boat."

"Ach, but I am sorry! And him so happy yesterday and dancing the best in the room," and her pleasant face clouded sympathetically.

"Meg, I'll go up to your room for a minute and finish my hair," said Hennie Penny. "I ran out just as I was—"

"It was very kind of you," said Charles Svendt, and the general sympathy seemed to comfort him somewhat.

"No good feeling too bad about it, old man, till you know all the facts," said Graeme, when the girls had gone off upstairs.

"It hits me, Graeme. Not financially, as I said. But in every other way it hits me hard.—Have you reached the point of seeing that it may hit her too?"—and he nodded towards upstairs.

"I suppose there was a glimmering idea of the chance of that at the back of my head somewhere, but we won't trouble about it just now. How about your mother?"

Pixley shook his head dismally again. "It will be a terrible blow to her. He was a bit hard and cold at home, you know, but she looked up to him as immaculate. Yes, it will hit her very hard. As to money, of course, she will be all right. I have plenty. But the talk and the scandal—" and he groaned again at thought of it all.

"Send her over here for a time—or bring her yourself. We have heaps of room here. Miss Penny is coming to stop with us next week. Your mother was always fond of Margaret, I believe."

"She was—very fond of her.... That's a good thought of yours, Graeme. Are you sure Margaret—?"

"Of course she would. She and Miss Penny will just take care of her, and no word of the troubles will reach her. That's the thing to do, and maybe you'll find things not as bad as you expect when you get back."

But, from the look of him, Charles Svendt had small hope of matters being anything but what he feared.

When the girls came down they made an apology of a meal, for, in spite of their hunger, the stricken look of their friend took their appetites away.

The thought that there might still lurk in their minds a suspicion that he had had some knowledge of his father's position, when he came across to stop their marriage, still troubled him.

"I do hope you will all believe me when I say that I knew absolutely nothing of it all," he said, when they had finished an almost silent meal. "When I said I had doubted him at times, I simply meant that his everlasting and—and—well, very assertive philanthropies palled upon me. It was a little difficult at times to believe in the genuineness of it all, for we did not see very much of it at home, as you know,"—he looked at Margaret, who nodded. "In business matters he could be as hard as nails, and it was not easy to fit it all together."

"Not one of us believes anything of the kind of you, old man. Just get that right out of your head, once for all. We're only sorry for your sake that the trouble has come, and I'm sure we all hope it will turn out not so bad as you fear," said Graeme heartily.

"What about your mother, Charles?" said Margaret. "I'm afraid she will feel this dreadfully. Hennie and I were talking about it upstairs, and we were wondering if you could get her to come and stop with us for a time—"

"You see!" said Graeme, with a smile at Pixley. And to Margaret—"I suggested exactly the same thing while you were up doing your hair."

"It's awfully good of you all," said Charles. "If you're quite sure—"

"We're quite sure. Send her to us at once as soon as you reach home, and Jock shall meet her in Guernsey."

"I think I'd perhaps better bring her across myself. I don't suppose there will be much I can do when I've heard the worst—if they've got to it yet. Things may be all tangled up, and it may take time. And for ten days or so, until folks have had time to forget, the name of Pixley won't be one to be proud of."

"Come if you can," said Graeme heartily. "You've seen nothing of Sark yet."

II

They all went down to the harbour to see him off—as is the custom when one's friends leave Sark. And when Charles Svendt had shaken hands with Margaret and Miss Penny—and had found a touch of comfort in the sympathetic droop of their faces—and had fancied Miss Penny's bright eyes were at once brighter and mistier than usual—and had thanked them again very humbly for all their kindness—he turned to say good-bye to Graeme.

"Come away, man!" said Jock cheerfully. "I'm coming too. Meg's given me a holiday, and I'm going to shake a free leg again in Guernsey—"

But Charles thought he saw through that.

"Don't you come on my account, Graeme"

"Not on your account at all, my boy, but the accounts of a good many shopkeepers over there which I've got to straighten out at once, while all the little differences are fresh in my mind. Something wrong in nearly all of them—some over, some under—and I'm still a bit of a business man though I do write books."

For, when Pixley went off to pack his portmanteau, Graeme had said to his wife, "Meg dear, what do you think of my going across to Peter Port with that young man? He'll have a bad black time all by himself. He's holding himself in before us, but when he's alone it'll all come back on him in a heap and he'll feel it."

And Margaret had said, "Yes, dear, go. You'll be a great comfort to him. I am very very sorry for him."

The last flicker of the waving handkerchiefs above the sea-wall, and their responsive wavings from the boat, had been abruptly cut by the intervening bastion of Les Lâches, but Charles Svendt still leaned with his arms on the rail and looked back as though he could pierce the granite cliff and see the girls still standing there, and Graeme stood patiently behind him.

He straightened up at last with a sigh.

"I'm glad I came," he said, "though if I'd had any idea what was going to happen I'd have drowned myself first. It's when one's in trouble"—as though this were a discovery of his own—"that one finds out how kind people can be."

"Yes, trouble has its uses. I had a deuce of a time for the first few weeks after I got here. Your dad had told me you and Margaret were to be married very shortly, and it knocked life into a cocked-hat for me—"

"That's what he would have liked. Do you know, Graeme, I've been thinking that it's just possible your marriage helped to precipitate matters with him. I don't know, of course; but if he has been juggling her money in any way, he may have been counting on a marriage between us to help straighten things. Then, when he heard nothing from me—"

"It's possible. But if it acted as quickly as all that, I'm afraid the chances for Margaret's portion are pretty small."

"Gad! That would hurt me more than anything. I shall do everything in my power—"

"I'm sure of it, my dear fellow. And you must understand that her money—whatever it is—has never entered into our calculations in any way. I knew nothing of it till Lady Elspeth Gordon told me, and I had it all settled on her before the wedding took place. If it is gone we can do without it."

And Charles Svendt, if he said nothing, thought all the more.

III

The two girls were standing in the outermost seaward corner of the breakwater, as though they had never moved, when the Assistance came nosing round Les Lâches next morning, and made for the harbour. And to Graeme, the sight of his wife, after a separation of eighteen hours, was like a life-giving stream to a pilgrim of the desert, or the blessing of light to a darkened soul. His heart swelled almost to paining-point for very joy of her. He took deep breaths of gratitude for this sweet crowning of his life. He wondered vaguely why he should be so blest above all other men. He vowed his vows again and his eyes were misty.

They saw him standing by the captain, and waved glad welcomes, and presently, his glimpse into the depths of Margaret's eyes as he kissed her, told him that he had been missed even as he had missed.

"I am glad I went with him," he said, as they climbed the steep Creux Road. "It did him good to talk. He's feeling it terribly."

He did not tell them that they had got the previous day's papers in St. Peter Port, and that their scathing comments on a peculiarly bad failure, and on the remarkable contrast between the profession and the practice of Jeremiah Pixley's life, had driven Charles Svendt almost crazy. The wound was raw in their hearts. There was no need to turn the knife in it.

"We shall see him back here with Mrs. Pixley before the middle of next week, unless I'm very much mistaken," he said. "He says there's nothing doing on the Stock Exchange, and he can fix things with his partner to get away for a time, and it seems the wisest thing to do."

"I have liked Charles better this time than I ever did in my life before," said Margaret. "And I am very very sorry for him and Mrs. Pixley."

"He's not half a bad fellow," said Graeme heartily.

And perhaps, if it had been put to Miss Penny, she would have improved even upon that.

"I hope you're not very set on being a rich woman, Meg," said Graeme, when they were alone together.

"Oh, but I am," she said, with a smile which all the riches in the world could not have bought from her, or brought to her.

"Yes, I know,"—and he gathered the smile with a kiss. "But in coarse material wealth, I mean."

"I'm just as set on it as you are. I want just as much as will make you happy. You mean Mr. Pixley has made away with it all?"

"I'm very much afraid so, but I guess we can get along all right without it."

"Of course we can—splendidly. I'm a famous housekeeper and you'll be a famous author. There couldn't be a better team. It will bring out the very best that's in us."

"We can never come to actual want anyway, for my little bit—which, by the way, Lady Elspeth once took the trouble to impress upon me was just about enough to pay Mr. Pixley's servants' wages—is in Consols, and they're not likely to crack up. And my last book brought me about fifty pounds—"

"It ought to have brought you five thousand. I'm sure it was good enough."

"Of course it was, but it takes time to work up to the five thousand point. Some get there, I suppose. But I should imagine more starve off at the fifty line."

"We could live like princes on a couple of hundred a year in Sark here."

"It would pall on you in time, I'm afraid."

"You've been here twice as long as I have. Has it begun to pall on you yet?"

"I don't think it would ever pall on me, if I lived here for a century. But then I've got my work, you see."

"And I've got you, my dear. When you and Sark begin to pall I'll promise to let you know. It's heavenly."

"Oh, I don't claim all that, you know. Don't expect too much—"

"Will Charles be involved at all, do you think, Jock?"

"I don't think so. They had not much to do with one another in business matters."

"I'm glad of that. Do you know"—with an introspective look in her eyes—"I've an idea—"

"Hennie Penny?"

Margaret nodded.

"That would be capital. She'd make him an excellent wife."

"I'm sure she would. She's just what he needs. She's as good as gold, and she has more genuine common-sense than anyone I know."

"Thousand thanks!"

"Oh, we're exceptions to all rules. But I do hope something—I mean everything—may come of it. And we would all have reason to bless this blessed little island all our days."

"Some of us will, anyway. It certainly shall not go unblest."

IV

On the Tuesday afternoon Graeme received a brief telegram from Charles Pixley—"Crossing tonight." And Wednesday morning found them all on the sea-wall awaiting the arrival of the steamer from Guernsey.

"There he is—in the front corner of the upper deck—keen to get here as soon as possible, I should say. I know just how he feels," said Graeme, with a laugh. "Looks a bit different from what he did the first time he came."

"That's Mrs. Pixley on the side seat," said Margaret, and they waved their welcomes.

There were two ladies on the side seat, and both stood up and waved vigorously in reply.

"Why—who—?" began Margaret. And then—excitedly, "Jock—I believe it's Lady Elspeth. I'm certain it is. It is. It is."

"Just like her! Hurrah for the Gordons!" and he sent them welcomes which a world full of Pixleys alone could not have excited in him.

"Now this is delightful," he said, as he sprang on board and rushed at Lady Elspeth.

"All right, my boy! Don't shake my hand right off, if you can help it. Here, you may give me a kiss, though it's contrary to the usages of my country. We'll pretend I'm your mother again. Now say how do you do to Mrs. Pixley. How's Margaret? I've got crows to pick with you young people—"

"Make it seven, or it's unlucky," laughed Graeme.

"Eh? What?"

"Tell you later. We're great believers in crows here. Mrs. Pixley, I am very glad indeed to see you here. Charles, old man, you've done splendidly."

Charles wrung his hand in silence. His face was sober, with a latent glow of expectation in it. When he had seen to the luggage he joined the group on the quay, and it was Miss Penny who was the first to see him coming.

"Welcome back to Sark!" she said cheerfully.

"I'm uncommonly glad to be here. Everybody all right? How's Mrs. Carré?"

"Everybody's first-rate, especially Meg and Jock. Their spirits are enough to inflate the island."

"It's good to be young," and the sober mask lifted slightly and let the inner light shine through.

V

"Go to an hotel?" said Margaret indignantly, in reply to a suggestion from Lady Elspeth. "Indeed you'll do nothing of the kind,"—and, as the old lady hesitated still,—"If you do I'll never speak to you again as long as I live."

"Oh well, I couldn't stand that—"

"Of course you couldn't. Neither could I. An hotel indeed!"—with withering scorn—"And we with four empty bedrooms crying aloud at night because two of their fellows are occupied and they are left out in the cold! An hotel! I'd just like to see you!"

"My guidness! Is she often like this, Jock?"

"Oh, always! I thought you knew her. Why couldn't you warn me in time?—No!" as Lady Elspeth attempted to speak—"It's too late now. We're bound for life. There's no cutting the bond. The Vicar told us so."

"You're both clean daft together," said the old lady, with dancing eyes. "Well, I'll stop in one of your crying bedrooms—on conditions. We'll talk about that later on. Where's the rest of the island, and how do you get to it?"

"Old ladies and luggage ride. We youngsters walk. There's Charles waiting for you at the carriage. There you are! Au revoir!"

As the young people breasted the steep, Pixley—forgetting entirely his vow never to do it on foot again—unfolded to them Lady Elspeth's idea, which simply was, that if the Red House could hold them all,—of which she had her doubts, in spite of his assertions,—they should all share expenses and such household duties as so large a party would involve.

"You see—if you don't mind it, Mrs. Graeme,"—with an apologetic look at Margaret,—"it will give the two old ladies something to do and will leave us young folks freer to get about."

"It's a capital arrangement if the old ladies don't mind. Mrs. Carré can get in another girl. It will keep them all busy seeing that we have enough to eat. But they'll soon get used to looking forward two or three days and ordering Friday's dinner on Tuesday."

"How long can you stop, old man?" asked Graeme.

"A fortnight—all being well," and there was a touch of soberness in it as he said that. "There's really nothing doing, and Ormerod's a good fellow and insisted on it."

"We can do heaps in a fortnight," said Miss Penny jubilantly. "However did you manage to catch Lady Elspeth?"

"She's a grand old lady. I found her with my mother when I got there. She'd been with her ever since— since the trouble. And when I proposed bringing my mother she said at once that she was coming too. She had crows to pick with you two, and so on. I expect she thought my mother would feel things less if she was with her."

"She's an old dear," said Margaret. "They shall both have the very best time we can give them."

"I shall take them conger-eeling," said Graeme,—"and to Venus's Bath"

"And down the Boutiques and the Gouliots"—suggested Margaret.

"And ormering in Grande Grève," laughed Miss Penny, who had spent a day there on that alluring pursuit and had come home bruised and wet and dirty.

"Oh, there's lots of fun in store for them," said Graeme, laughing like a schoolboy out for a holiday. "And, as Hennie Penny says, we can do heaps in a fortnight."

VI

Having made up their minds that there was no earthly reason why Charles Pixley and Hennie Penny should not be as happy as they were themselves, Margaret and Graeme saw to it that nothing should be awanting in the way of opportunity.

Miss Penny's natural goodness of heart impelled her to the most delicate consideration towards Mrs. Pixley. Hennie Penny, you see, had come bravely through dire troubles of her own, and tribulation softens the heart as it does the ormer. She anticipated the nervous old lady's every want, soothed her bruised susceptibilities in a thousand hidden ways, tended her as lovingly as an only daughter might have done,—and all out of the sheer necessity of her heart, and with never a thought of reward other than the satisfaction of her own desire for the happiness of all about her.

Not that the others were one whit less considerate, but, in the natural course of things, Miss Penny's heart and time were, perhaps, a little more at liberty for outside service, and in Mrs. Pixley the opportunity met her half-way.

It is safe to say that the old lady had never in her life been so much made of. Margaret had always been gentle and sweet with her; but the cold white light of Mr. Pixley's unco' guidness had always cast a shadow upon the household, and Margaret had got from under it whenever the chance offered.

"You are very good to me, my dear," Charles heard his mother say to Hennie Penny, one day when they two were alone together and did not know anyone was near. "If I had ever had a daughter I would have liked her to be like you. How did you learn to be so thoughtful of other people?"

"I think it must have been through having come through lots of troubles of my own," said Hennie Penny simply.

"Troubles abound," said the tremulous old lady. "You have drawn the sting of yours and kept only the honey," which saying astonished Charles greatly. He had no idea his mother could say things like that. She had had time to think plenty of them, indeed, but there had never been room for more than one shining light in the household and that had cast strong shadows.

Charles had gone quietly away smiling to himself, and had been in cheerful spirits for the rest of the day.

The first night, when the ladies had gone chattering upstairs to make sure that all the arrangements were in order, Graeme and Pixley sat out on the verandah smoking a final pipe.

The ladies' voices floated through the open windows as they passed from room to room, and Graeme laughed softly. "What's up?" asked Pixley, gazing at him soberly.

"I was thinking of the changes here since the first night I slept in this house all by myself, and heard ghosts creeping about and all kinds of noises."

"Much jollier to hear them," said Charles, as Miss Penny's and Margaret's laughter came floating down the softness of the night.

"Ay, indeed! Very much jollier," and they smoked and listened.

No word had so far passed between them as to the troubles that lay behind. There had, indeed, been no opportunity until now, and Graeme had no mind to broach the matter.

But Pixley had only been waiting till they could discuss things alone, and the time had come.

"It will take them months to get to the bottom of things over there," he said quietly. "I saw the accountants, and they say everything's in a dreadful mess. He must have been involved for years. It makes me absolutely sick to think of it all, Graeme, and him—"

"I'm sure it must, old chap. Why think of it? It's done, and it can't be undone, and everyone knows you had nothing to do with it."

"I know. Everyone is very kind, but I can't get rid of it. It's with me all the time like a dirty shadow."

"We'll chase it away. No place like Sark for getting rid of bogeys and worries."

"How things will come out it's impossible to say. I made special enquiries into Margaret's affairs, and it's quite certain he's tampered with her money, but they could not say yet to what extent. On the other hand, certain of her securities are intact, so everything is not gone. But what I wanted to say was this. I am determined that Margaret shall not suffer, whatever may have happened. Any deficiency I shall make good myself."

"My dear fellow, she would never hear of it."

"That's why I'm talking to you."

"Well, I won't hear of it either. As I told you before, it was a trouble to me when I heard she had any money. Whatever she had I settled on herself, and we can get on very well without it."

"All the same I'm not going to have her lose anything through my—through him. Neither you nor she can stop me doing what I like with my own money."

"We can refuse to touch it."

"That would be nonsense."

"Not half as bad as you crippling yourself for life to make good what you'd never made away with."

"It wouldn't do that," said Charles quietly. "Ormerod's a long-headed fellow, and we made some pretty good hits before the bottom dropped out of things. You must let me have my own way in this matter, Graeme, if it's only for my own peace of mind. I'm going to ask Miss Penny to be my wife. Do you think—"

"My dear fellow," said Graeme, jumping up and shaking him heartily by the hand, "that's the best bit of news I've heard since Meg said 'I will' in the church there. She's an absolutely splendid girl, is Hennie. Except Meg herself, I don't know any girl I admire so much. She's as good and sweet as they make 'em, and for sound common-sense she's a perfect gold mine."

"And you don't think—?"

"I've never heard a hint of anyone else. Like me to ask Meg? She'd be sure to know. Girls talk of these things, you know."

"I don't know. Would it be quite—"

"Everything's fair in love and war,—proverbial, my boy. But I'm pretty sure you've a clear field, and I congratulate you both with all my heart. Come to think of it, she's been as dull as a ditch since you went away"

"Really?"

"Fact! I was trying the other night to prove to her that she'd got influenza coming on, or hay-fever, or something of the kind. She's as different as chalk from cheese since eleven o'clock to-day. It's you, I'll bet you a sovereign."

Charles did not respond to the offer. He sat smoking quietly and let his thoughts run along brighter paths than they had done for days.

VII

At breakfast next morning Graeme soberly suggested to Lady Elspeth that she should go conger-eeling with him that day. And the shrewd brown eyes looked into his, and twinkled in response to the deep blue and the brown ones opposite, and she said, "I mind I was just a wee bit feather-headed myself for a while after I was married. I caught congers before you were short-coated, my laddie, but I'm not going catching them now."

"They are a bit rampageous when they're grown up," he admitted. "We got one the other day about as thick round as one's leg, and it barked like a dog and tried to bite."

"And does he make you go congering, my dear?" she asked Margaret.

"Make?" scoffed Graeme. "Make, forsooth? How little you know! I'd like to see the man who could make that young person do anything but just what she wishes. Why, she twists us all round her little finger and—"

"Ay, ay! Well, discipline is good for the young, and you're just nothing but a laddie in some things."

"I'm going to keep so all my life. So's Meg! Well, suppose we say ormering then, if congering's too lively. Hennie Penny's an awful dab at ormering. If you'd seen her the other night when she came home! A tangle of vraic was an old lady's best cap in comparison—"

"And how many did I get, and how many did you get?" retorted Miss Penny.

"I got six and you got seven—"

"Seventeen, and you stole four of your six from Meg."

"Oh well, I found the mushrooms, coming home, and they were worth a pailful of ormers."

"You didn't beat them long enough. Ormers take a lot of beating," she explained to Lady Elspeth.

"Thumping, she means. My mushrooms beat them hollow,—tender and delicate and fragrant"—and he sniffed appreciatively as though he could scent them still.—"Your ormers were like shoe-soles."

"And as to the mushrooms," continued Hennie Penny, "you'd never have found them if I hadn't tumbled into them, and then you thought they were toadstools."

"Oh well!—Who can't take a hook out of a whiting's mouth? Who was it screamed when the lobster looked at her?"

"It nearly took a piece out of me."

"Who nearly upset the boat when a baby devilfish came up in the pot? And it wasn't above that size!"

"I draw the line at devil-fish. They're no' canny."

"Do they generally go on like this?" asked Lady Elspeth of Margaret.

"All the time," said Margaret, with a matronly air. "They're just a couple of children. I keep them out of mischief as well as I can, but it's hard work at times."

"She's just every bit as bad, you know, when we're alone," said Miss Penny. "But she's got her company manners on just now. You should see her when she's bathing."

"Ah—yes! You should see her when she's bathing," said Graeme, with a smack of the lips. "All the little waves and crabs and lobsters keep bobbing up to have another look at her. In Venus's Bath the other day—"

"Now, children, stop your fooling. Where shall we go to-day?" laughed Margaret, and Lady Elspeth could hardly take her eyes off her, so winsomely, so radiantly happy was she.

"We old folks will stay at home and talk to Mrs. Carré," said Lady Elspeth. "You young ones can go off and do what you like."

"Oh no, you don't," said Graeme. "You didn't come here to loaf in a verandah. When you come to Sark you've got to enjoy yourselves, whether you want to or not. Suppose we take lunch along to the Eperquerie, and the elders can bask and snooze, and we'll bathe three times off that black ledge under Les Fontaines. And if the Seigneur's out fishing perhaps he'll take some of us with him, those who don't scream when the poor fish gets a hook in its throat. And you'll see Margaret out on the loose. She always goes it when she's swimming."

"I hope you won't venture too far out, Charles," said Mrs. Pixley, with visions of his limp body being carried home.

"Miss Penny and I are sensible people when we're bathing," said Charles. "We don't lose our heads—"

"Nor any of the rest of you,—nor touch of the stones," laughed Graeme.

"That's so," said Charles. "We like to know what's below us and that it's not too far away."

"It's very wise," said Mrs. Pixley plaintively. "One hears of such dreadful accidents. I'm very glad you're so sensible, my dear," to Miss Penny.

"Oh, I'm dreadfully sensible at times, especially when I'm bathing. But that's because I can only swim with one foot at the bottom."

"Any beach about there?" enquired Charles forethoughtfully.

"Nice little bit just round the corner, with a cave and all,—capital place for children. Paddle by the hour without going in above your ankles."

And so they wandered slowly up the scented lanes past the Seigneurie, laden with the usual paraphernalia of a bathing-lunch, and came out on the Eperquerie.

They established the old ladies in a gorsy nook, built a fireplace of loose stones, and collected fuel, and laid the fire ready for the match, which Lady Elspeth was to apply whenever they waved to her.

"If She isn't fast asleep," said Graeme.

Then they pointed out all the things that lay about, so that they might take an intelligent interest in their surroundings,—Guernsey, and Herm, and Jethou, and Alderney, and the Casquets, and the coast of France, and the Seigneur in his boat, and then they trooped off like a party of school-children.

And presently the old ladies saw them scrambling down the black, scarped sides of the headland opposite, and then they disappeared behind rocks and into crannies. Then a pink meteor flashed from the black ledge, followed in an instant by a dark-blue one, and both went breasting out to sea. And in front of the cave two less venturesome figures beguiled the onlookers and themselves into the belief that they were swimming, though they never went out of their depth and sounded anxiously for it at every second stroke.

And up above, the larks trilled joyously, and the air was soft and sweet as the air of heaven; and down below, the water was bluer than the sky and clear as crystal, so that they could see the great white rocks which lay away down in the depths, and they looked like sea-monsters crawling after their prey. And the shouts of the swimmers came mellowly up to them, and they could see their little limbs jerking like the limbs of frogs.

"It is good to be here," said Lady Elspeth enjoyably.

"It is very very good to be here. I am very glad we came," said Mrs. Pixley, with a sigh that was not all sadness.

VIII

Many such days of sheer delight they had, and kept the dark cloud resolutely below their horizon. They accommodated their activities to the limited powers of the elders, and took them wherever it was reasonably possible for them to go. They chartered a boat for the day, and took them and all the luncheon-things round from Creux Harbour to Grande Grève, subjecting Charles to long-unaccustomed labours at the oar. In the same way they introduced them to Dixcart Bay, and Derrible, and Grève de la Ville; and, choosing a fit day, they circumnavigated the island again in three boat-loads, landing for lunch on an even keel on Brenière, and penetrating into every accessible cave they came to,—Mrs. Pixley enjoying the wonders in fear and trembling, and breathing freely only when they were safely out in the open once more. And Graeme and Margaret watched the approximating of Hennie Penny and Charles with infinite delight. It needed only a full understanding between these two to complete their own great happiness.

But the dark cloud was there, though they might refuse to look at it, and clouds below the horizon have a way of rising, especially dark ones.

The post-office in Sark is a cottage, or the part of a cottage, turned from private to public use. In former times the service was of a very perfunctory character, Providence largely taking the place of post-master while that official attended first to his fishing and then to his duties, and any who had good and valid reason to expect a letter came down to the mail-bag where it lay on the beach and went through it for themselves.

The advent of visitors accustomed to more exact and business-like methods, however, has done away with this Arcadian simplicity, and now each day when the boat is in, all who prefer not to wait for the tardy delivery at their own houses, collect gradually round the official cottage, and in due course, and after the exercise of virtues, receive their mail across the counter. And some tear their letters open at once, regardless of spectators, and devour them on the spot, but the wiser carry them home for private consumption. For one never knows for certain what of heartbreak and disaster the most innocent-looking envelope may contain.

Graeme and Margaret and Miss Penny, however, being in retreat, and having cut the painter with the outside world, had not cultivated the post-office until Charles and Lady Elspeth arrived. But, as Charles had to keep more or less in touch with Throgmorton Street, they had now got into the habit of calling with him for his letters, except when the doing so interfered with the programme for the day. And many an amusing, and sometimes touching, insight did they get there into human nature. Graeme said it was worth while the trouble of going, just to sit in the hedge opposite and watch people's faces, especially the faces of those who tore open their letters and those who got none.

They were sitting so in the hedge one morning, quietly watching and commenting silently, and by looks only, on the vagaries of the letter-scramblers, and Charles had pushed into the crowded little room to antedate the delivery by a few minutes if possible.

As he came out, with his letters in his hand, they all saw at a glance that something had happened. His face, which had been gradually relaxing to its old look of jovial good-fellowship and satisfaction with the world, was tight and hard, and yet they saw that he had not opened a letter. He turned up the road with a mere jerk of the head, and they followed wondering, and all, as it came out afterwards, with the same dim idea as to the possible cause of his upsetting.

He handed Margaret a couple of letters for Lady Elspeth, and made an attempt at conversation as they went along, but the cloud they had been keeping out of sight was visible now to all of them. Among the unopened letters in his hand was one which disturbed him even before he knew what was in it, and they could only wait, with troubled minds, for developments.

Charles went straight to his room, as he usually did when business matters claimed his attention, and from the look on his face Graeme judged that the scramble, fixed for that day on account of a specially low tide, round the Autelets, whose rock-pools and phosphorescent seaweeds and beds of flourishing anemones were a perpetual delight, would be off for the time being at all events.

But Pixley came down presently and intimated that he was ready, and they trooped away, leaving the elders at home for a day's rest, since rock-scrambling was outside their limits.

Their progress, however, was not the usual light-hearted saunter enlivened by merry jokes and laughter. The lanes were fragrant as ever, the air was full of larks and sunshine, but the cloud had risen and overshadowed them, and Graeme guessed why Charles had come. There was something he wanted to discuss with them alone, out of the hearing of his mother and Lady Elspeth.

He was not surprised—when they had scrambled down into Port du Moulin, and had passed through the arch, and were sitting on the rocks above the first of the sea-gardens,—when Charles said, "There's something I want to consult you about, and I couldn't do it at the house, as I want it kept to ourselves. I got this, this morning. Will you read it?" and he handed Graeme a letter. Graeme opened it and read it out.

"99A HIGH STREET, ALDERNEY.

"MY DEAR CHARLES,—I will not at the moment attempt any explanation of the calamity which has befallen our house. If you knew all, you would not blame me as I fear you must be doing. Let me say, however, that I have every reason to hope that in course of time I may be able to redeem the position by making good all deficiencies and so clearing our name of reproach. To do so, I must get away—to

Spain in the first instance, and for that I need your assistance. The end came unexpectedly and took me unawares, and I am almost penniless here. In asking your help, I do so the more confidently as, in the path I have indicated, lies the only hope of redemption. In assisting me you will not only be doing what a prosperous son might reasonably be expected to do for his father in his day of misfortune, but you will be acting for the general weal in putting me into a position to make good what I have all unwittingly become responsible for, and to that sacred end the remainder of my life shall be most solemnly dedicated.

"I came here from Cherbourg, and am for the moment safe from oversight. As soon as you place me in position to do so, I shall get away and begin my new life-work, which I am earnestly desirous of doing at the earliest possible moment.

"Address me as above—Revd. J. Peace.

"Your affectionate FATHER."

Graeme kept the humorous wrinkles about his eyes and mouth in order with difficulty as he read this very characteristic effusion, but Margaret was the only one who saw it. Charles had kept his eyes intently on the pool below, and Miss Penny had been regarding him sympathetically.

"What do you make of it?" said Charles. "It makes me sick."

"He evidently needs your help," said Miss Penny.

"Yes, but have I the right to give it him? That's the question."

"He says—" began Graeme.

"Oh, he says!" growled Charles. "Trouble is, he's been saying for the last twenty years, and it has all been a lie. This is probably all a lie too. Not all"—he added grimly. "As I read it, he has got funds stowed away somewhere and he's anxious to get to them."

"So that he may make restitution," urged Miss Penny.

"Yes, that's what he says," said Charles, in a tone that showed no slightest tincture of conviction. "What would you do," he asked, looking up at Graeme, "if you were in my place?"

Graeme filled his pipe thoughtfully.

"Let us look at it quietly all round," he said, and lit up and puffed away contemplatively.

"From what he says,"—checking off his points on his fingers,—"if you don't assist him, he may be taken, and the—the unpleasantness of the situation be thereby increased.... I do not see that his punishment would help anyone—except maybe as a deterrent, and that is problematical.... I gather from this, as you do, that he has funds awaiting him somewhere.... You have no great faith in his promises—"

"None," growled Charles.

"And I presume, as a business man, you would count a bird in the hand worth several in the bush—in other words, you would sooner have what he has stowed away—somewhere, than what he hopes to make some time—"

"Sight sooner!"

"Then, I should say, offer him such assistance as he needs to get away, and, if you can see your way to it, a bit to live on afterwards, on condition of his placing in your hands everything he has got stowed away, so that you can pass it on to the receiver."

Charles shook his head. "I couldn't trust him."

"Then there's only one thing to do if he agrees, and that is to go with him and bring the property back with you."

Charles groaned. "It may mean the Argentine. Spain's no place for investments these days."

"It's rough on you, old man, but it's the best I can think of," said Graeme.

"And supposing he tells me to go hang?"

"Then," said Graeme, with a shrug, "I don't see that you can help him. I have no personal feeling against him whatever, but I cannot see how you can help him except on some such lines as I've indicated. How does it strike you, Meg?"

But Margaret shook her head. "I feel very much as you do. If he is caught and punished it will only add to Mrs. Pixley's and Charles's trouble, and benefit nobody. But he is very obstinate. He has evidently planned out his future. I doubt if he'll turn from it."

"And you, Hennie?" asked Graeme.

"I think you should help him if you possibly can. It's horrible to think of him hiding there and in fear of being caught—"

"Helping him in any case is against the law—"

"Blood is thicker than water," said Hennie Penny earnestly.

"—But if some present benefit was to come to his creditors I should consider it right to do it, not otherwise."

"Suppose you go across, and see him, and talk it over with him, Mr. Pixley?" said Hennie Penny.

"I suppose that's the only thing to be done," groaned Charles. "How do you get there?"

"The Courier would call here by arrangement—up at the Eperquerie," said Graeme. "She can't come in, of course. It means lying out in a small boat and waiting for her. What do you say to us all going? In fact, unless we do, how are we going to explain Charles's going to Mrs. Pixley?"

Charles nodded.

"You could go and see him and we could talk it over again afterwards. I'm inclined to think that he won't accept, you know."

"I don't believe he will, and it'll be a bit hard to refuse him any help, if he really is on his beam ends."

"He wouldn't have written to you if he could have done without, you may count upon that."

"Is he as safe there as he seems to think?" asked Charles.

"Yes, I think so. Safer probably than in Cherbourg. It's an out-of-the-way place, from all accounts."

Discuss it as they would, they could not get beyond Graeme's proposal, and so at last they went back home, decided on the visit to Alderney on the morrow, but all feeling doubtful, and some of them distinctly nervous, as to the outcome of it.

IX

The little party that lay in wait for the Alderney steamer in old Jack Guille's boat off the Eperquerie, next morning, was eminently lacking in the vivacity that usually distinguishes such parties when the sea is smooth and the sky is blue. In fact, when they got on board, the Captain decided in his own mind that they must all have quarrelled before starting. There was no sign of anything of the kind about them now, it is true, but that might just be their good manners. For English people are not like the Sark and Guernsey folk, who, when they do quarrel, let all the world know about it.

These four had apparently little to say to one another and less to anyone else. If they had been going to a funeral they could hardly have been more reserved.

And to something very like a funeral they were going, with the added anxiety of very grave doubts as to the result of their visit.

They had had no difficulty in persuading the elder ladies that Alderney was not for them. The steep path down to the Eperquerie landing, and the tumbling about in a small boat until the steamer came, did not greatly appeal to them. Moreover, Lady Elspeth's clear eyes had noticed the signs of their clouding, in spite of their efforts after naturalness, for to experienced eyes there is nothing so unnatural as the attempt to be natural. If Mrs. Pixley noticed nothing it was probably because her faculties had not yet fully recovered from the shock to which they had been subjected. If she noticed she said nothing, having no desire, perhaps, to add to the weight of her already heavy burden.

"Now, my boy, what is it?" Lady Elspeth asked, when she had persuaded Graeme to take her for a stroll in the evening, under plea of cramp through overmuch sitting.

"Jeremiah Pixley is in Alderney and has written to Charles begging his help to get on his way."

"Ah! And what are you going to do about it?".

Graeme outlined their ideas on the matter.

"He's an old rascal," said Lady Elspeth softly. "I doubt very much if you'll get anything out of him."

"Can you suggest any better way of dealing with the matter?"

"I don't know that I can at the moment, but I doubt if you'll get any satisfaction out of him. He'll stick to all he can, and his promise of restitution is all bunkum, I should fear."

"And would you help him to get away in any case?"

"Personally, I think a course of penal servitude would be of the greatest service to him. But, for Charles's sake and his mother's, the sooner the whole matter is buried the better, and so I should be sorry to hear of him being taken. It would only revive the scandal."

"That's just what we all feel;" and he saw that the problem of Jeremiah Pixley was too much even for Lady Elspeth.

And so the party of four on the Courier lacked vivacity, and found no enjoyment in the lonely austerity of the Casquets or Ortach; and the frowning southern cliffs of Alderney itself, as the steamer raced up the Swinge to Braye Harbour, seemed to them but a poor copy of their own little isle of Sark, lacking its gem-like qualities. But then their minds were intent upon the business ahead and their outlook was darkened.

X

"Would you like me to come up with you, Charles?" Graeme asked, as the steamer rounded the breakwater.

"Yes, I'd like it," said Charles gloomily. "But I think I'd better go alone. I don't believe anything's going to come of it."

"I'm afraid not—as far as we're concerned. You'll just have to keep a stiff upper lip and stick to what you believe the right thing to do." To which Charles replied only with a grim nod, and they went ashore.

"We'll walk up to the town with you," said Graeme, when they got outside the harbour precincts. "When you've got as far as you can with him, come down to the shore due West. You'll find us by that old fort we saw from the boat;" and presently they branched off towards the sea, while Charles went doggedly on into St. Anne on as miserable an errand as ever son had.

He tramped on along the hot white road, till he found himself in the sleepy little town, where the grass grew between the granite sets in the roadways and a dreamy listlessness pervaded all things. He sought out No. 99A High Street and knocked on the door.

It was opened by an elderly woman who seemed surprised at sight of a visitor.

"Mr. Peace?" asked Charles, feeling thereby particeps criminis.

"He's inside. Will you come in?"

She opened a door off the passage, said, "A gentleman to see you;" and Charles went in and closed the door behind him.

His father had started up from a couch where he had been lying. There was a startled look in his eyes and his face was pale and worn, but a touch of colour came back into his cheeks when he saw who his visitor was.

He had shaved off his bit of side whisker. His face was grayer and thinner and his body somewhat shrunken, even in these few days. He wore a white tie, and his coat and waistcoat were of clerical cut. On the table was a pair of gold spectacles and on the sideboard a soft billycock hat. He looked the not-too-well-off country parson to the life. The only outward and visible sign of the old Jeremiah was the heavy gold pince-nez which lay between the top buttons of his waistcoat, which he hauled out and fingered as of old the moment he began to speak.

"Ah, Charles! This is good of you. I hardly expected a personal visit. I was beginning to fear you had not got my letter, or that you had decided not to answer it."

"It followed me to Sark."

"Ah! you are back in Sark?"

"I thought it well to take my mother there, to be out of things for a time."

"Quite so, quite so! That was very thoughtful of you. This is a terrible calamity that has befallen us. But, as I said in my letter, I have every hope of being able to redeem matters if I can only get to where that is possible."

"Where's that?"

"Well, in the first place to Spain—"

"And afterwards?"

Mr. Pixley hesitated. "Perhaps—for your own sake—it would be as well you should not know—for the present, at all events. You may be asked questions. If you don't know, you can truthfully say so."

"I gather that you have funds put away somewhere."

"If I can get to where I want to go, I can at all events make a fresh start. And I am prepared to devote the rest of my life to the one object I have named.... The last few years have been very wearying. I have had trouble with my heart at times;" and he put his hand to his side to emphasise it. "But if I can get quietly away I shall soon pull round and be ready for work again, now that the strain is over."

"You know you're asking me to do what I've no right to do?" said Charles gloomily.

"I know, my boy, and it is very bitter for me to have to ask it. But I can't get away without your help, and the alternative is not pleasant to think of—for either of us.... I do not ask more than I would willingly have done for you if the positions were reversed.... On the whole, I do not think I have been a bad father to you. Circumstances, indeed, have been too strong for me at the end, but—"

"I am willing to do what you want—and more, on one condition."

"What is that? Anything in reason—"

"I will provide you with funds to get away, and I will send you three hundred pounds each year—"

"Good lad!"

"On condition that you hand over to me all the property you've got stowed away—"

"Damn!"

"So that I may hand it over to your creditors."

"Why not write at once to Scotland Yard and tell them where I am? But, after all, I'm not sure that even your world would applaud so filial an act as that."

"I'm prepared to make sacrifices myself to help right some of this wrong—"

"I had to make many for you, my boy, before you were old enough to understand it—before my own position was assured. Ay, and since too. I would have flung it all up years ago but for you. I wanted you to be set firmly on your feet before the crash came. It has been killing work. I'm glad it's over—whatever the end may be. If you can't see your way to help me, the end is obvious and close at hand. I have, I think, something under two pounds in my pocket. If I'd waited to get more I should not be here. The end came unexpectedly. Old Coxley called for some securities which I had—which I couldn't give him at the moment, and I had to go at once or not at all."

Charles stood up. He would have liked to tell him all he felt about the matter. How the tampering with securities hit him more hardly than almost anything could have done, since straight dealing in such matters is the very first of Stock Exchange tenets. How, if he had come to him, he would have strained himself to the utmost to set things right.

But, facile talker as he was on matters that were of no account, he found himself strangely tongue-tied here.

"Well?" he asked. "Will you let me help you?"

"As you will, my boy ... If you do, it offers me a chance—my only chance. If you don't—" he shrugged his heavy shoulders meaningly.

"Do what I ask," urged Charles. "It is the only possible amends you can make."

Mr. Pixley shook his head. "It is out of the question. I could do nothing with three hundred a year—"

"You could live quietly on that in many places."

"I don't want simply to live. I want to work and redeem myself."

"You have worked hard enough and long enough," said Charles; and he might have added, as was in his mind, "And it has all ended in this."

"I would like to help you," he said, as he moved slowly towards the door, striving hard to keep the stiff upper lip Graeme had enjoined on him. "But I don't think you should expect me to do what I know to be wrong. I'll do what I said—"

Mr. Pixley shook his head. His face was gray, his lips pinched in. Charles went out and closed the door behind him.

But he could not leave him so. He had known from the first that he would have to help him, right or wrong.

He opened the door again quietly and went in. His father was sitting at the table with his head in his hands. Charles laid down the money he had, with Graeme's assistance, prepared, laid his hand on his shoulder for a moment, and went quietly out again, and out of the house.

It was a miserable business altogether. He never forgot that last sight of him sitting at the mean little table in the mean little room with his head in his hands.

XI

Charles went soberly down the green slopes towards the sea, and presently discovered the dismantled fort they had seen from the steamer as they ran up the Swinge that morning. And sitting on the broken wall of a gun platform was a figure which he knew by the dress to be Miss Penny.

She had evidently been on the look-out for him. She stood up and waved her hand, and he waved his in reply, and plunged down the slope. His heart was sore at what had just passed. It turned gratefully to one whom he knew to be full of sympathy for him.

When he reached the foot of the hill, they were crossing the causeway which led from the fort to the shore.

"Well, old man, you've got through with it?" said Graeme; and all their faces showed the anxiety that was in them to know how he had prospered.

He nodded. "Let's go back and sit there for a few minutes. I feel like a whipped dog;" and they all went back to the fort, which, in its dismantlement and ruin, whispered soothingly of the rest and peace that sometimes lie beyond broken hopes and strenuous times.

"Well, how did you find him?" asked Graeme, as they seated themselves on the broken wall again, with the fair blue plain of the sea dimpling and dancing in front.

"Very broken, but as obstinate as ever," said Charles gloomily. "Wouldn't listen to my proposal, says he's set on redeeming himself, and so on. I offered him all I could, but it was no use. So I left him—"

"You never did—" began Miss Penny, with a pained look on her face.

"I did. But I couldn't leave it so. I went back, and he was sitting with his head in his hands.... I just gave him all I had brought and came away.... I know it was all wrong—"

"It wasn't. You did quite right," said Miss Penny vehemently.

"I don't suppose any of us would have done differently when it came to the point. I don't really see what else you could have done," said Graeme.

"He reminded me of all he had done for me when I was a boy, and so on, and told me that if I didn't help him there was no hope for him. I did my best—"

"You have done quite right, Charles," said Margaret. "I do hope he will get away all right."

As he gave them the details of his interview, their quiet sympathy restored him by degrees to himself. The bruised, whipped soreness wore off, to some extent at all events, and there remained chiefly a feeling of thankfulness that the matter was over, and that, in doing the only thing possible to him, if he offended against the law, he had still done what commended itself to his own heart and to those whose good opinion he chiefly valued.

If there were no signs of merriment about them as they wandered quietly about the strand, if they still bore something of the aspect of a funeral party, it was at all events the aspect of a party after the funeral. Their corpse was laid, so far as they were concerned, and their thoughts and hearts were more at liberty to turn to other matters.

They have none of them ever cared greatly for Alderney, and they always speak of it as a remote, unfriendly, melancholy, and slow little place, lacking the gem-like beauty and joyous vitality of Sark. But then one's outlook is always coloured by one's inlook, and an overcast mind sees all things shadowed.

They lunched at the Scott Hotel, in the garden, and felt better than they had done for two days when their feet once more trod the deck of the Courier.

The southern cliffs were filmy blue in the distance, Ortach and the Casquets were dim against the horizon, and Charles and Miss Penny stood together in the stern looking back over the long straight track of the boat, and thinking both of the lonely one in the mean little house in St. Anne. Margaret and Graeme had stood watching for a time, and had then stolen away forward. Their outlook was ahead, where Sark was rising boldly out of the blue waters.

"I doubt if we'll ever hear anything more of him," said Charles, with a sigh at thought of it all.

"You will always remember that you have done your duty by him. You could not have done more."

"You have been very kind to me all through, very kind, all of you. And you especially.... Hennie—will you marry me?"

And she looked up at him with a happy face, and said quietly, "Yes, I will. I believe we can make one another very happy."

"I'm sure we can. Come along and tell the others;" and they also turned from the past and went forward.

John Oxenham — A Concise Bibliography

God's Prisoner (1898)
A Princess of Vascovy (1899)
Under the Iron Flail (1902)
Barbe of Grand Bayou (1903)
Bondman Free (1903)
Hearts in Exile (1904)
John of Gerisau (1904)
A Weaver of Webs (1904)
White Fire (1905)
Giant Circumstance (1906)
Profit and Loss (1906)
The Long Road (1907)
Carette of Sark (1907)
In Christ There Is No East or West (1908)
Pearl of Pearl Island (1908)
The Song of Hyacinth (1908)
My Lady of Shadows (1909)
Great Heart Gillian (1909)
A Maid of the Silver Sea (1910)
The Coil of Carne (1911)
The Quest of the Golden Rose (1912)
The Gate of the Desert (1912)
Bees in Amber (1913)
Broken Shackles (1914)
The King's High-Way (1916)
All's Well (1916)
The Fiery Cross (1917)
The Vision Splendid (1917)
High Altars (1918)
Hearts Courageous (1919)

The Wonder of Lourdes: what it is and what it means (1924)
The Hidden Years' (1927)
Gentlemen - the King! (1928)
God's Candle (1929)
Hearts in Exile (1930)
The Splendour of the Dawn (1930)
The Man Who Would Save the World (1930)
The Pageant of the King's Children (1930) (with his son Roderick Dunkerley)
Cross-Roads: The Story of Four Meetings (1931)
A Saint in the Making (1931)
Christ and the Third Wise Man (1934)